WHISPERING PINES

WHISPERING PINES

Heidi Lang & Kati Bartkowski

Margaret K. McElderry Books

NEW YORK   LONDON   TORONTO   SYDNEY   NEW DELHI

MARGARET K. McELDERRY BOOKS
An imprint of Simon & Schuster Children's Publishing Division
1230 Avenue of the Americas, New York, New York 10020
Text copyright © 2020 by Heidi Lang and Kati Bartkowski
Jacket illustration copyright © 2020 by Diana Novich
All rights reserved, including the right of reproduction in whole or in part in any form.
MARGARET K. McELDERRY BOOKS is a trademark of Simon & Schuster, Inc.
For information about special discounts for bulk purchases, please contact Simon & Schuster Special Sales at 1-866-506-1949 or business@simonandschuster.com.
The Simon & Schuster Speakers Bureau can bring authors to your live event.
For more information or to book an event contact the Simon & Schuster Speakers Bureau at 1-866-248-3049 or visit our website at www.simonspeakers.com.
Jacket designed by Tiara Iandiorio
Interior designed by Mike Rosamilia
The text of this book was set in Adobe Caslon Pro.
Manufactured in the United States of America 0720 FFG
First Edition
2 4 6 8 10 9 7 5 3 1
Library of Congress Cataloging-in-Publication Data
Names: Lang, Heidi, author. | Bartkowski, Kati, author.
Title: Whispering Pines / by Heidi Lang and Kati Bartkowski.
Description: New York City : Margaret K. McElderry Books, 2020. | Summary: "When otherworldly forces descend on their town of Whispering Pines, conspiracy theorist Rae, who's searching for her lost father, and Caden, who's haunted by the ghost of his brother, must band together to save their home"— Provided by publisher.
Identifiers: LCCN 2019059084 (print) | LCCN 2019059085 (eBook) |
ISBN 9781534460478 (hardcover) | ISBN 9781534460492 (eBook)
Subjects: CYAC: Supernatural—Fiction. | Ghosts—Fiction. | Conspiracy theories—Fiction. | Missing persons—Fiction. | Monsters—Fiction.
Classification: LCC PZ7.1.L3436 Whi 2020 (print) |
LCC PZ7.1.L3436 (eBook) | DDC [Fic]—dc23
LC record available at https://lccn.loc.gov/2019059084
LC eBook record available at https://lccn.loc.gov/2019059085

For Lyn and Bruce, the best mother-in-law and father-in-law in the world. Thank you for welcoming me into your home and your lives, and for reading everything I write with such enthusiasm.
—H. L.

———◆◆———

And for Nick and Ember. Your patience and support were exactly what I needed to make this book happen.
—K. B.

PROLOGUE

{ LATE JUNE }

Jasmine clung to the edges of the hall. They were less likely to creak, and in this old house she needed all the help she could get. The weight of her flashlight was nice and comforting, but she kept the light off so no one would see her, even though the shadows here were so dark someone could be sitting in the middle of one and she wouldn't notice them unless they tripped her.

She crept into the living room, quietly searching behind the television stand and under the couch. She even felt around the cushions. No one was there.

Her brother, Jake, always forced her to be *It* first, just because she was the youngest. It wasn't fair, but if she complained, the others might not let her play anymore. And she loved playing hide-and-seek. She and Jake had been playing every night this summer with their cousin and the neighbor next door. She'd gotten pretty good at it; even though she wasn't as fast as the others, she was definitely sneakier. So far she'd managed to tag everyone except their neighbor Stephanie.

But that was about to change.

Jasmine stood in the middle of the room and listened.

Creak. Creak. Creaaak.

She smiled and snuck toward the source of the noise: their front door, hanging slightly ajar. The wood had warped from the humidity of the summer, so it wouldn't shut all the way now unless you slammed it. Which meant someone—Stephanie—had snuck outside.

It wasn't technically cheating. They were allowed to hide in the yard, but yesterday Jasmine had noticed Stephanie crouching where the edge of the yard met the forest out back, in that space they kept arguing was out-of-bounds.

Jasmine pushed the door open wider and slipped outside into the cool night air.

She stood alone on the porch of her family's old colonial house, which sat right at the edge of the Watchful Woods. Night bled across the sky like ink, transforming the forest into tangled tree limbs and disturbing shadows.

Jasmine shivered. Normally she could hear peepers, bugs, and bats, but everything had gone still tonight, like the rest of the world was waiting for her to make the first move.

She stepped off the porch and walked silently toward the

woods in search of Stephanie, her eyes darting left and right, tracing the shapes of trees, the rusted remains of the fort her mom had built for her and Jake when they were little, the long curving driveway . . .

There. Something moved at the edge of the forest, a darker shadow. It paused beneath the tree line, then slunk deeper into the woods.

Jasmine looked at those trees all clustered together, the space beneath them super creepy, then glanced back at her nice, safe house. She could head inside and tag Jake or Teresa. She didn't have to go out there.

But then Stephanie would win. Again. And it wasn't fair. It was definitely her turn to be *It* for once.

Jasmine crept into the woods. A few feet in and she could barely see, the dying light from the sky blotted out by tangled branches overhead. She hunched her shoulders and kept going, leaves crunching underfoot no matter how carefully she tried to walk.

Long minutes passed with no sign of Stephanie. Jasmine glanced over her shoulder. She couldn't see the house anymore. She hesitated, then noticed something gleaming white just ahead, a spot of brightness in all the gloom. Jasmine eased her way closer, squinting, until she made out Stephanie's long blond hair. *Got you*, she thought triumphantly.

Stephanie didn't move, even though she had to have heard Jasmine coming.

Jasmine paused a few feet away, unease prickling up and down her back. She clicked the flashlight on like a spotlight, illuminating

Stephanie bent forward, her face in her hands, her shoulders shaking like she was crying. "Stephanie? Are you—"

Stephanie spun, one pale, grasping hand catching Jasmine by the wrist, another latching around her upper arm, yanking her close so fast Jasmine didn't have time to resist. Her fingers were still clenched around the flashlight, its beam bathing Stephanie's face, and the numbness of horror spilled through her.

Jasmine barely felt Stephanie's too-tight grip, or the wet from the grass seeping through her shoes, or anything. She couldn't feel *anything*.

Stephanie's mouth moved, open and shut, open and shut, almost like she was gnawing on an invisible bone. And her eyes . . . oh, her eyes . . .

Where her eyes should have been, there was nothing. Nothing but two deep pits full of night.

Jasmine made a low animal sound deep in her throat. She wanted to scream, but her voice had shriveled away to nothing.

Stephanie leaned in closer, and now Jasmine could see how filthy her face was, streaked with mud and crisscrossed with angry red welts, like she'd been running headlong through the branches. "Eyes," Stephanie rasped, right beside Jasmine's ear. "He said I have lovely eyes. Lovely, lovely eyes." She released Jasmine as abruptly as she'd caught her.

Jasmine scrambled away, slipping in the damp grass. She knew she should stay, should somehow help Stephanie, but fear pulled Jasmine, sprinting, back to the safety of the house.

The front door stood wide open, but Jasmine barely noticed

as she raced through it, running down the hall and into the dining room. And then stopped.

Her brother cowered under the table, his knees drawn to his chest. He had his cell phone out, the light of the screen turning his face a pallid, sinister blue, his eyes dark pockets of shadow.

"Jake?"

He looked up, and Jasmine's flashlight reflected off the whites of his eyes. She wanted to sob in relief. For a second, she'd been picturing Jake with empty eye sockets just like Stephanie, and she'd been so afraid.

"Shh," Jake hissed. "There's *something* in the house."

"What?" Fear came back, sharp and throbbing.

"We thought it was you, but it . . ." His voice choked off in a sob. "It went after Teresa."

"What did?" Jasmine demanded.

"I don't know. It . . . it had no eyes, Jas. It had so many teeth, but no eyes."

No eyes . . . like Stephanie.

This was a nightmare. This wasn't real. Jasmine couldn't believe any of this was happening. But then she heard screams. *Teresa's* screams. They seemed to echo all through the house, high and shrill and terrified before stopping suddenly. As if someone had just turned the sound off.

Jasmine clicked off her flashlight, listening hard. Her heart beat too loud in her ears, her breath rasping, but beneath that she thought she heard the creaking of footsteps. Behind her? Above her? It was too hard to tell in this old shifting house. She should go get help, but she didn't want to go outside, in the dark, alone. She didn't want to pass Stephanie. She was afraid to go, and terrified to stay.

"I'm trying to call Mom, but it's not going through." Jake's whisper was too loud. Jasmine felt like he was shouting. And his phone screen was so bright. For some reason, this was the only room in the house that got cell reception, but it wasn't always reliable even in here.

The footsteps grew louder.

Jasmine whimpered. "Close the screen, Jake."

"I need to reach Mom."

"We need to hide." She could hear something at the other end of the hall, moving toward them. Closer.

Jake's phone made a noise, and it sounded like someone picked up, the voice muted and garbled.

"Jake," she sobbed. "We need to go."

He put the phone to his ear. "Voicemail."

"Jake!"

He looked up. "You go, Jas. Go hide. And don't come out, no matter what you hear."

Jasmine shook her head.

"Go!" He punched at the phone again, and she knew he wouldn't leave this room. So she went.

She couldn't stop crying, silent little gasps, but somehow she made it to the kitchen. She opened the cabinet doors below the sink, folded herself against the cold pipe, and pulled the doors shut.

Outside, all was silent.

And then the screams began again. Jake's screams this time. Jasmine pressed her face into her knees and wept, and tried not to listen as they went on and on and then, abruptly, stopped.

In the sudden silence, Jasmine could hear footsteps creaking across the old wooden floor, stopping only a few feet in front of her hiding place. She tried to keep her breathing shallow, quiet, the scent of mold and bleach and that awful fake orange cleaner filling her nostrils. Her knees were crammed practically to her face, the cold pipe of the sink pressing into her back. Would it think to look under here? Jasmine was small for her age, and flexible. Most other ten-year-olds wouldn't be able to fit.

"I know you're in here," the *thing* said.

Blood roared in Jasmine's ears, and she bit down on her fist to keep from gasping. She squeezed her eyes shut and waited, counting slowly until the noise in her ears faded. Nothing happened.

She opened her eyes, blinking in the dim light filtering through the cabinet doors. It must have been bluffing.

Creak. Footsteps somewhere else in the house. The sound of a door opening and closing.

Jasmine relaxed, her foot bumping a bottle.

The cabinet doors flew open.

Jasmine couldn't scream, her throat one tight knot.

"Hello, little girl." The monster smiled, the skin of its face stretching around all those teeth like a badly made mask. "What lovely eyes you have." And as it reached for her, Jasmine found she could scream after all.

1.

RAE

{ THREE MONTHS LATER }

Rae Carter had never run away from anything in her twelve
years, no matter what. She believed in always finding out
the truth and facing it head-on, even when it cost her all
her friends. But now, as her mom's minivan rumbled into their
new town, she realized that running away was exactly what she
was doing. And it felt . . . okay, actually.

Although she wasn't so sure about the place they were running *to*.

"'Welcome to Whispering Pines,'" Rae read off the large
sign posted at the edge of town. "'Mind the goats.'" She frowned.
"Really? Goats?"

"Goats must be important around here," her older sister, Ava,
said in that irritatingly superior tone she'd been using lately, like it
was all so obvious.

"Don't try to pretend that's not weird," Rae said. "Most other town signs just tell you the population."

Ava shrugged. "*I* happen to like it. You like it, right, Mom?"

"It's definitely different," their mom said, slowing down to match the speed limit as they cruised down the main street. Twenty-seven and a half miles per hour. Rae had never seen a decimal point in a speed limit sign before, but this time she kept that to herself. Ava would probably claim she liked that, too.

Rae scowled at the back of her sister's head. Ava was five years older than her, which hadn't mattered all that much before. But this past year, Rae had felt each and every one of those years piling up between them.

Don't be such a child, Rae . . .

Rae shook off the memory of the worst day of her life, the day she'd really needed her sister's help and instead got a condescending lecture. If Rae was finally running away from something, it might as well be *everything*. She could leave her old self behind, and be someone new here. Someone who wasn't overly focused on strange things. The kind of girl who made friends easily—and kept them—and was able to let the little things go.

But then she thought of her dad and knew she couldn't actually abandon everything.

They left the small downtown area behind and turned onto a tree-lined street. *All* of the streets here were tree-lined. They'd had plenty of trees back home in Sunnyside, California, too, but not like this. It was as if the houses and businesses of this town were battling the forest for space.

A few more turns, even more trees, and up ahead Rae spotted a moving van parked on the street in front of a rectangular white house. Her mom pulled up behind the van and cut the engine, the car filling with quiet as the three of them just sat there, staring out at their new home.

It was definitely larger than their old place but looked older, the paint a bit weathered, the bushes lining the walk slightly over-grown. Otherwise, it seemed normal enough. No goats anywhere. Rae was a little disappointed.

She glanced at her mom in the rearview mirror. Her mom wore one of those looks that meant her mind was a million miles away, her eyes wide and unfocused. It was a look she'd worn way too often this past year, ever since Rae's dad had vanished.

Been taken, Rae corrected herself. That was one truth she couldn't forget, not for a second. "Mom?" she asked.

No response.

"Should we go in?" Ava asked, a little louder.

Their mom gave herself a little shake and smiled. "I sup-pose we'd better," she said. Of *course* she responded to Ava. She always did.

Rae crossed her arms, remaining in the back seat as her mom and sister got out and headed toward the house. Neither of them looked back, though, and after a minute Rae got tired of being sulky and climbed out of the car too. She took a deep breath.

The air smelled different here, like pine needles and dirt. The trees nearby had just started to change color, clumps of red and orange bursting out from behind all that green. Rae had heard that nothing beat autumn in Connecticut. So far it seemed like it was off to a slow start.

"You coming in?" Ava called, poking her head out the front door.

"Yes, yes," Rae grumbled. But she hesitated at the bottom of the driveway. Once she went inside, that would be it. The end of the old Rae, the start of the new. She wasn't sure if she was ready.

She looked at the moving van looming in front of her, packed full of everything from her family's old life, and realized she didn't really have a choice.

Movement behind the van caught her eye. Someone was walking through the yard of the house across the street. Rae glanced at the open front door behind her, then took a step away from it. She wasn't stalling. She was investigating.

She stepped past the van so she could see the house across the street better. It sat up on a hill, its own driveway long and unpaved, and at the bottom a large square sign read, GOT A GHOST PROBLEM? NAME YOUR PRICE! in bold orange letters. Below that, written in black, it said PARANORMAL PRICE: SPECIALIZING IN EXORCISMS, TAROT READINGS, AND HOUSE CLEANSINGS, followed by a phone number.

Rae scratched her head. Maybe it was a joke?

She looked past the sign, through a thin layer of trees and up the driveway, where a boy with messy dark hair moved slowly backward through the yard. He was tall and skinny and wearing all black—probably a requirement if his family actually specialized in ghost hunting—and he was tossing handfuls of something into the grass as he walked.

"Hello?" Rae called loudly. If they were going to be neighbors, she might as well be friendly.

The boy looked up at her.

She waved.

He turned away, tossing more of whatever it was into the grass behind him and ignoring her completely.

Rae slowly lowered her hand to her side, her heart sinking. Maybe things wouldn't be any different here for her after all.

"Don't mind him," a voice said behind her.

Rae whirled, coming face-to-face with a girl about her age wearing jeans and a gray T-shirt with the words "Seeking Samantha" printed on it.

"Caden Price doesn't really like people." The girl tossed her long dark hair back over her shoulder. "I mean, we live on the same street, and I think he's spoken to me once."

"What's he doing?" Rae asked.

"Drawing a line with salt."

"Salt? Why?"

"I have no idea, and frankly, I'm scared to ask. But he does it a lot. Especially lately."

"Great," Rae muttered. She was living across from a ghost-hunting weirdo with a condiment problem.

"I'm Brandi, by the way," the girl said. "You must be Rae, right?"

Rae's eyes widened. How could this girl possibly know that?

"I promise I'm not some creepy stalker," Brandi said quickly. "We just don't get many new people here, so as soon as the moving van showed up, I *had* to investigate."

"Spoken like a true stalker," Rae said, the words slipping out. She immediately regretted them. They belonged to the old Rae, the one who had ended up friendless and alone. "I mean . . ."

Brandi laughed. "No, that's fair. My mom tells me I'm too nosy for my own good. Claims it'll get me in trouble someday." She shrugged. "Anyhow, you'll be in my school, good ole Dana S. Middle School. Seventh grade, right?"

Rae nodded.

"I'm a grade above you, but I like helping new students get settled in, and since you're, like, only the second one we've had in a year, I can totally show you around if you want."

"Show me around? You mean, here? Or at school?"

"Both." Brandi grinned. She had chapped lips and a small gap between her front teeth, but somehow they made her smile look better.

Rae wanted to grin back, but embarrassingly, she could feel tears building in the back of her eyes. It had been a long time since anyone had been so nice to her. Not since her ex–best friend had cut all ties at the beginning of sixth grade. "I'd like that," she said, turning a little away and blinking rapidly.

"Cool beans." Brandi studied the moving van. "You probably want to get started unpacking, huh?"

"Not really," Rae admitted. She wasn't looking forward to going through all those boxes.

"Oh good! Want to get ice cream with me instead? I'm supposed to be cleaning, but if I'm showing the new girl around, my mom can't really get mad at me."

"Oh, so you're using me?"

"Just a little." Brandi flashed another gap-toothed smile. "Want to come anyhow?"

This time Rae managed to smile back. "I'd love to. Let me just check with my mom."

"I'll wait."

Rae turned and hurried up the driveway, her earlier hesitation gone.

It was time to reinvent herself here in this strange little town. Out with the old Rae, and in with the new.

2.
CADEN

Caden Price walked carefully backward, tossing handfuls of salt in a line around his house and muttering the protection spells he'd memorized years ago. He usually liked doing this chore—it made him feel safer—but his thoughts kept slipping away from words of power, sliding instead toward the new girl across the street.

She'd seemed nice. He should have waved back.

Caden gritted his teeth and kept going. His mom had worked with him on shielding spells when he was in first grade, and since then he'd become pretty good at them. The key was a focused mind. He couldn't keep out negative energies if he was planning what to eat for lunch, or worrying about homework, or running through what-if scenarios. Like . . . what if he'd been more friendly and gone over there, like Brandi?

Stop it, Caden told himself firmly. It wouldn't have mattered how friendly he was anyhow. As soon as the new girl got to school and heard all the rumors, she would want nothing to do with him. Better not to even try.

He took the remaining three steps back until the end of the salt line met the beginning. It reminded him of the ouroboros: the ancient symbol of a giant serpent eating its tail. His mom had told him that it represented the endless cycle of life, death, and rebirth. He used to believe that cycle encompassed everything. Now he knew better.

He closed up the large leather sack with the remaining salt just as an unfamiliar car pulled up his driveway. Caden paused near the front door and watched as a middle-aged couple got out. The man walked to the back of the car and opened the trunk, moving slowly and stiffly, his dark suit hanging on him as if he'd recently lost a lot of weight. The woman waited by the front of the car in a dark green dress that fit her perfectly, her graying hair carefully styled, but Caden was close enough to see the mascara smeared beneath her red-rimmed eyes. And he could feel the grief surrounding her in swirls of a bruiselike bluish purple.

They must be new clients, which was good. Business had slowed down for the Prices this year. Caden wasn't sure if it was because of the rumors around him—nothing like having the police come by your house multiple times to make people suspicious of you and your family—or if it was because his mom had stopped trying to get more work, but she'd gone from very busy to maybe one or two visits a week in the past nine months.

The man pulled a cardboard box out of the trunk and shut the door, then strode toward Caden. "Hello," he said, his voice deep and scratchy. "We're the McCurleys. We had an appointment?"

"My mom is—" Caden began, just as the front door opened and his mother stepped out, her silver-and-blue striped skirt swirling around her bare feet, her black hair tumbling long and loose down her back. She must be really trying to make an impression; she was even wearing a pair of large dangling pentagram earrings that Caden knew gave her a headache.

"Laura," she said, clasping the woman's hands. "And Rob. Please, come inside." She didn't even look at Caden, just left him there on the doorstep.

Caden ran a hand over the pendant he always wore around his neck. His mom had given it to him for protection on the day he'd realized he was different from other kids, back in first grade. It had been one of the worst days of his life, but the pendant reminded him that even if no one else wanted to be around him, he'd at least always have his family. Only now his brother was gone, his father was working increasingly long hours, and his mom . . .

His mom wanted nothing to do with him. Caden couldn't blame her.

He glanced across the street. The new girl had already gone. He took a deep breath, then headed inside.

". . . has it been since your son disappeared?" Caden's mom was asking the couple as Caden entered the kitchen.

"Nine months to the day tomorrow."

Caden stumbled, catching himself on the coatrack. Nine months tomorrow? It had to be a coincidence. When he glanced at his mom, her face gave nothing away, but he noticed a flicker of deep, dark brownish red hovering around her, like an old bloodstain. It felt like guilt, or something deeper. Shame.

She met his eyes, and the color vanished so completely Caden could have been imagining it. "Don't you have homework to do?" she asked him.

"Just making some tea first." There was no way he was leaving now, not after that. He walked around her and started up the kettle.

"Thirteen?" Laura asked Caden.

He nodded.

"Our boy, Peter, is the same age." She smiled, her lip quivering. "You probably didn't know him. We homeschooled."

"Oh," Caden said. Then after a beat he added, "I'm sorry he's missing."

Laura sniffed. "The police have stopped looking. They think he just ran away."

"But you know he didn't," Caden's mom said carefully. A statement, not a question. She'd taught Caden about the importance of that kind of phrasing, back when she'd been training him and his older brother to help with the family business.

People come to us when no one else in their life believes them, she had said. *Therefore you never want them to think you doubt their story.*

"It was the first snowfall," Laura explained. "Peter wanted to test out his cold weather camping gear. He wasn't going far, just to the woods in back of our house."

"He loved the outdoors," Rob added. His wife shot him a look, and he amended hastily, "*Loves* the outdoors."

"He's not dead. He's *not*." Laura's voice caught. Caden's mom handed her a box of tissues. She took one, dabbing gently at her eyes and nose. "You—your family, you're our last hope. If you can somehow find him." She held out her hands to Caden's mom. "Please."

"I promise to try. Do you have anything of his? Something he valued?"

Rob opened the cardboard box he'd carried inside and pulled out a battered navy blue baseball cap with a picture of a large white dog balancing a basketball on one paw on the front.

"The Malamutes are his favorite team," Laura said, her voice a little stronger. "He never went anywhere without that hat. He wouldn't have left without it."

"The police found it out in the woods," Rob added, with another sidelong glance at his wife.

She pressed her lips together and didn't say anything.

"I'll need some time," Caden's mom told the couple. "Give me a week, and I'll see what I can discover."

"Thank you." Laura clasped her hands together. "And if you need anything else, anything at all . . ."

"Laura," her husband warned. "Remember what they said about making promises that—"

"I don't care! I know our Peter is hardly the first child to go missing in this town, but . . . I just want him back," she sobbed.

"I understand," Caden's mom said quietly. "I would do anything to get my son back too."

Caden felt the full weight of her gaze on him and wondered if she knew the truth: that he was the reason his brother, Aiden, wasn't here.

Silence filled the small kitchen until the shriek of the kettle shattered it. Caden turned off the stove. "Tea, anyone?" he asked.

3.
RAE

Rae waited in the front office of Dana S. Middle School, reading the bulletin board and trying to pretend she wasn't nervous. She'd never been the new student before. And everything in Whispering Pines seemed so . . . *alien*. Including this place. Fifth graders were in middle school here, and the hallways were all enclosed like some sort of prison instead of being open to the sunlight like her school back in California. And then there were the school rules.

A small sign in the corner of the bulletin board read: PLAY IT SAFE, AND "LEAF" THE WOODS ALONE. Next to it the rules were written in black Sharpie:

Curfew begins at sunset. No students out after dark.
Parents or recognized guardians MUST pick up students
from school following any after-school activities.

Garlic is to be eaten, not worn.

Absolutely no chalk allowed.

The second field is closed due to a sudden sinkhole appearance. All outdoor activities will now be scheduled on the first field only.

No wearing red. This includes shirts, pants, hats, and lipstick.

No cell phone use within school grounds.

Rae frowned at them. They seemed a little random, with the exception of the cell phone rule.

Below the rules was an announcement about an upcoming assembly with something called "Green On!" followed by the caption, "Join the Green family, best deals in clean energy!"

"Rae Carter?"

Rae turned. A tall woman with short, ferociously styled blond hair and a perfectly pressed navy blue pantsuit came out from behind the office in back. She carried a clipboard in one hand, and everything about her screamed careful control, from the thin line of her mouth to the rigid way she stood.

"I'm Ms. Lockett, the vice principal here at Dana S. Middle School. Welcome to Whispering Pines."

"Thank you," Rae said. Even though that "welcome" had been said with about as much warmth as a New England blizzard.

"We don't generally *get* new students . . . and especially not a month into the school year. It makes things messy. However, I understand our principal made an exception for you." Her lips twisted, like she'd bitten into something sour.

Rae wasn't sure if she should apologize. But then, it was hardly her fault.

"Seventh grade is a tough year," Ms. Lockett continued. "Particularly at our school. We expect a lot from our students. You'll need to work hard to catch up."

"That's fine. I'm not afraid of working hard."

Ms. Lockett studied her. Rae hated when people looked at her like that, like they were digging into her brain and running their fingers through all her thoughts. "I'm sure you're eager to prove yourself somewhere new," Ms. Lockett said finally. "Especially considering what happened with your father." She shook her head. "Sad business."

Rae's heartbeat pounded in her head, and she dug her nails into her palms. No one here was supposed to know about her father.

After he'd disappeared at the start of sixth grade, she'd told her best friend, Taylor, the truth about what happened to him. Taylor hadn't believed her. Even worse, she'd told everyone Rae's secret, turning it into a joke. Rae could still hear Taylor and the other kids in her school laughing while she cried in the bathroom, could still see the horrible pictures they'd drawn and stuffed in her locker and remember the names they'd called her. Rae had spent the rest of sixth grade alone.

But this was a new school, and she was a new Rae. One who had learned to keep her secrets to herself. "I don't know what you heard," she said, her voice barely shaking. "But it wasn't a big deal."

Ms. Lockett's eyebrows lifted.

Rae made herself shrug. "Lots of people's dads run off. It sucks, but it happens." It hurt to say the lie, but she kept her face blank, her tone casual. She'd practiced this before they moved. She'd practiced lots of things.

She planned to blend in here. She wasn't going to be the school outcast again.

Ms. Lockett sniffed. "Well." She glanced down at her clipboard like she was looking for a script to tell her how to respond.

Someone coughed.

Rae looked up.

A girl as tall and slim as a javelin leaned against Ms. Lockett's open office doorway, her shiny blond hair pulled up in a high ponytail, her arms crossed. She was staring hard at Rae, her eyes like two ice chips.

Rae shivered.

"This is my daughter," Ms. Lockett said. "Alyssa, meet Rae Carter."

"Hey." Alyssa bared her teeth in the world's most unfriendly smile.

"Alyssa will be showing you around today," Ms. Lockett continued.

"Oh, that's okay," Rae said quickly. "My next-door neighbor said she'd do it."

Ms. Lockett frowned down at her clipboard. "And who might that be?"

"Brandi Jensen?" Rae said. "She's an eighth grader here."

"Brandi . . . isn't here right now." Ms. Lockett tapped her clipboard, her lips pursed.

Not here right now? Rae tried not to be too disappointed. She'd really liked hanging out with Brandi this weekend, and knowing she'd have a friend to ease her in on her first day had made the prospect of school much less terrifying. Now she was on her own.

"Do you have any other questions?" Ms. Lockett asked.

Rae shook her head.

"Good. Because I'm very busy. And I doubt you'll stick around here for long."

"What? Why?" Rae asked.

"Most outsiders move back out within a few months. If they get the chance, that is."

Rae blinked. Now *that* didn't sound ominous or anything.

First bell rang outside, loud and obnoxious.

"And you're about to be late," Ms. Lockett added.

"Let's go." Alyssa opened the office door and waved Rae through it. Other students had begun slowly trickling into the school, their noise echoing off the painted brick walls. Rae glanced at the mural next to her. A giant diving eagle, drawn cartoonishly. "Eighth-grade art," Alyssa explained. "They get to paint all the walls."

"Oh." Rae looked at the next mural. This one depicted a vampire complete with dripping fangs. It reminded Rae of the weird rule about garlic. "So . . . what's up with those school rules?" she asked.

"What about them?"

"Like, not wearing garlic?" Rae said.

"Oh, you know. It doesn't smell very good."

Rae couldn't tell if Alyssa was mocking her, but she forged on.

"I mean, did you have a lot of people wearing garlic, then? Enough that you needed a rule against it?"

"Yeah, it was a problem for a while. Last year, Terence showed up at school with bite marks on his neck, and then Sophie the day after, and people went a little bonkers. Especially after someone found Emmett totally drained of blood and stuffed in a locker."

Rae stopped walking. *"What?"*

Alyssa didn't stop. "You don't want to be late on your first day," she called over her shoulder.

Rae hurried to catch up. "Who is Emmett?"

"Emmett *was* a rabbit. The fifth-grade science classroom pet." Alyssa shrugged. "They haven't replaced him. Pets don't seem to do well here . . . kind of like new kids."

Rae frowned. It almost sounded like Alyssa was threatening her. Fantastic. Her first day of school and she'd already somehow made an enemy. "I don't plan on getting my blood drained," she said.

"I'm sure Emmett didn't plan on it either."

Rae had to admit, that was probably a good point.

"Alyssa! Hey, wait up!" a girl hollered after them.

Alyssa and Rae turned as a short, slender girl with long black hair and a truly enormous backpack sprinted over to them. "Whew, you were booking it!" the girl said. "I could barely catch you!"

"Only because you insist on carrying that thing." Alyssa poked at the giant backpack. "Why, I'll never know."

"And I'll never tell." The girl flashed her a smile, then turned it on Rae. It was such a wide, easy expression that Rae found herself smiling back too. "I'm Vivienne. You must be the new girl. The mysterious Rae."

"That's me," Rae said. "Super mysterious."

"Marvelous. I love a little mystery. Makes things exciting." Vivienne looped her arms through Rae's and Alyssa's, like the three of them had been besties forever, and started marching them down the hall. "I hear Ms. Lockett stuck you in our homeroom. You are in for a treat!"

"Really?" Rae said, letting Vivienne pull her along.

"No, not really. We have Mrs. Murphy, and she. Is. The. *Worst.*"

"She's not the *worst*," Alyssa said.

"Whatevs, lady. You just like her because her son is hot."

Alyssa tugged her arm free, her face scrunched. "I don't care about her son."

"Oh, sorry," Vivienne said. "Too soon? Please tell me you're not still pining after Jeremy, are you?"

"Jeremy?" Rae tried to keep up with all this gossip. She used to be good at this sort of thing, but a year without friends had definitely slowed down her social reflexes. "Is he, like, an ex-boyfriend or something?"

"Or something," Vivienne agreed. "He's over there to the left—no, don't look!"

It was too late. Rae had already looked.

A lanky boy with large brown eyes, curly blond hair, and a green plaid button-up shirt looked back at her, his expression bored. "'Sup?" he said.

"Oh, stop trying to pretend you're cool, Jeremy," Vivienne

huffed, pulling Rae past him. "We don't talk to him," she said.

"I think Alyssa talks to him," Rae said.

Vivienne whirled around. Alyssa was standing in front of Jeremy, her arms crossed awkwardly. She laughed at something he said, and Vivienne sighed and pulled Rae farther down the hall. "She's lost to us. Poor lovesick fool. But don't worry, I'll take good care of you."

"Um, thanks, Vivienne."

"Anytime. You can call me Vivi, by the way. I heard you wanted to join cross-country?"

Rae blinked. "Um, yeah." She'd always been good at running; she'd planned on trying out for the team back at her old school before everything went bad. "How'd you know?"

"Alyssa heard her mom talking to your mom about it before you arrived. And news travels fast around here." Vivienne grinned. "Alyssa and I are both on the team."

"But I thought tryouts weren't until Saturday."

"Yeah, but I'm pretty much a shoe-in. No brag, just fact."

Rae laughed. Alyssa might not like her, but Vivienne seemed like someone she could be friends with.

Vivienne kept up a near-constant stream of chatter as they headed down the hall, stopping only briefly at the lockers to drop off their backpacks. Rae mostly just listened, allowing Vivienne's conversation to carry her along. It made things much easier, and before she knew it, they were in homeroom. "You can sit there," Vivienne said, pointing at the desk next to hers.

Rae took it, and a few seconds later Alyssa hurried inside,

stopping when she saw Rae. "Um, that's actually my seat," she began, just as second bell shrieked down the hall.

"Take your seats," the teacher at the front ordered. "That means you, Miss Lockett."

Alyssa frowned but took a seat at a desk a few rows over.

"Whoops," Rae said. "She looks a little mad."

"She'll get over it." Vivienne waved a hand casually. "It's your first day. You should be comfortable!"

But Rae could practically feel Alyssa glaring at her from the back. Comfortable. Yeah, right.

A boy stepped inside the classroom. Rae sat up straighter, recognizing him immediately as her neighbor from across the street. Once again he was wearing all black, from his T-shirt to his skinny jeans. The only color on him came from his beat-up grayish-white sneakers and the gemstones on his thick silver rings. Even his hair was black. It was spiked up around his head, but not like he styled it intentionally, more like he ran fingers through it instead of a comb.

He met Rae's eyes across the room. When she didn't immediately look away, he raised both eyebrows, like some kind of challenge, and stared until Rae turned away, her face burning.

"That's Caden Price," Vivienne whispered.

"He lives across the street from me," Rae said.

"Oh. You'll want to watch out, then. He's . . . well. Kind of a weirdo."

"Weirdo how?" Seemed sort of ominous in a town where everything appeared to be a little weird. "I mean, I did see a sign in his yard for Paranormal Price."

"Oh yeah, that. His mom has a ghost-hunting business."

"A what?"

"She does exorcisms, house cleansings, stuff like that." Vivienne said it as casually as someone back home might have said, "His mom's an accountant."

"Okay . . . ," Rae said.

"This town is super haunted," Vivienne added.

Rae laughed awkwardly.

"You'll see," Vivienne said, all cryptic. "But anyhow, about nine months ago, his older brother vanished. Just poof! Gone."

Rae frowned.

"Lots of people think Caden did it," Vivienne continued. "Chopped his brother up and stuffed him in the walls. Especially since the police questioned him. Multiple times."

"Is that what you think?"

Vivienne shrugged. "Hard to know."

The announcements crackled on, long and droning. Rae barely heard them, her attention focused on the back of Caden's head. She knew what it was like to have a family member vanish mysteriously—the way rumors would pile up around you higher and higher until you were buried in them, and even you weren't sure what the truth was anymore. For one treacherous second, her heart ached, and she wanted to get up and talk to this boy. Find out his truth. Tell him she understood . . .

But she turned away from him.

She'd made her choice to blend in when she moved here, and she wasn't about to look back now. "So, what class do you have first?" she asked Vivienne, once the announcements ended.

"I have—"

Bzzt! Bzzt! Bzzt!

The alarm sounded, loud and jarring, then was replaced by a new message blaring at top volume from the loudspeaker. "Warning. This is a code yellow. All students to stay in homeroom for a head count. I repeat, every student to remain where they are."

Students looked around, as if they were doing their own head count, checking on their friends. Whispers filled the room like waves crashing, and Rae could practically feel the anxiety rising around her. "What's a code yellow?" she asked.

Vivienne looked worried, her eyebrows drawing together. "It means another student has gone missing."

"Does that, um, happen often around here?"

"No, not very often," Vivienne said. "We only usually lose a student or two each year."

"*What?* You lose students every *year*?" Rae gripped the edges of her desk.

"Yes, but this year?" Vivienne said, leaning closer. "This year it's been worse."

4.
CADEN

Caden had never really loved school. Even before Aiden vanished, it had been something to endure. And today, with yet another student missing, it was worse than normal. He could feel the rumors flowing all around him, thick and sticky like blood.

No one said them to his face, of course. They were all too scared of him. But that made it worse.

At least today was almost over.

He sighed and sank lower in his seat as the bus rumbled down the road. Behind him, someone whispered the most recent rumor to their friend, that Caden wore his brother's ashes in a pouch around his neck.

Caden's hand brushed the small leather pouch tied around his neck, resting next to the pendant he always wore. *Not ashes, just salt,* he wanted to say. But that wouldn't really make him less weird, even for this town, so he just stayed quiet and pretended he couldn't hear. It was harder to ignore the feeling of everyone's emotions pressing in on him like people in a too-crowded elevator. Suspicion like a wire-haired brush scraping relentlessly against his skin; glee at this next bit of gossip like tiny soapy bubbles; fear vibrating around him in small, chaotic waves.

For as long as Caden could remember, he'd always been able to sense people's emotions. Sometimes it was a flash of color, other times almost a physical sensation. He used to think everyone could do it. After all, when he was little, no one else seemed to notice there was anything different about him. But that all changed in first grade.

Caden touched his pendant, remembering the day he'd learned that his abilities scared other people.

He'd burst into his mom's study, sobbing so hard he could barely breathe. His mom had taken one look at him and put her tarot cards aside, listening as he told her how no one wanted to play with him anymore. First Josh Hemlock had shoved him during math class after he told everyone about Josh's fear of the buttons they were counting. And then Emily Windsor had officially sworn never to speak to him again after he let slip that she had a secret crush on Jeremy Bentley. She'd called him a freak and a mind reader and warned everyone from getting too close to him.

After that, no one wanted anything to do with him. He'd spent recess playing by himself.

His mom had dried his cheeks on the sleeve of her sweater.

My poor boy. She'd pulled him into her lap and wrapped her arms around him like he was a baby. *Remember what I said about secrets?*

But it's not a secret. It's obvious.

To you, maybe. But that's because you have a special gift. She'd brushed his hair back from his forehead. *A very rare and wonderful gift.*

Do you and Aiden have it too?

No, we don't. The only other person I know who could feel people's emotions the way you can is my mother.

Caden had only met his grandmother once. If she was the only other one, then he was practically alone. *Can I get rid of it?*

No, honey. It's a part of you. And someday you'll appreciate it.

Caden had thought of how everyone had played basketball without him at recess. Even though he was one of the best players in the class, no one had wanted him on their team. What if they never wanted him on their teams now? What if he always got picked last, or worse, not at all? *I just want to be like everyone else,* he had said, frustrated. *Why can't I be like them?*

Because you're a Price. It's a heavy burden. She'd sighed. *Someday you'll understand exactly how heavy. But for now, your dad and I can teach you to shield yourself so you can keep most of those emotions out.* She'd worked with him on a few exercises, and then she'd given him his talisman. *To help you focus your energy, and for protection. And to remind you,* she'd said.

Remind me of what?

Of who you are. And who you belong to.

Caden dropped his hand, letting the memory fade away. He didn't need the reminder; he'd learned how to block out the emotions of others, but the damage had already been done. No one wanted to be friends with the kid who could read minds. And so even though he was very careful about what he said and he didn't give away any other secrets, he still spent recess playing alone.

The only kid who wanted to hang out with him was his brother. He'd been the one to teach Caden how to block out people as well as emotions. *You don't need other people*, he'd said. *You have me.*

Only now his brother was gone too. And Caden was completely alone.

He didn't want to think anymore, especially about his brother, so he pulled a sketchbook out of his backpack and emptied his own emotions out, turning his mind as blank as the page in front of him. He doodled idly as the trees blurred past. First just shapes: swirls and lines forming strange patterns that twisted out to the corners of the page. Then objects: a moving van, a ring of salt, a girl with large brown eyes . . .

The bus driver stopped in front of Caden's house. He closed his sketchpad and hurriedly stuffed it into his backpack, then stood up.

"Both of you, be careful," the driver warned.

Caden glanced at the new girl hovering just behind him, her hands clenched around the straps of her backpack.

"Code yellow," the driver added. As if they hadn't been told that all day. Ever since Brandi hadn't turned up for breakfast with her family that morning. She already had a reputation for sneaking out in the evenings—Caden had even seen her do it multiple times from his porch swing—so everyone figured she'd slipped out of the house after dinner to meet some friends, and then vanished.

That wasn't too unusual for Whispering Pines; their school had a reputation for losing the occasional student. But last year they'd lost *four* students, including his brother. And even though the other three were found again eventually, according to the news, they'd been mutilated and were still being treated for some kind of trauma.

Now Caden knew there'd been a fifth disappearance: thirteen-year-old Peter McCurley, missing since late December. And with the attacks on those three kids this summer, and then Brandi's disappearance today, people were beginning to worry that things here were getting worse. Which meant they'd start looking for a scapegoat. Since Brandi had lived on his street, Caden knew he'd be looked at with extra suspicion.

The bus door opened, and Caden stepped out into the muggy afternoon air. There was a strange heaviness to it, almost a physical weight. It made him uneasy, like the sky was pressing down on him.

The new girl followed him out, and the door shut, the bus pulling away.

Caden carefully kept his shields up, but he could still feel a hint of grief from the Jensen home down the road. He turned away, trying to block it all out, and caught the new girl staring at him, like he'd caught her several times today. Not as if she was afraid, but more like he was a puzzle she was trying to solve.

He wasn't sure how he felt about that.

"What?" he asked.

"I was just wondering if you really murdered your brother and stuffed him in the walls of your house."

Caden raised his eyebrows. Bold. That was a refreshing change. "Well, I would have," he said casually, "but our walls were too thin."

To his surprise, she smiled. She had an interesting mix of wide, gentle brown eyes, like a deer's, with an angular jaw and very defined chin. But when she smiled, it took all the hardness out of her face. "I'm Rae," she said.

"Caden."

Her smile wavered, then slipped off her face. "What do you think happened to Brandi?" she asked.

"I don't know."

"Do you think they'll find her?"

He glanced back at Brandi's house. The lights were off, shutters pulled closed, like the whole house was in mourning. He knew what her family was going through. "I really hope so."

"Me too." Rae adjusted her backpack. "Well, I'll see you around, Caden." She lifted one hand in a little wave, then turned and headed across the street. He stood there, watching until she disappeared behind the trees that lined the front of her house. And then he stood a little longer until he heard the sound of her front door opening and closing, just to be sure she made it in.

It was a code yellow day, after all.

He turned and headed up his own driveway. It was long, unpaved, and steep, a real fun thing to shovel in the winter. Every year his dad talked about getting it paved, and every year he didn't.

Maybe this year, since they wouldn't have as many people around to help. This past winter had been pretty hard on them.

Aiden had vanished just after the first big snowfall exactly nine months ago today. The same day as Peter McCurley.

Caden reached his front door and paused. Something didn't feel right. It reminded him of a few years ago when he'd argued with his brother, and later discovered that Aiden had moved all of the furniture in his bedroom exactly one inch to the left. Not enough to be obvious, just enough to make Caden feel off-balance.

Around the house, the trees seemed to still, their branches quiet, their leaves no longer rustling. There was no wind at all.

Caden swallowed, one hand snaking up to rest against the pendant around his neck. It felt warm, and he couldn't tell if the heat was from his skin or something else.

He glanced at his mom's car sitting alone in the driveway, then eased the front door open. The house smelled like sandalwood and lavender, and immediately the hairs on the back of his neck prickled. His mom burned that incense to help clear her mind and mentally prepare herself before summoning a spirit. He left the door open, slid his sneakers off without untying them, and hurried silently past the kitchen.

Caden fought to keep his emotions calm so his presence wouldn't be obvious to . . . whatever might be there. Because it certainly felt like *something* was in the house. Something that didn't belong. As he crept down the long hall, his eyes on the closed door of his mother's study at the far end, he felt like he was wading deeper into the ocean, the temperature dropping with every reluctant step. The space directly in front of the door seemed as cold as if he'd arrived at depths so far beneath the surface, the sunlight never reached them.

He grasped the doorknob, bracing for ice. But instead, the metal felt hot against his fingers. Painfully hot. The gemstones on his rings flashed and sparked, and he snatched his hand back. He gritted his teeth and gripped the knob again, this time ignoring the pain as he turned it sharply.

The door flew open. Caden almost fell into the room before he caught himself.

It was dark, the shades drawn thick over the windows, only a single candle burning in the center of the room for light. Caden's mom was sitting in front of it, chanting something too soft for him to hear. She held a small brass bowl cupped between her hands. Her chanting rose and she lifted the bowl, tipping it gently over the candle, the flame sputtering and dancing as the liquid inside dripped slowly into it.

A sharp coppery smell filled the air. Blood.

Unease curled in Caden's gut like a snake as the pressure in the air built, growing thick and heavy. He looked past his mother at the tall dark mirror looming behind the candle. The dancing flame reflected in the glass was all *wrong*, the fire stretching, forming lines, slowly outlining a silhouette . . .

Caden darted forward before his mind had even registered what he'd seen. Dimly he heard the study door slam shut behind him, his mom's voice growing louder. The candle in front of her sputtered and roared, the flames changing from yellow and orange to a deep, dark purple, the outline in the mirror growing clearer, hands reaching, glass rippling—

"No!" Caden yelled. "Go away, you are *not* welcome here!" And he stepped past his mother and blew out the flame, plunging the room into total darkness.

She went quiet immediately. They both did. And in the ringing silence, Caden thought he heard footsteps, soft and close, and a whisper of laughter. Invisible fingers traced through his hair, then were gone.

He felt his mom get up, and a second later the lights turned on, flooding the room. "What," she said slowly, furiously, "do you think you're doing?"

"What am *I* doing?" Caden rose from his crouch by the still-smoking candle. "What are *you* doing?"

"You know better than to interrupt in the middle! You know how dangerous—"

"Dangerous?" Caden stalked toward her. Now that it was over, his fear had been snuffed out like the candle's flame, replaced by a cold, hard anger. "Yes, I *know* how dangerous it is! Isn't that why you promised you'd be more careful?"

"I *am* being careful!" she insisted, but her cheeks had gone pink, and she wouldn't meet his eyes.

"You're using blood magic," Caden said quietly. They both looked at her left arm, where blood was still oozing from a shallow cut. She turned away from him, going to her dresser and pulling out a length of white cloth, then pressing it against the wound. Caden wondered if she was going to ignore him now, pretend this conversation was over. He widened his stance. He wasn't going any-where. This was too important to gloss over.

"I'm looking for Peter," she said finally. "His parents deserve to know what happened to him."

What happened to him. That sounded depressingly final. Caden looked down at his mom's setup, noticing the blue hat sitting next to the bloodstained bowl. "And did you find out?"

She glanced at him, then away again, her expression troubled. "Not yet," she whispered. Caden tried sensing her emotions, but she had them tightly shielded. She was hiding something.

"What are you really doing?" he asked. "This isn't a spell for seeking. It's a summoning spell." He indicated the mirror, the candle, and the ring of salt his mom had poured around both of them. It was as if his mom had deliberately set up a beacon so any-thing out there could find her. With her blood augmenting the sig-nal, it would be very powerful.

Her lower lip trembled, her black hair tumbling loose around her face and shoulders. At thirteen, Caden was already a few inches taller than her, and for a second he felt almost like their roles had flipped. Like *she* was the child. "I *am* seeking," she said. "I just . . . I need to find him." They both knew she wasn't talking about Peter anymore. She took a breath that sounded dangerously close to a sob.

Now it was Caden's turn to look away. He had told his mom what he saw happen to his brother . . . He had told both his parents. But since he still wasn't sure exactly what he'd seen, it didn't help much. And it wasn't information the police believed either.

And there were a few details he'd left out too. Like why his brother hadn't come back.

His eyes trailed over the protective salt circle, meant to keep the spell—and the things it might call—contained. It was smudged, a small gap in one side. Caden's heart clenched like a fist, but he forced himself to relax. His mom had probably broken the circle when she stood to turn on the lights. It was nothing.

But he remembered the feel of those ghostly fingers in his hair, that laugh, and hunched his shoulders.

His brother was gone. He *knew* Aiden was gone.

But he didn't know if it would be forever. He was afraid Aiden would somehow make it back.

And when Aiden did, Caden was sure he'd want revenge.

5.

RAE

After dinner Rae made a beeline for her room. She checked the time—a little before seven—and sat down at her desk. They'd sold most of their furniture when they moved and bought new things out here, but Rae had begged and pleaded to keep her same desk. It wasn't just that it was the exact right size, or that she liked the faint piney smell it still gave off, or even how solid it seemed, like it would be able to survive an earthquake with barely a scratch. She did love those aspects, but mostly she loved how easy it was to hide things inside it.

She studied the corkboard attached to the back of the desk. Even though she'd finished unpacking most of her room, her board was still pretty sparse. She used to have tons of photographs of her and Taylor, and a few of their other friends, but she'd ripped those into the smallest pieces she could long ago. Now all she had up was a photo of Ava dressed as a pirate, and another of her and Ava with their mom and dad standing in front of the Grand Canyon, their last big family trip together. Aside from those, she'd pinned up a couple articles about running, and a picture of baby foxes she'd cut out of a magazine because they were just too cute.

She glanced at her closed bedroom door, then ran her hand along the cork backboard. Her fingers found the hidden latches on the sides, and with a soft *click*, she slipped them down and pulled the board free, setting it aside on the floor.

Her *real* corkboard stared back at her now, cluttered with articles that had nothing to do with running.

Rae believed that any good, solid investigation needed a paper trail. Articles online could vanish; computers could be wiped clean. Or worse, her mom could decide it was time to snoop through her files again. So Rae was careful to erase her browsing histories, and she kept a hard copy of anything important hidden away here.

Like the article detailing the disappearance of two engineers last year from a small northern California town. Engineers who had both been assigned to the same contract, working on a project called Operation Gray Bird. The article wasn't clear what, exactly, their objective had been. No one seemed to know.

Rae knew, though. Her dad had talked about it, probably more than he was supposed to.

He told her they were working on something top secret, some kind of aircraft, trying to reverse-engineer its technology. Specifically, her dad's team had been in charge of figuring out its energy source, trying to see if they could take it apart and replicate it. But something had gone wrong, and her dad went from being very excited about the project to abruptly deciding he needed to quit.

Rae had her theories about why. Just as she knew what had happened to him afterward, even if she couldn't prove it. Yet.

Can you even believe what Rae thinks happened to her father? She's, like, some kind of conspiracy freak. I always knew it. She's so weird.

I heard her father ran off and found himself a new family. I would too, if I were him.

So, so weird.

But Rae knew what she'd seen.

She looked at that article, and all the ones she'd found that were at all related. Rumors of unidentified flying objects, of abductions, of bizarre phenomena. Stories of people vanishing from their homes and lives. Accusations of government cover-ups and secret military technology. These were the stories she cared about. Her secret obsession.

She might be a new Rae out here, but that didn't mean she was giving up on her quest to eventually find her dad. She'd never stop searching until she did. She only hoped that if her dad found his own way back, he'd be able to trace them to Whispering Pines.

She looked at the single photograph pinned to this board: a picture of her standing with her dad, his arm around her shoulders. They were both smiling, but not like a posed, camera-ready smile. More like they'd been sharing an inside joke. Her dad was wearing his favorite shirt, the ugly green-and-purple plaid that Rae and Ava had picked out for him together a year before he disappeared.

There was another picture pinned behind it, but even here, in the safety of her room, she didn't dare pull it out. It was the only proof she had. Instead, she thought of Brandi. Brandi, who liked strawberry ice cream and owned a ferret and planned to be a pilot when she grew up so her family could travel wherever they wanted. Brandi, with her chapped lips and her gap-toothed smile and her warm brown eyes. Brandi, who was missing.

But missing did not mean gone for good. Rae *had* to believe that. She might not be able to search for her dad right now, but she *could* search for Brandi.

She didn't know enough about this town yet to know where to look, so she started her search with the day's paper.

The front page had a feel-good piece about Green On!'s donations to a homeless shelter and an animal rescue agency. Beneath that was an article about a local playground closed on account of squirrel activity, which seemed weird. And then a whole write-up on the local university basketball team, the Malamutes, and how they were already gearing up for the new season. Rae flipped to the next page, and stopped on one of the strangest articles she'd ever seen. And that was really saying something.

SERIAL EYE SNATCHER IN OUR MIDST?

Whispering Pines, CT. Three months ago, four children, ages 10, 12, 13, and 14, were playing an innocent game of hide-and-seek when they were viciously attacked. Someone targeted the oldest child first, removing her eyes before moving on to the others. Only the 10-year-old escaped unscathed. Although she claimed to have seen the attacker, she was unable to provide credible information, and authorities are no closer to discovering the cause of this brutal and unexpected assault.

While only the eyes were taken, the mental trauma has been so great that none of the victims have been able to give any information that would help identify the perpetrator either. Doctor William Anderson, who gave an initial assessment of the injured parties, stated, "Eyes are the windows to the soul, and I'm afraid both of those were taken from them."

This isn't the first attack of this nature. Six months ago, the same phenomenon struck three other children. For now, all those affected are being treated at a private lab owned by Green On!, where it is hoped they will eventually make some sort of recovery. However, despite the company's history of excellent medical and scientific achievements, there are some, like Doctor Anderson, who believe these victims should be treated elsewhere.

"We have no idea what they're doing with these kids up in their labs," claims Anderson, who has a history of opposing Green On! and the good work they are doing for this community—good work like providing free, clean energy to any Whispering Pines resident willing to take part in their energy monitoring system.

Alan Dietrich, head of PR for Green On!, had this to say: "There will always be those few misguided individuals who don't understand or appreciate what we are trying to do. But that's fine. We know that most of the citizens of Whispering Pines are behind us."

Meanwhile, local law enforcement will be implementing a strict curfew for everyone under eighteen. "If it's getting dark, you need to head inside," says police chief Paul Moser. "And honestly? I'd recommend those over eighteen stay indoors too."

When asked who or what he believes is doing this, Moser had no new insights at this time.

Rae carefully cut out the article and pinned it to her board, then continued through the rest of the paper. There were several other articles of note, like one about a sinkhole that had opened over the summer behind Dana S. Middle School. She skimmed through it, stopping on the quote in the middle:

"It appears to be bottomless," claims one source who refused to be named. "I've been throwing my garbage into it every day since it appeared, and so far no one has noticed a thing. It's great."

Rae shook her head and flipped to another article, this one about the strange unreliability of cell service near the Watchful Woods. Several townsfolk had complained. There was a petition to get to the bottom of it.

Rae cut that article out too, and pinned it to her board with the others.

Eye snatchers, bottomless sinkholes, and missing students. Just what kind of place *was* this?

Brandi had been the first person to be nice to Rae in a year, and Rae was determined to help find her if she could. But now the first hint of worry crept in with her resolve. Because Brandi wasn't just a friend. She was also her next-door neighbor. Her next-door neighbor who had been taken from her home.

Rae sat back in her chair and stared out her bedroom window at the trees just visible outside, and felt like they were somehow staring back.

6.
CADEN

Dinner that evening was an exercise in torture for Caden, with his family acting like everything was totally normal. His mom pretended she was the perfect housewife, serving him and his dad a slightly burnt casserole, while his dad pretended to be the perfect working stiff, rambling about some boring programming problem he was having, and how the guys at work wanted him to come golfing with them this weekend. And Caden pretended to care, and pretended to eat, and counted down the moments until he could escape back to his room.

Later, he did some of his homework, but his thoughts kept drifting back to Aiden.

He used to adore his older brother. Smart, good-looking, talented. Aiden had been everything Caden wanted to be. Everyone in school admired him. The teachers loved him, the other boys all wanted to be friends with him, and he'd started dating by the time he was thirteen. Those relationships never lasted, but that didn't really matter to Aiden.

That was the thing that Caden hadn't realized at first. None of it mattered to his brother. He didn't care about the people at his school, about his so-called friends or girlfriends, his grades, nothing. All he cared about was the magic. The power.

We are so much better than all of them, he'd say. *These sheep, they have no idea what's out there. But you and me? We get it.*

It made Caden feel like he didn't even need friends. He had his brother, and both of them were better than the others. And someday the two of them would take over the Price family business together.

But everything changed when Caden got to middle school. His brother was in eighth grade, the top of the school, and Caden was in fifth, the bottom. And he did see all the things he'd expected to see around his brother: Aiden's adoring fans, the students who followed him around, his amazing basketball wins. But Caden also noticed the whispers, the fear. The rumors that bad things happened to the people Aiden didn't like.

Like when Vanessa Sanchez broke up with him . . . and that afternoon the brakes in her mom's car stopped working on the way home from school, and they ended up plowing into a snowdrift and almost dying. Or when Mark Peterson got in a fight with Aiden over a pickup basketball game . . . and his house caught fire that night.

Gossip. Lies. Caden was sure of it. All of those things were just coincidences. There was no way his brother had anything to do with any of them.

But then there was the incident with Zachary Mitchell.

Caden hated thinking about it. Even now, two years later, he burned with humiliation. After first grade he hadn't bothered trying to make friends, even when the rumors about his mind reading faded and his classmates started inviting him to play on their teams at recess again. By then he'd decided he didn't need any of them; he preferred to do things by himself. So people learned to leave him alone.

But Zachary Mitchell was different. He'd moved to Whispering Pines in the summer before fifth grade and had taken an instant dislike to Caden. Zachary didn't believe in ghosts—his grandfather had been a famous skeptic—and he told everyone often and loudly how Caden's family was taking advantage of people.

Caden dealt with Zachary's subtle taunts, his attempts at tripping him, his jeering looks. It wasn't that big a deal, and mostly Caden ignored them.

But Aiden had noticed. And one evening, after Zachary caught Caden in the face with a well-timed soccer ball, Aiden had cornered Caden in his room. At first Aiden hadn't said anything, just looked at the bruise on his brother's face.

It's nothing, Caden had insisted.

And Aiden had been furious. *That* worm *hurt you. That's not nothing. So what are you going to do about it?*

I don't know.

Let me give you some advice, Aiden had said. *If someone hurts you, you don't just take an eye for an eye. You take the whole head.*

Caden had shrugged that off. And then a week later, on a cold November morning, he'd heard people yelling and laughing down the hall. When he'd turned the corner, there was Zachary, slapping himself in the face.

It had been funny. Everyone was laughing. Even Zachary, at first. But then he kept going. It was like his hand had been possessed; he couldn't stop. Each time, the hit was harder, the sound echoing down the hall as the students around him grew quiet.

Caden put down his pen.

He didn't want to think about it, but the image of Zachary's face floated in his mind. Puffy and bruised and red, like raw hamburger, his eyes swollen shut, his lip split. He'd been sobbing, begging someone to stop him. And standing nearby, smiling, was Aiden.

Aiden never admitted that he was responsible. But Caden had known. Somehow his brother had done it, because he could do anything.

Part of Caden had been happy, because Aiden had done this to protect *him*. But Caden was ashamed of that part, and sickened by the gleeful way Aiden had dispensed his version of justice. It finally made Caden see his brother for who he really was. And when Aiden started talking about another dimension, and how he wanted to tear a hole into it and steal its energy, Caden had known he'd be able to accomplish that, too. Just as he'd known his brother should never be given more power.

Caden sighed and pushed his books away from him. He wasn't

going to get any homework done tonight. His thoughts were too distracted. He'd be better off getting some extra sleep and tackling the work in the morning.

He left the desk lamp on and checked that his windows were shut and locked. Then he crawled under the covers, closed his eyes, and drifted to sleep.

Caden walked down a long, dark wooden stairway. He hugged the walls, trying to still his noisy breath. Why was his breathing so loud? And *painful*, each gasp wheezing from his ragged lungs. His legs shook as he took a tentative step down, hoping there was another exit—a door or an unboarded window—even as he feared there would be nothing there but darkness and a dead end.

Creeeeak.

His heart hammered against his rib cage, sweat trickling down his spine. He knew he shouldn't look, but he had no control over his body, and he turned anyhow. A shadow stood at the top of the stairs, outlined by a trickle of dim light filtering in from above. It didn't move, and Caden shrank lower against the wall, praying the darkness of the stairwell would hide him. He tried holding his breath, but tiny gasping wheezes still slipped out.

Please, please, he thought at that shadow, *just walk by. Don't come down here* . . . He reached a shaky hand for his protective talisman, but it wasn't there, his hand closing on nothing. Shock rippled through him. It felt like he'd tried to take another step, and missed the stair.

"I know you're there," the shadow said, seeming to grow larger until it blocked the whole top of the stairwell. "You can't hide from me any longer, Rae."

Rae?

Caden sat up in bed, sweat soaking his T-shirt. He fumbled for the pendant sitting warm against his chest, his fingers closing over it gratefully. "Just a dream," he whispered. "A dream."

But it wasn't. Not entirely. Caden had prophetic dreams only occasionally, but he recognized one when he had it. They ended when he noticed that he was in someone else's perspective. And the dreams were always a warning.

He blinked in the darkness of his room before realizing how that was wrong too. He'd left a light on. He *always* left a light on. It must have burned out in the night. He closed his eyes and opened them, trying to blink away the darkness, but the shades blocked out all the moonlight.

"Caden."

A singsong voice breathed his name, no louder than the wind.

Caden froze, every nerve in his body instantly plunged in a wash of icy fear. He wanted to pull the blankets over his head and hide, like he used to do when he was little. But now that he was older, he knew blankets couldn't save him from the things in the dark. So he lunged forward instead, his fingers grasping for the reading lamp on his desk. They hit the firm porcelain, and the lamp slid to the floor.

Crack!

Cursing, Caden stumbled toward the thick curtains at his window, frantically shoving them, almost ripping them down in the process. Beautiful, glorious moonlight filled the room, illuminating the fact that he was completely alone.

It took a few more minutes before his breathing slowed, his racing heart easing back into its normal rhythm. He looked at his sad, cracked lamp and shook his head. There was no hope for it; he would just have to get another one.

He flipped the light switch next to his howling wolf poster, squinting against the sudden brightness, and glanced at his bed. A tangle of blankets lay beside it, his comfy pillow spilled next to them on the floor. He picked those up, and then he turned and made himself check the perimeter of his room. He'd placed protective gemstones in all four corners, and three of them were exactly where they should be.

But the fourth, the one that was supposed to sit in the corner between his closet and his shelf of horror novels, had moved. Someone or some*thing* had rolled it several inches farther into the room.

Caden's heart sounded unnaturally loud in his ears as he bent and picked up the rose quartz. It was surprisingly warm, and he curled his fingers around it, then gently laid it back in its corner where it belonged.

7.
RAE

Rae woke up all at once, the way she did lately in this new place, in this new room. The light hit her window strangely, and her bed didn't feel right, and the air smelled different. Just little things, but enough to make her feel like a pebble in a jar of marbles.

She sat up, pushing that thought away. She would make herself fit in. Yesterday no one at school had called her names or chased her down the hallway, so she was already way ahead of where she'd been at her last school. In fact, thanks to Vivienne, she'd sat in the middle of the most crowded table at lunch and was quickly becoming friends with a handful of other girls.

That made her think of Brandi, her first almost friend here. Rae glanced at her desk, her decoy corkboard firmly in place over her research. Then she got dressed and headed downstairs to the kitchen, where she could hear the water running and the low hum of her mom's new favorite oldies station, Big C 103.

Her mom stood in front of the sink wearing baggy jeans and a faded blue T-shirt, her hair pulled up in a messy bun, a dish towel clutched in one hand and a dirty dish in the other. She could have been posed like that for one minute or several hours, her brown eyes fixed on some invisible speck straight ahead.

"*And now, back to the greatest hits of the eighties, nineties, and—*"

Rae clicked the radio off. "Maybe you should save some of that water? You've probably destroyed a whole fishy habitat by now."

Her mom blinked, then blinked again, finally focusing on Rae. She smiled. "Sorry, love. Good morning. You ready for school?"

"Mostly," Rae said.

Her mom nodded and began scrubbing at the dish, as if she were a show that had been temporarily set on pause. After it was spotless, she set it inside the dishwasher. Rae used to argue with her that the whole point of a dishwasher was so you wouldn't have to wash your dishes yourself, but her mom did it anyhow. By now, Rae had given up trying to stop her.

"Cross-country tryouts are on Saturday," Rae said, wanting to break the silence.

"That's nice." Her mom picked up another dish. Scrub, scrub, scrub, rinse, and into the dishwasher.

"Assuming they aren't canceled. You know, because . . . because of Brandi." Rae swallowed.

"Hmm."

Rae was suddenly irritated. She'd told her mom about Brandi.

After all, it wasn't very often that she made a friend. At least, lately. "You know, Brandi?" she demanded. "Our next-door neighbor?"

"Uh-huh."

"She vanished yesterday. No one knows what happened to her."

"Good to make new friends."

Rae sighed. It was going to be one of those conversations. Sometimes Rae felt like she was her own radio station with the volume turned slightly too low. Her mom pretended to hear her without actually listening to what she said. She'd been like that ever since Rae's dad went missing, almost like part of her had gone with him.

"Morning!" Ava chirped, skipping down the stairs. "Mom, mind if I take the car tomorrow?" She grinned. "I'm asking preemptively. As requested." It had been a constant fight ever since Ava got her driver's license last year; she would ask for the car last minute and then get mad when it wasn't available.

"Aren't you becoming responsible?" Their mom smiled, her attention snapping back into focus now that Ava was around, and Rae realized it wasn't that part of her mom had left with her dad at all. It was more that her mom acted like maybe *Rae* had left with her dad. Like she wasn't really there either.

Rae scowled.

She missed the way her family was like before. When her dad disappeared, it was as if the glue holding them together had gone too, and they were all drifting further and further apart from one another. When she found her dad again, would they be able to go back to what they'd been? Or had her family changed forever?

"And sure, you can take the car," their mom continued, "as long as you take your sister to her appointment tomorrow afternoon."

Rae's scowl deepened. "My what?"

"With your new psychologist." Her mom went back to scrubbing another plate. "We talked about this."

"Yeah, we did! And I said I didn't need to see a therapist anymore."

Her mom shrugged. "Humor me."

"Mom. Seriously."

"Go for a month, okay? Just during this transition. Please, love?"

Rae shook her head. Therapy sessions belonged to the old Rae, the one who hadn't known to keep her mouth shut about what she'd seen. Here she was supposed to be a new person. How could she go talk to someone if she didn't plan on actually talking?

"Meet at Kat's Café tomorrow after school?" Ava asked Rae. "That way I can avoid the unwashed masses of middle schoolers."

"Only some of them are unwashed," Rae grumbled. "And I don't know where that place is."

"It's just across the street from your school. You can't miss it." Ava glanced at their mom, but she was into her dishes again. "Tell you what. You agree to meet me there, and I'll give you cash to pick us both up a drink and a sandwich."

Rae hesitated, but in the end, she did love a good mocha, and her mom almost never let her have one. "Fine, whatever." Rae turned her back on her sister and rummaged in the cupboards for a bowl, spoon, and box of cereal. It wasn't that long ago that Rae would have been excited to meet her sister at a café. But these days she wasn't really speaking much to Ava. Their mom might have made them move, but it was Ava who'd dragged them so far away. All because she just *had* to go to WestConn University next year. As if there weren't perfectly good universities much closer.

Rae knew it was really because her sister had given up on their dad. She hadn't been quite as close to him as Rae had been, so she'd written him off and gone on with her life, and now she wanted everyone else to do the same thing. It made Rae so angry. She jabbed her spoon into her cereal and took a bite.

"Don't you want milk with that?" Ava asked.

Rae chewed the dry stuff and swallowed it down. "No," she lied. "I like it this way." She took another bite, even though it tasted like sugary sawdust.

"If you say so. See you later. Bye, Mom!"

"Bye, honey."

Rae waited until her sister was gone and then grabbed the milk. Her mom didn't say anything else to her as Rae poured it and ate the rest of her cereal. Instead, the kitchen filled with the sounds of Rae's crunching and her mom's dish washing.

Rae finished eating as quickly as possible, silently handed her mom the bowl and spoon, and headed out to wait for the bus.

The worst part about her mom's lack of interest was that her dad would have been so excited to watch her try out for cross-country. Rae's vision blurred, the trees all running together. She squeezed her eyes shut, breathing slowly through her nose. The last thing she wanted was to be crying when the bus came, but she missed him so much.

He was the one who introduced her to running.

Every year for Thanksgiving, Rae, her sister, and her parents would go on a sunrise hike together. They'd been doing that tradition for as long as Rae could remember, since she was small enough to be carried in a pack.

Four years ago, when she was eight, she'd asked her dad why they only really did hikes once a year.

We hike other times, he said.

Like when?

Like . . . tomorrow. And so the next day, he and Rae had headed out to a park to hike while Ava and her mom slept in. Her dad let her pick the trail, and afterward they'd gone for milkshakes at a nearby diner.

You know, this was a lot of fun, he said. *How about we do it again sometime?* He grinned, his teeth flashing in his beard. He always let it grow in the winter. Rae's mom hated that, but Rae liked how it made him look like a nerdy mountain man, what with his glasses and his tendency to wear too much plaid.

Can we run the downhills? she asked.

Soon they were running every Saturday, and sometimes once or twice during the week too, until her dad got too busy with work. And at the end of fifth grade, when she told him she was thinking of trying out for cross-country the next year, he was delighted. Before he disappeared, he'd already marked all the meets on his calendar so he could make sure he got the time off to go to them.

Rae had taken that calendar from his office the night he didn't come home. It was one of the only things of his she had left.

"Hey," Caden said.

Rae jumped, her eyes flying open.

"Oh, sorry," he said quickly. "I didn't mean to scare you. Apparently, I often have that effect on people."

Rae tried to smile.

Caden's eyebrows drew together, his forehead creasing. "Are you okay?"

"Me? Yeah, totally." She ran the back of her hand over her eyes, trying to be casual about it.

"Because if you want to—"

The bus rumbled to a stop in front of them, the door creaking open. Caden gave her a quick, inscrutable look and then headed on, leaving Rae to follow him.

She paused at the top of the steps, staring out across all those seats. Everyone was looking at her, and she wasn't sure where to sit.

Caden shifted over, leaving space next to him.

Rae looked at that empty seat and hesitated. Caden seemed all right, but he was the school loner. If she sat with him, would she be treated like a loner too? She already knew exactly what that felt like; she didn't want to end up in that same place at this school too. Immediately she felt guilty for being so shallow, but—

"Rae! Over here!" Vivienne waved at her from the middle of the bus.

Rae hurried down the aisle and sank gratefully onto the padded bench next to Vivienne just as the bus began moving again.

"You looked a little lost," Vivienne said. "It was like staring at a baby deer."

"I felt a little lost," Rae admitted. "Thanks for making space for me."

"Oh, anytime. Usually no one sits next to me because of this." Vivienne patted her humongous backpack, wedged in between them. "But you're small enough, I figured we could all fit."

"What do you carry in there?" Rae asked, fascinated by all the bulging pockets. She'd never seen a backpack so full.

"Stuff," Vivienne said casually. "A girl can never be too prepared."

"So, have you heard anything else about Brandi?" Rae asked. "Did they find her?"

"Not yet."

Rae's heart sank. That meant Brandi had been gone for at least twenty-four hours. She knew from her own research that the first forty-eight hours were the most crucial; after that, potential leads dried up as people's memories faded, their information becoming less reliable. And after seventy-two hours, there were usually almost no leads at all.

"Don't look so worried," Vivienne said. "She might turn up tomorrow, or a week from tomorrow." She launched into the newest theories, that Brandi had decided to live in a yurt in the woods— "It's happened before. Not with Brandi, but we've definitely misplaced students that way. Sometimes a yurt, sometimes a tree house, once there was a cave . . ."—to the theory that she'd run off with the lead singer of Seeking Samantha, a local high school band. "I know for a fact she was a huge fan."

"What about the sinkhole?" Rae asked, thinking of the articles she'd read and those bizarro school rules pinned up in the office.

"Which one?" Vivienne asked.

Rae blinked. "Is there more than one?"

"Oh yeah. We have a couple that pop up every once in a while. You know that cave in the woods I mentioned? Supposedly there's a whole cave system attached to it right below the town, and sometimes it gets unstable and the ground will just collapse."

Rae's jaw dropped.

Vivienne laughed. "Relax. It's just a rumor. I mean, it's also totally true, but no biggie."

"So there *are* caves under us?"

"At least a few that I've seen." Vivienne picked at her backpack.

"And . . . and there *are* random sinkholes?"

"Oh yeah, that's indisputable fact."

"So there are random sinkholes, and you said yesterday that one or two students go missing every year," Rae said slowly.

Vivienne nodded.

"And people still live in this town because . . . why?"

Vivienne laughed. "You can't beat the cost of living here. At least, that's what my mom always says. Plus, our schools are really good."

"As long as you make it to graduation day," Rae muttered, wondering if her own mom had done any research at all before moving here. Did she know what a strange place this was?

"Besides, there are a ton of well-paying jobs in the area. I mean, most of them are with Green On!, but still."

"What is Green On!?" From yesterday's paper, Rae knew they had some kind of science lab, but that was it.

"It's this super-large company devoted to coming up with renewable energy sources," Vivienne said. "They employ, like, half the town in some way or other. My mom works for them, in fact. She's kind of a big deal there."

"Oh yeah? What does she do?"

"She heads the nuclear division."

"Oh," Rae said, impressed.

"You know, when she's not working in one of their secret labs." Vivienne said it so offhandedly, Rae couldn't tell if she was joking, but it still sent shivers down her spine. Secret labs? Energy research? It reminded her too much of her dad's project, even though this was on the other side of the country. There was no way any of this had anything to do with him.

"So, this company . . . ," Rae began, right as the bus stopped and Alyssa got on.

"Alyssa! Yoo-hoo!" Vivienne yelled.

Alyssa grinned over at her, but the moment she saw Rae sitting there, her grin slid away, and by the time she reached them, she looked a little annoyed. "I thought you didn't like sharing your seat?"

"No, no." Vivienne waved a hand. "I said my bag doesn't like sharing. But it's okay with Rae-Rae here. She doesn't take up much space."

Rae smiled, sudden happiness filling the cold spot inside her and spilling out.

"You can sit back here with us," a boy called.

Rae craned her neck, recognizing Jeremy a few seats back. He was sitting next to another boy with pale blond hair and dark eyes, his nose long and straight. He was almost too good-looking, like he belonged in a television show. He caught her looking and smiled at her.

Rae looked away, strangely uneasy.

"Don't do it," Vivienne warned Alyssa. "You've been down that road before, my friend. It's ugly and unpaved."

Rae laughed.

"I think I'll take my chances," Alyssa said, shooting them both a look and then heading down the aisle.

Vivienne sighed. "That girl."

"Well, at least you still have me," Rae said, feeling bold.

Vivienne grinned. "I'm glad you moved. I think you'll like it here."

"I think I might," Rae said. And for the first time in over a year, she almost forgot about her missing dad and relaxed as Vivienne chatted away, the rumble of the bus a soothing undercurrent beneath her feet.

8.

CADEN

Caden sat on the bus with his sketchpad open on his lap and listened to Rae chatting with Vivienne Matsuoka like they'd been friends forever. Part of him was envious; what must it be like to move to a new school and make friends with one of the most popular kids so quickly? To fit in immediately?

He didn't care about things like that. He didn't need friends. He was totally fine on his own.

"Sure you are."

Caden glanced around. No one was there. For a second, he could have sworn he heard his brother's voice. He started reaching for his pendant, then caught himself and clasped his hands in his lap instead. Because it was ridiculous to be afraid. His brother was gone.

"Maybe I'm not as gone as you think. Or . . . as you wish."

Caden let himself grab his pendant this time, holding it so

tightly the stone dug into the palm of his hand. He was just tired, and imagining things. He squeezed his eyes shut and desperately hoped that was true, trying not to remember the feeling he'd had last night. That his brother was in the room, watching him.

For one trembling second, he pictured Aiden the way he'd been in that final moment: face full of triumph, dark eyes reflecting back a pulsing sickly yellow light. Caden remembered how his brother had turned toward him, holding his arms wide. He couldn't resist gloating. *I told you I'd do it.* But he never should have turned his back, because he didn't see the creatures coming up behind him.

Only Caden saw them.

"And you didn't warn me."

This time Caden was sure he heard his brother. He slowly, slowly opened his eyes and turned his head to look, tensing. Nothing. Just empty air. He sagged back against the window, heart still beating way too fast. "I *did* warn you," he whispered. "You just didn't listen."

"Hey, kid!" the bus driver barked, and Caden jumped. "You getting off here, or what?"

Caden glanced out the window. Everyone else was already off the bus. "Sorry," he mumbled, standing and hurrying outside. He could hear a few kids laughing as he walked past them, but that didn't matter.

Caden ducked into homeroom just as the final bell tolled.

"Cutting it close there, Mr. Price," Mrs. Murphy said as he slipped into his usual seat near the front. He didn't answer her. His head ached, the vein in his temple throbbing like it was trying to escape. He dropped his face into his hands and tried to focus.

"What a weirdo," he heard Alyssa mutter.

He tried not to take it personally, especially since he actually felt a little bad for Alyssa. She was like an actor desperate for more lines, always pretending she knew the most sensitive information, that she was in on everything, when really she just wanted approval. Whose approval, no one really knew, and Caden doubted that Alyssa knew either. And meanwhile, her best friend was slowly drifting away from her.

"Oh, stop with all that empathetic nonsense. You hate her." His brother ran ghostly fingers over Caden's forehead, cool and soothing. *"This has always been your problem. You are never honest, even with yourself."* The fingers dug into his temple, pressing against his pulsing vein, and he gasped and sat up.

The kids around him shifted their chairs slightly away, giving him strange looks.

"Leave your things," Mrs. Murphy instructed. "We'll be returning here before your next class."

"We'll be . . . what?" Caden asked, confused as everyone stood and filed out the door.

"We're having an assembly," Rae said, stopping by his desk. "Someone from Green On! is talking to us."

"Weren't you listening, ghoul boy?" Alyssa demanded. "Or were you sleeping?" She looped her arm through Vivienne's and swept out the door.

Rae started after them, then paused. "Are you okay?" she asked.

Caden blinked, surprised and strangely touched. It had been a long time since anyone had asked him that, and even longer since they actually seemed to care about his answer, but he could tell Rae did. Her concern buzzed around her like tiny gnats. "I'm okay. Like your friend said, just sleeping." He thought of the dream he'd had of her.

But Rae was already leaving, and the moment to tell her its warning was lost.

Caden stood slowly, his body aching almost like he had a fever. He looked around at the empty room. No Aiden. Maybe he *had* fallen asleep, and all of that was another dream.

"You'd better hurry," Mrs. Murphy told him. Then she frowned. "Unless you need to see the nurse? You're looking a little—"

"I'm fine," Caden said. "But thanks." He hurried into the hall-way, following the crowd of seventh and eighth graders into the auditorium. Like the rest of the school, the auditorium wasn't par-ticularly big, but it was well taken care of. Green On! put a lot of money into the community and had paid for extensive renovations to Dana S. Middle School a few years ago. Probably the reason they were able to put on assemblies whenever they wanted.

Caden tried finding a seat near the back, but they were all taken, so he ended up sinking into a chair all the way up in the third row just as the lights dimmed. A few seconds later and the lights over the stage turned on, highlighting Ms. Lockett chatting with a well-dressed young man. Caden couldn't hear them, but it was obvious Ms. Lockett approved of the visitor, which was highly unusual for her. Maybe it had something to do with his expensively tailored dark suit or his expensively styled dark hair. Ms. Lockett reached up to fix her own hair three times while talking to him, before turning to the audience.

She blinked as if surprised to see them all sitting there, watching her.

"Hello, everybody," she said into the stage lectern's microphone.

"Is it me, or is your mom's voice higher-pitched than normal?" Vivienne whispered.

Caden glanced behind to see her sitting sandwiched between Rae and Alyssa.

"Shh!" Alyssa hissed, which only made Vivienne giggle.

"He *is* awfully handsome," Rae added.

"That's not funny," Alyssa said.

"It's a little funny," Vivienne said.

"You are in for a wonderful treat," Ms. Lockett continued, and Caden had to admit, her voice did sound a little higher and girlier. "Patrick here is a senior consultant at Green On!, and he's here to talk to you about a wonderful opportunity with his company." She beamed at him. "So let's all bring our hands together for Patrick and Green On!, because *it's never too soon to think about the future.*"

The clapping was half-hearted. Every kid there was tired of hearing that same old slogan. Most of them knew people working there. It was another way that Caden stood out: he was one of the few kids in Whispering Pines who didn't have a single family member working for or with Green On!.

Patrick moved up to the lectern and smiled out at all of them. "Thank you for that . . . warm welcome."

That got a chuckle.

"I'm guessing most of you know a thing or two about Green

On!," he continued. "Probably have heard way too much of it now from your moms and dads, neighbors and cousins, right?" Patrick unhooked the microphone from the lectern and walked to the front of the stage. "Which means you know that we believe the future should be left in the hands of the smartest, most capable minds. It's why we employ the top engineers, scientists, doctors, and more from not just Whispering Pines, not just the United States, but the whole world."

All of this was part of Green On!'s very common marketing spiel. Caden could feel everyone around him getting bored. Whispers started in the back of the room, giggles in another corner.

"What if I told you," Patrick continued, not seeming to notice the distraction, "that this won't be enough to save us?"

Sudden quiet filled the room.

"That's right. All the smartest adults in the world might not be able to fix the earth's problems. Which is why we have decided that it's time to look at other avenues to advance humanity." He paused, looking from face to face. Caden shrank down in his seat, not wanting to be noticed.

"Specifically, we are looking at *you*." Patrick's voice dropped practically to a whisper, his words only carrying because of the microphone in his hand. Caden could see kids leaning eagerly in their seats, trying to catch his every word. "We want to give kids—smart, talented kids with *unusual* gifts—a chance to work with us." At that, Patrick looked right at Caden.

Caden froze, caught beneath that dark gaze like a butterfly on a pin. He didn't generally feel for other people's energy since their emotions wrapped themselves around him all day, every day. But curiosity made him reach out for Patrick's. Instantly he knew he had made a grave mistake. Where emotions normally bounced around like sunbeams and raindrops, Caden felt himself being sucked into a cold, black pit with Patrick. There was nothing there, nothing inside Patrick but emptiness echoing on forever, so cold Caden couldn't breathe. The room faded around the edges, spots flickering in his eyes, his lungs burning . . .

And then Patrick's gaze shifted away, and Caden sagged against his seat, gasping. No one else seemed to notice.

"What does this mean for you?" Patrick asked. "It means opportunity. Over the next few weeks we'll be selecting a few of you for our new program. Those chosen will team up with our scientists in our labs as part of an after-school internship and will be eligible for a chance at a full-ride scholarship to a university of their choice. Not only that, but these interns will be working with us to help better the world. Because like Joan Lockett said, it is never too soon to think about the future."

This time the applause was loud and enthusiastic. Caden couldn't bring himself to join in, no matter how much it made him stand out.

There was something very wrong with Patrick. Something *inhumanly* wrong.

Caden wasn't sure how he got through the rest of the day. He spent all his energy trying to sense Aiden and ignoring all the talk about Patrick and Green On!, so by the time he was on the bus headed home, he felt like an overused dishrag.

"Hey, Caden," Rae said as she passed his seat.

Caden looked up at her, and for a second the bus disappeared, and he saw her instead the way she'd been in his dream: crouched on the stairs in the dark, terrified.

"Or not," Rae said, frowning slightly.

Caden blinked, and the vision was gone. "W-wait," he called, but it was too late; Rae had already slid into a seat in the back of the bus, next to Vivienne. *Great*, he thought. *The one person who doesn't seem to think you're a psycho, and you go and ruin it.* He tried not to care, but he couldn't help it. Rae seemed nice.

And someone wanted to hurt her.

Caden didn't want to think about his dream, because he wasn't sure what to do about it. If he told Rae about it, she would probably freak out. It would be just like first grade all over again. But if he didn't tell her, and something happened . . .

She's fine, he told himself firmly. She didn't need his help. Besides, what was he even supposed to say? "Hey, Rae, I had a dream about you last night. Don't worry, not the creepy kind, but the kind where someone was stalking you in an old dark mansion . . . Never mind, I guess that *is* creepy."

Sighing, he ran a hand through his hair. He'd only had a handful of prophetic dreams, the last one being about the old science classroom's pet rabbit, so he had no way of knowing how far into the future this one was predicting. Or even if it would *actually* happen. The future was weird like that, all twisted and looping. It was like a braid, all those different strands running side by side, heading in roughly the same direction.

His brother had been convinced the present was the same way. Just as he'd been sure he could somehow hop from one strand to another.

And he'd been right.

When the bus stopped, Caden made up his mind. He'd warn her once and then leave it alone. He waited until she got off first, then followed.

"Can I walk you home?" he asked as the bus pulled away.

"Uh, why?" Rae asked, obviously already uncomfortable. This was exactly why Caden didn't talk to people.

"I just . . . I need to talk to you."

"Okay," Rae said slowly. "That's not ominous at all." She started walking across the street, Caden trailing after her. A light breeze built slowly around them, moving the hot, muggy air and replacing it with something fresh. It tasted like future rain, and the trees around Rae's house rustled in excitement, leaves lifting eagerly toward the sky.

"Yes?" Rae raised her eyebrows.

Caden forced himself to stop stalling and launched into a recounting of the dream. Immediately he knew it was a mistake; Rae's whole face closed in on itself, and he could feel her suspicion stabbing out at him like thousands of tiny needles. But he kept going until he finished. By then they were at her front door, and she had her hand on the doorknob like she wanted to escape.

"Why would you tell me this?" she asked. "It's super creepy."

"I told you it was a creepy dream."

"Oh, I'm not talking about the dream." She gave him a pointed look.

Caden felt his cheeks flare hot. "I thought you should know. But you do whatever you want with it." He walked away from her, his shoulders stiff. He never should have told her.

His brother was right. Better to ignore everyone, and only focus on himself—

He paused at her driveway. The afternoon didn't feel right. The air no longer tasted like future rain, but something else. Almost rancid, a hint of that same sour-fear smell that had seeped out of the place his brother had opened.

Something was out here that did not belong.

He turned slowly, scanning the trees. Like all the other houses in this area, Rae's house was built practically into the forest. The line between the edge of her yard and the start of the Watchful Woods had blurred beneath layers of fallen leaves and pine cones and dirt. Even the front yard had a few trees trailing around it, so it felt almost like they were surrounded.

"What are you doing?" Rae asked.

"Shh."

"Don't *shh* me in front of my own house! I—" She stopped abruptly.

"What?" Caden looked at her, then followed her frightened gaze to the woods.

Someone stood just at the edge, swaying gently like one of the trees. She looked familiar, short and slender with long, dark hair cascading around thin shoulders.

"What's wrong with her?" Rae moved toward him, standing so close he could feel her shaking.

"I don't know."

The girl took a small step toward them, then another, before stopping again, still swaying, her face bent forward too far to see clearly.

"H-hello?" Caden called.

The figure shuddered but didn't say anything.

"I'm calling for help." Rae slid her backpack off one shoulder and rummaged inside, pulling out her phone. As if Rae's movement was some kind of cue, the girl suddenly staggered toward them, moving fast, hands outstretched.

Rae gasped as the girl lunged right at her.

Caden dove between them, catching the girl by her skinny wrists and pulling her hands away from Rae's face.

The girl twisted in his arms and tossed her head back, giving Caden a clear look at her face. Her gaunt, pale face, mouth open slightly, cheeks smeared with blood and dirt, and where her eyes should have been, nothing but two hollowed-out pits.

Fear rose like bile in his throat, and he couldn't move, his brain screaming at him in horror.

And then, abruptly, it was like he was back in that room again, watching his brother laugh as a sickly yellow light pulsed around him. Behind him, the edges of the doorway hung in jagged shreds. Only it wasn't a doorway at all. It was reality itself, as if his brother had somehow slashed a knife across the world, tearing it open and revealing something horrible underneath.

Silhouetted in the glow, terrible shapes moved and jerked and twisted.

Aiden didn't see them. He was too busy laughing, his arms out wide, blood running down both hands, his chest bare. *I told you I'd do it.* He looked right at Caden, his eyes wide and triumphant. *I told you!*

Aiden! Watch out! Caden could see the things lurching closer, moving fast. Some of them had tentacles, or too many limbs, their bodies too thick or too thin. And one of them was a thing with teeth, so many teeth that its mouth took up its whole face, leaving no room for the eyes.

Aiden turned, but he was moving slowly, too slowly. The things were almost out. And Caden knew with cold, deadly certainty that if they escaped into his world, they would kill him, and his mom, and his dad. And maybe everyone.

Aiden dropped his arms, looking uncertain for the first time in his life. A ghostly tentacle slithered across his bare chest, tracing the lines of blood, slowly taking on more shape, more substance. Another tentacle joined the first, and then a misshapen hand reached out to run too-long fingers down the side of Aiden's face. Suddenly the first tentacle dug itself into the cut in his arm, and drank.

Aiden screamed.

Tentacles seemed to come from all directions, all wrapping around Aiden, tearing at his skin, slurping at his blood. Other things moved closer, and as Aiden staggered back, he seemed to pull the awful light of that world with him, widening that gap. Giving them room to escape.

Caden wasn't sure exactly what happened next. It was all a blur— his brother screaming, those tentacles tearing at him, and then—

And then the feeling of his hands hitting Aiden's back, shoving him forward. Shoving him into the rift. It was the only way Caden knew to seal it. But he remembered the feeling of movement past him as he'd pushed his brother in, the sense that something else was sliding out at the same time. . . .

9.
RAE

Rae looked anxiously down the street, clutching her phone. She hoped the ambulance would be here soon. Caden was just sitting there. He was still holding on to the girl, but his eyes had rolled back in his head and he wasn't responding. And the girl kept making these awful moaning sounds. Rae didn't know what to do.

She hated that feeling.

"Caden," she tried again. She was afraid to touch him, terrified that whatever had happened to him could somehow happen to her, but she screwed up her courage and gently shook his shoulder. "Caden, *please*." Her voice broke at the end.

He looked up. His eyes stared right through her, as if she were some kind of ghost. Then he blinked, and his vision cleared. "Rae?"

Relief coursed through her. "Thank goodness," she breathed.

"For a second I thought . . ." She stopped, not sure what she was going to say. That she thought he'd been somehow magically affected? That was ridiculous. But as she gazed down at the girl still struggling weakly in his grip, it didn't seem so silly. The girl's mouth opened and closed like a zombie's, her body shook with tiny tremors, and her eyes . . .

Panic clawed its way up Rae's chest, and she didn't want to look too closely. But if she wanted to find her dad someday, she had to be strong enough to deal with things like . . . like missing eyeballs. So she forced herself to crouch and really study the girl.

She started at her chin, small and dainty, the chapped lips above it, then the sharp nose, and finally, the hollows where the eyes should have been. They were perfectly smooth. No eyelids, no extra skin, no blood or scratches or anything. It was as if something had just scooped the eyes out and then polished the area left behind.

Rae stood abruptly, horrified. "No," she whispered, hugging herself. "No, no, no, no."

"What?" Caden said. "What is it?"

"That's Brandi." Rae didn't even recognize her voice anymore. "That can't be. What happened? How? Who would—" She stopped, took a deep gulp of air, felt it swell up inside her. "Do you think . . . can someone help her?"

"I don't know," Caden said softly. "It's not just her eyes. There's something else wrong with her. Something internal."

"How can you know that?" Rae wanted to lash out and shake him. She didn't know where the anger came from, but it was better than feeling so afraid.

"I just do."

Rae glared at him, then turned away, blinking rapidly, trying not to cry. It wasn't fair. Brandi had been the first person to be kind to her in a long time. She was funny and she liked helping people and someday she was going to travel the world.

Rae bit back a sob.

"Are you okay?" Caden asked.

She ignored him, focusing on evening her breathing, and then she turned back. Kneeling, she took one of Brandi's limp hands. It felt as cold as a corpse. Rae had no idea who would do something like this, but she would find them. Somehow she'd track them down. And then she'd make them pay.

She squeezed Brandi's hand gently. "I'm so, so sorry," she whispered. "You didn't deserve this. I promise, I'll—"

Brandi shuddered and raised her face as if she were trying to see. "Eyes," she murmured.

"What was that?" Caden leaned closer.

"Lovely eyes." Brandi lifted one trembling hand, pointing. But not at him.

Rae realized Brandi was pointing right at her.

10.
CADEN

Caden watched Rae freeze beneath that accusatory finger, those empty eye sockets trained right on her face as if they could somehow see her. Dread pooled in his stomach in a thick, sticky layer, and it felt like something awful was coming together here. It was like one of his prophetic dreams, that feeling that he could see what would happen, but that he wouldn't be able to stop it.

A van tore down their street and screamed to a stop at the bottom of Rae's driveway, lights flashing and sirens blaring.

Brandi dropped her arm just as three men hopped out of the van and hurried over. One of them wore an expensive-looking black suit and shiny black shoes. He was movie-star handsome, with thick dark hair styled just slightly so it pulled back from a tanned face and dark blue eyes.

Rae gasped. "You're Patrick. From the assembly."

Caden froze. He remembered Patrick all too well. Slowly he built up his protective wall, picturing a ball of white light all around him, pulling in all his senses. He didn't want to touch whatever was inside Patrick. Not again.

"That I am." Patrick smiled at Rae. Even with his senses pulled in, Caden could see her relaxing. She actually trusted this guy.

Caden rubbed his thumb against one of his rings and looked past Patrick at the van. It was bright green with the words GREEN ON! stenciled along the side in large blocky letters. "I thought you called the police," Caden said.

"I did," Rae said.

"Oh yes." Patrick flashed that smile again. "And *they* called *us*. As I said this morning, we have the best scientists and doctors in the world working for us. If anyone in this town can help this poor girl, it will be us." He whistled, and the other two men hurried forward. Unlike Patrick, neither of them wore suits. Instead, they had on bright green one-piece outfits that almost looked like hazmat suits, minus the helmets.

"We'll take her from here," one of them said.

Caden looked down and realized Rae was still holding Brandi's hand.

"What will happen to her?" Rae asked. "Will she be all right?"

"We'll do what we can for her," Patrick said. "Trust me, she'll be in good hands."

Rae let go of Brandi, and the two men stepped forward, carefully guiding her back toward the van and out of sight. Caden forced himself to watch her go.

If this was his fault . . .

"This is a delicate situation, as I'm sure you can understand," Patrick said. "We don't want to cause a panic. Can I trust you both to exercise discretion?"

"You mean . . . you don't want us to tell anyone about this?" Caden crossed his arms, frowning. "You want to keep this a secret?"

"Oh, word will get out. Undoubtedly. But the longer we can keep it under wraps, the better chance we'll have of catching whoever is committing these heinous attacks. You wouldn't want to interfere with an ongoing investigation, would you, Mr. Price?"

Caden stiffened. Whoever this Patrick was, he obviously knew *him*. And knew he'd been involved in a recent police investigation. Caden didn't like to think of all those interviews, the cops asking him the same questions over and over again. Questions he couldn't possibly answer. *Yes, I was with my brother the night he disappeared. No, I don't know where he went.*

Patrick caught his eye, waiting a beat, like he wanted to make sure the full import of his words had soaked in. Then he turned to Rae. "And . . . I'm sorry," he said. "I don't think I know you?"

"I'm Rae. Rae Carter."

"Rae Carter." Patrick said her name slowly, as if he were memorizing it. "The new girl? Pleasure, Ms. Carter. I'm sure I can count on you to be discreet."

Rae nodded, but she looked uncertain. *Good*, Caden thought at her. *Don't trust this guy.*

"What about her parents?" Caden glanced back at the Jensens' house. It seemed dark, too dark. Caden wondered if anyone was even home.

"They'll be notified. Don't worry, we are very thorough. We'll take care of everything." He flashed both of them another perfect smile. "Have a good night. Stay safe." And then he hopped into the front of the van, and it drove off.

Caden stood there for a long moment, listening to the sounds of the woods. Birds chirping, the wind rustling the leaves of the trees, a car door slamming somewhere farther down the street. The soft rhythm of Rae's too-fast breathing.

"How did you know?" she asked suddenly.

"What?" Caden said.

"In your dream, you talked about my lungs. How did you know I have asthma?"

"I didn't."

"Lucky guess? Or have you been spying on me?" Rae's face took on a look Caden remembered all too well, an equal mix of suspicion and fear disguised beneath a mask of anger.

"No. I told you, I have these dreams sometimes. But you don't have to believe me. I know it's easier to lash out than to accept the impossible."

"That's *not* what I'm doing."

"If you say so."

Rae scowled. "I'm going home."

"Please do. And Rae?" He waited until she was looking at him again. "Make sure you lock your doors. And windows." He glanced past her, back at the forest to the left of her house. The night felt calm now, all the danger past. But only for the moment. He knew there would be more attacks, and soon.

And he was pretty sure whoever was doing these attacks was not human.

11.
RAE

Rae wanted to yell at Caden, but instead she turned and stomped back inside her house, very aware of him standing there, watching her. Anger simmered inside her in a tight, controlled wave. *It's easier to lash out than to accept the impossible.* Caden had no idea what he was talking about. He didn't know her. He didn't know a *thing* about her.

She'd accepted the impossible before.

The night before her dad disappeared, she'd eavesdropped on a conversation between him and her mom. An impossible conversation.

I tell you, that thing is not of Earth origin. Her dad had been almost shouting. *It's alive, and it's not going to want to stay locked up in an underground lab!*

Shh! You'll wake the girls, her mom had warned. *And you don't know for sure, do you? I mean, Chris, honey . . . this sounds . . .*

I know what it sounds like. But I saw it. With my own eyes. I wasn't supposed to. He'd sighed, a long, defeated sound. *But I did. And now? I can't unsee it.*

Rae blinked the memory away, her anger fading with it. Her dad had sounded angry that night too. But now, thinking back on it, she realized he'd actually been scared.

She was scared.

She pulled her front door shut and locked it. Then she turned the deadbolt for good measure. It didn't seem like enough. Not even close.

Rae wandered through the next day at school like a zombie. She couldn't stop thinking about Brandi. But since no one else knew what had happened to her, Rae had to keep her thoughts to herself.

"Wait, wait, I haven't given you your homework yet!" their science teacher, Ms. Reed, called as final bell rang. But it was too late; Rae tumbled out of science class with everyone else, all of them laughing and talking excitedly around her.

"Are you feeling okay?" Vivienne asked.

Rae pasted on a smile. "I'm fine. Just didn't sleep well."

"Maybe your neighbor is casting weird spells on you," Alyssa said.

Rae turned and saw Caden trailing behind them. He met her gaze, and it was like he was silently reminding her of everything that had happened last night, his brown eyes dark and way too intense.

She turned away from him. She couldn't think about any of that stuff right now. Later, when she was safely back home and at her desk, she'd continue her research. She would find Brandi's attacker, but right now she wanted to pretend everything was normal.

"He's been looking at you all day," Alyssa added, side-eyeing Caden as he walked past them. "I think he might have a little crush." She smirked.

"I doubt it," Rae said.

"Yeah, you always think everyone has a crush," Vivienne said. Alyssa's smirk withered and turned into a scowl as Vivienne turned to Rae and asked, "What are you doing after school?"

"After school?" Rae hesitated. She was supposed to see the psychologist today, which wasn't something she wanted to tell Vivienne. *Especially* in front of someone like Alyssa, who would totally use that knowledge as a weapon. "Um . . ."

"If you're free," Vivienne continued, "Alyssa's mom is taking a few of us to the movies, and—"

"And I'm not sure we have room for another person in my mom's car," Alyssa said quickly. She flashed Rae an insincere little smile. "Sorry."

Rae was surprised how much that hurt, since she didn't particularly like Alyssa. But it was too similar to how everything started at her old school. After Taylor stopped hanging out with her, suddenly everyone else did too. At first, there were the little excuses. Not enough room in the car. Could only invite a certain number of people. Decided to have a party last minute. But all of those little excuses added up to one big fact: no one wanted anything to do with Rae anymore. She was officially on the outs. And then came the mean comments, the laughter, the taunts . . .

"Okay," Rae said. She kept walking to her locker, keeping her pace casual. That was the big thing she'd learned from before; never let them know you were upset.

"Really, Alyssa?" Vivienne asked. "Isn't your mom driving an SUV these days?"

"Yeah, but there's stuff all over the back seat."

"What kind of stuff?"

"Um, important vice-principal stuff."

"Ah," Vivienne said. "Well, I can see how that would be impossible to, I don't know, move to the trunk?"

"Uh," Alyssa said awkwardly. "I mean, I *could* ask. I guess."

"That's okay," Rae said, stopping in front of her locker. She gave Alyssa her own insincere smile. "I get it." She was rewarded by the red flush spreading across Alyssa's face, turning her fair skin a splotchy pink.

Alyssa looked away. "It's not that I don't want—"

"Really, it's fine," Rae said, suddenly tired of this game. "I'm actually meeting my sister at the café now anyhow." She got her backpack and closed her locker. "See you tomorrow," she told Vivienne, and then she headed for the exit.

"Why are you being like this?" she heard Vivienne say behind her.

"Being like what?" Alyssa asked, and then Rae was outside and couldn't hear anymore. Probably for the best. She really didn't want to listen to Alyssa make up more excuses.

The buses were already loading up, but it wasn't hard to snake around them and scurry across the street to the shopping plaza.

There were a few restaurants here, including a bagel shop, a pizza parlor, and the café. Vivienne had complained at lunch that day about the unfairness of trapping all of them in the school for meals and forcing them to eat regurgitated corn products when there were all these better options mere feet away. But during school hours they weren't allowed to leave the grounds, and Ms. Lockett patrolled the area like some kind of Doberman, making sure all the students complied. Considering how often students seemed to go missing around here, Rae thought maybe not letting them wander around too much wasn't the worst idea. Not that it seemed to be keeping them safe.

She ducked into Kat's Café, pausing just inside the door. It was a larger café than she'd been expecting, the lighting dim. Tables of various sizes were scattered around the middle of the space, while large, worn-down couches had been pushed to the walls on the side closest to the door. Across the room sat a small stage with a hand-made poster reading: FRIDAY NIGHTS, AMATEUR MUSIC NIGHT, next to a homemade sign talking about an alien graveyard.

There were a few groups of high school students already in here, and Rae could feel the weight of all their eyes staring at her. She hunched her shoulders and moved closer to the front.

"What can I get you, honey?" the woman behind the counter asked.

Rae tried to look confident, like she came in here all the time. But her voice squeaked when she gave the woman her order, and she didn't know she was supposed to move down to the other side of the counter to wait until the person next to her practically shoved her over there.

Red-faced, Rae hugged the wall until the woman thrust two coffee cups and two sandwich plates at her. Rae managed to stack the sandwiches on top of each other, carrying them in one hand and tucking her mocha under the other arm so she could carry Ava's coffee. She made her way toward the couch closest to the stage.

Her cell phone vibrated before she got there, and she jumped, spilling hot coffee all over her hand.

"Great, just great," she muttered, putting her drinks down on the nearest table. The girl sitting there gave her a dirty look. "It's just for a second," Rae told her.

Sighing, the girl went back to her book. Rae grabbed a wad of napkins from the center of the table and wiped off her hand and the outside of the cup, then dug her phone out of her pocket and glanced at it, hoping it was Ava telling her she was there.

Instead, it was Vivienne.

VIVI: Sorry about Alyssa. Hope you're not mad.

Rae stared at that message, then typed: Not mad. Totally fine. Enjoy your movie!

VIVI: Oh, I'm not going. Text me later if you want to hang.

Rae started typing a response, then stopped. She wasn't sure what to say. Part of her felt really happy that Vivienne had obviously decided to ditch Alyssa. But she also felt guilty about it too. In the end, she just sent a quick, ambiguous smiley face. Then she stuffed her phone back into her pocket and went to grab the drinks again.

And paused, her hand hovering. Someone was standing next to the table, staring at her. She glanced around. But no, he was definitely staring right at her. A boy with short, pale blond hair and very dark brown eyes. She recognized him from the bus. Jeremy's friend. "What?" she asked him.

"You look like you have your hands full." He moved closer. "Let me help you with those." He reached for her coffee, and she pulled the cups away, almost spilling a second time.

"I've got it . . . but thank you."

"Really?" He raised his eyebrows. "You don't look like you've got it." He indicated her hand, which was already developing a nice red mark from her earlier spill. "I'll take one, you get the other." He reached for her cup again.

Rae hesitated.

"I'm just trying to help," he said. "If you show me where you want to sit, I'll drop off your drink for you and then head back to my table."

The girl sitting at this table gave Rae another impatient look over her book, and this time Rae let the boy take one of her cups.

"That table there." Rae jerked her chin at a small table perched near the emergency exit.

The boy followed her toward it. "I haven't seen you around school before this week," he said as they walked. "You're new, right?"

"Um, yeah. Just moved here."

"I'm pretty new too. Got here last year."

"Oh," Rae said. She felt like she should say more, maybe ask him how he liked it here, but she didn't want him to keep talking. She wanted him to go.

"It's a hard place to be the new kid," he continued, obviously content to keep the conversation going on his own.

They reached the table, but he continued to hold on to her cup. She wasn't sure if she should reach for it or wait for him to put it down. She put her own down firmly and looked at him, but he didn't seem to get the hint. So she put down her plate of sandwiches next to it and pulled out her chair. "Thanks for your help. I'm good from here."

"Are you waiting for someone?" he asked.

"Yes. My sister should be here any minute."

"Mind if I sit with you while you wait?" He sat down before she could answer, still holding her drink hostage. It was her own mocha, probably going cold. And cold mochas were the worst.

"If you give me my drink back," she said.

"Sure thing." He placed it on the table between them. "I'm Ivan, by the way."

"Rae."

"Nice to formally meet you, Rae." Ivan smiled. "I was wondering if, maybe later, you wanted to—"

"There you are," Ava said.

Rae and Ivan both looked up. Ava was standing over them, frowning slightly. "Who are you?" she asked Ivan.

"A friend from school. But I was just leaving." He glanced back at Rae. "I'm sure I'll see you around again soon."

Rae didn't say anything back as he got up and left, but her stomach was in weird knots, and she wondered if he'd been about to ask her out. Then she wondered why that idea made her so uncomfortable. Maybe because she didn't really know him?

Ava watched him go. "What was that all about?"

"Oh, uh, nothing." Rae took a sip of her mocha.

"Rae," Ava said warningly.

"Ava," Rae said back. Then she sighed. "Fine. He's just some boy who wanted to talk to me."

Immediately Ava's expression shifted from annoyed and suspicious to sly. "Oh he did, did he?"

Rae shrugged. "It's not a big deal."

"I don't know. He was *awfully* cute."

Rae could feel her face growing hot. "I don't want to talk about it," she said quickly. "Also, your sandwich is getting cold."

Ava took it, studying the label. "Didn't realize hot egg salad sandwiches were a thing."

Rae laughed, and it was only a little forced. Thankfully, Ava dropped the whole cute-boy thing and let her finish her mocha in peace.

12.
CADEN

When Caden got home from school, he found his dad sitting on their porch swing, wearing his favorite obnoxiously bright blue button-down shirt. Caden preferred to wear black for protection, but his dad had always put more faith in blue. He claimed it helped keep him safe *and* brought out the color in his eyes. Caden's mom taught him that blue was used for mental clarity and focus, but maybe that was exactly what his dad needed to feel safe.

"You're off work early," Caden said. His dad helped out with his mom's Paranormal Price business, but his main job was working as a computer programmer.

"Yeah, didn't feel like being there anymore," his dad said, grinning.

"So why are you sitting out here?"

"Your mom has a client over for a consultation. Mr. Murphy."

That explained the extra car Caden had seen at the bottom of their driveway on his walk up. "Any relation to my homeroom teacher?"

"Possibly. They have a vacation home up in New Hampshire that may be haunted, and he wanted to get your mom's advice on it."

Caden tentatively dropped his emotional shields and felt around the house. Everything seemed normal . . . or at least as normal as it ever did, which meant that his mom was probably doing nothing more than a simple tarot reading.

His dad patted the swing next to him. "Come. Sit with me."

Caden hesitated. He was pretty sure his dad had been purposely waiting to talk to him. Never a good sign.

But then Caden could sense the sadness lurking beneath his dad's cheerful words and wide smile. It made him think of a recently cleaned room with a closet jammed full of stuff, as if his dad had taken all of his messy emotions and just hidden them out of sight. So Caden dropped his backpack on the porch and settled back on the swing's cushions.

Caden and his dad gently rocked back and forth. Today the mugginess in the air had evaporated, the wind finally cool and crisp with the hint of autumn. Leaves drifted slowly down from their branches to coat the grass, and the afternoon sky burned that brilliant shade of blue that only seemed to happen at this time of year. It felt strangely peaceful.

Caden knew it wouldn't last. It never did.

"It's been exactly nine months this week," his dad said abruptly.

"Nine months since your brother—" He stopped as suddenly as he'd started, the silence thickening between them. They never really talked about Aiden—at least, not after that first frantic month when it was all anyone could talk about. Caden remembered all the interviews with reporters, the increasingly desperate searches. And the endless police interrogations. He knew they wouldn't believe him if he told them the truth, so he'd had to lie, again and again.

You wouldn't want to interfere with an ongoing investigation, would you, Mr. Price?

Caden's hands clenched at his sides. It still bothered him that Patrick had known exactly who he was. Just as he'd known the police had talked to him several times after his brother vanished, those "talks" becoming more and more serious, until even his class-mates heard about them. It was one of the reasons why so many of them believed he'd been the one to murder his brother. And Caden couldn't even blame his classmates, or the police. Since he'd been the last person to see Aiden alive, he was the obvious choice. And really, they weren't wrong.

It had all happened during a routine exorcism. Just a normal Sunday night for the Price family.

Hey, kids, Caden's mom had said that evening. They were eating her favorite dinner recipe: a slightly burnt green bean casserole. *After dinner, your dad and I are heading out on a house call. We have some negative energies to cleanse and possibly a spirit or two to deal with. Want to come along and help out?*

I don't know, honey . . . , Caden's dad started. He never really liked to involve Caden or Aiden in any of the fieldwork. "I don't know, honey" used to be his catchphrase. *It's not the best idea to bring them. I mean, on a school night and everything too.*

Caden's mom smiled. *This will be a safe, easy job.*

And at first, it *had* been.

The house was a cute little cottage painted a cheerful sky-blue with yellow rosebushes overflowing by the front door. It looked like a house from a magazine. The doctor met them outside and explained that he'd been hearing noises and catching glimpses of things that weren't there. Caden still remembered how he'd joked about it. *It's a really bad sign for someone in my profession.* But when Caden's family stepped inside, everything seemed fine. No trace of paranormal activity. Still, they lit their smudge sticks, the sharp scent of burning sage filling every room, his dad trickling out lines of salt, putting rose quartz in the corners, his mom lighting her candles.

While their parents worked, Aiden and Caden had gone deeper into the house. And then Aiden had discovered the door to the cellar.

It was painted the same off-white as the surrounding walls, and Caden could still remember the sense of *wrongness* when they opened that door. It crawled all over him like a nest of bugs that he couldn't shake off. The owner of that house had definitely been messing with energies he shouldn't have, and some of them had stuck to the cellar the way static electricity stuck a balloon to a wall.

Aiden, Caden whispered, afraid of attracting anything hanging around. *Let's go get Mom.*

But Aiden wasn't listening. His eyes were closed, his head

thrown back. *Can you feel it?* He took a deep breath, pulling in the negative energy. *This*, he said, *will be* perfect. And he'd seemed so excited that Caden had gone along with him.

Caden should have known then that Aiden's plan had nothing to do with cleansing negative energies . . .

"We've been back to that house, you know," his dad said now, bringing Caden back to the present. "Your mother and I. But there was no trace of your brother." He scowled. "And now the owner won't let us in anymore. Claimed we were hurting his business."

"I remember," Caden said. His parents had been furious about that, especially after the police told them they'd be charged for trespassing if they continued going back. In the end, his parents had decided there was nothing remaining at that house that would actually help them find Aiden, and they'd let it go.

"As if it wasn't his fault in the first place, with his meddling with the dead. As if *he* wasn't the one who invited us there." His dad's scowl had twisted into something strange and ugly.

Caden put a hand on his dad's arm. "Dad," he said gently.

His dad tensed, then relaxed. He scrubbed his hand down his face. "I'm sorry. I just . . . I'm not really sure what else to do. We never should have taken you with us that night. Your mom's work is too unpredictable. We shouldn't have involved either of you. Maybe then . . ." He took a deep, shuddering breath.

Caden couldn't bear to look at his dad's anguished face. This was why his parents hardly spoke to each other these days. All of the "shouldn't have"s hovered constantly between them, haunting them worse than any ghost.

"Oh, there are far worse ghosts to have."

Caden froze, as if going still would save him. Dimly he heard his dad start talking again, his regrets, promises that they were still looking, but Caden couldn't really pay attention. All of his focus was on the space next to him, just beside the edge of the swing.

That space was cold, and growing colder. And Caden couldn't pretend he didn't know what that meant anymore. The hairs on his arms and neck rose, all of them lifting as if he'd just built up a charge of static electricity. The telltale signs of paranormal activity, indicating a ghost was nearby.

Aiden's ghost.

Caden thought of his mom's sloppy summoning spell yesterday, and the feeling that something had been in his room afterward. She'd been looking for Aiden; apparently, she'd found him. Or *he'd* found *them*.

Caden swallowed. He knew how his brother could get when he felt like he'd been wronged. Now, at least, Caden could admit that Vanessa Sanchez's car crash and Mark Peterson's house fire weren't accidents. And there had been other incidents too. Whispers that Caden had tried to ignore.

But Caden had wronged Aiden more than anyone else ever had. And Caden had seen his mom deal with enough ghosts to know that they could hurt. They could even *kill*. He'd never meant to hurt his brother, but there was no way Aiden would believe that. So now that he'd found them again, what was Aiden planning to do?

"You mean, how am I planning to get my revenge?"

Caden shivered, instinctively looking around, but of course he saw nothing.

"I'll be seeing you around, little brother . . ."

Caden felt the space near him vibrate, and then abruptly that sense of presence vanished. He put a hand out, and the cold was gone.

13.
RAE

Neither Ava nor Rae said much as they drove to the psychologist's office. It was times like these when Rae felt the distance between her and her sister like a physical pain. She would never admit it, but she missed Ava. She missed the sister she used to have, the one she lost the week their dad vanished.

Rae closed her eyes, remembering that day. She'd come home from school expecting to find her dad waiting for her, like he'd promised, and instead finding several men in dark suits swarming around her house. Her mom was talking to two of them, her voice tight and high-pitched.

What's going on? Rae had asked.

Nothing, her mom had said. *Go to your room.*

Where's Dad?

I said go to your room, Rae. Her mom had sounded so anxious that Rae hadn't asked any more questions, just hurried past them down the hall. Three more men in suits were ransacking her parents' bedroom, tearing through their dressers, their closet, rifling through bedding. She slipped past them to her dad's home office, where another man was rummaging around in her dad's desk.

Rae watched him grab notebooks, USB drives, and even photos still in their frames, tossing them into a large cardboard box. She cringed at the sound of shattering glass as he dropped her parents' wedding photo into the cardboard depths. She looked around, spotting her favorite photo—one of her and her dad—perched precariously on top of a bookshelf, half-hiding the small wall calendar behind it. Then she eyed the man. He had his back to her as he went through a desk drawer.

She darted forward and snagged the photo. At the last second, she tore the calendar off the wall too, smuggling both of them into her room. She didn't know what those men were doing in her house or why they were taking her dad's things, but she was terrified of what they'd do to her if they noticed she'd stolen these items. They scared her, these men with their identical dark suits and identical blank looks.

She opened her thick math notebook and tore out a chunk of pages from the middle, then slipped the calendar inside, tucking the whole thing back into her schoolbag. The photo she decided to hide behind her decoy corkboard. But when she popped the frame open, she saw that her dad had taped another picture to the back.

At first it looked almost human. Two eyes, nose, mouth. But

the eyes were too large, and all pupil, the nose nothing more than a pair of slits, and the mouth barely visible. And its skin was gray. It was undeniably an alien. And it was peering out from behind some kind of weird cage.

Her dad must have taken this picture.

Rae's hands trembled as she studied it. It was probably the reason those men were searching his office.

Somehow she'd known in that moment that her dad wasn't coming back home. He was gone, but he'd left this picture, this *proof*, hidden behind a photo of her, which meant he'd wanted her to have it. Carefully she tucked it back behind that photo and hid both of them away.

But it was a secret too big to keep, and she had to tell someone. . . .

She managed to keep it to herself for almost a whole week, until she heard the rumor that her dad and another engineer from his team had run away together, and she finally went to her sister with the truth.

You're being a child, Ava had told her. *There's no such thing as aliens, and no one took Dad.* She'd had so much scorn in her voice, it had been worse than a slap. *Grow up, Rae. Lots of people's dads run off. You don't have to invent some big fantasy around it.*

I have proof, Rae had said.

No one will believe it. You should just let it go.

And then Ava had just gone on with her life, as if nothing had changed.

The worst part was that later, when Rae lost all her friends after she told Taylor that the government had abducted her father, she couldn't go to her sister. Ava would have said "I told you so," and Rae couldn't take that. She couldn't tell Ava anything anymore, and she'd felt so very alone.

"So," Ava said now.

"A needle pulling thread," Rae answered.

"Ha ha. Very clever." Ava checked her mirror, slowed down. "Do you see this?"

"What?" Rae said.

"The goats?"

Rae frowned out at the road. A man, looking very ordinary in jeans and a T-shirt, was casually strolling down the side of the road with a pack of nine goats. They were all on leashes, like dogs, the ends clipped to a fanny pack he wore snug around his middle. "Huh," Rae said. "Maybe these are the goats we're supposed to mind. Whatever that means."

"This is an odd place," Ava said.

"Yeah, well, you picked it."

Ava sighed. "I suppose so."

"I still don't see why you had to apply to a college as far across the country as possible." Rae crossed her arms. Ava was extremely smart and very motivated. She'd applied to WestConn University in her junior year of high school, less than a month after their dad's disappearance, and they accepted her provisionally; once she completed her high school degree, she was in. Rae hadn't even known it was possible for a junior to do that, but apparently for Ava, everyone was willing to bend the rules a little. Even universities. Clearly her sister could have gone just about anywhere. She didn't need to leave their dad so far behind.

"I've told you," Ava said exasperatedly, "it's one of the only schools that offers a degree in astrobiology."

"But why do you need *that* degree?"

Ava pressed her lips together.

Rae turned her back on her sister and glared out the window at the trees blurring past. Of course Ava wasn't going to answer. She didn't tell Rae anything these days either.

Ava drove the rest of the way in silence, pulling up in front of Eastbury Mall. It looked more like a strip plaza with delusions of grandeur than any mall Rae had seen before. "Doctor Anderson's office is at the end," Ava said.

"Doctor Anderson?" Rae thought that name seemed oddly familiar.

"Your therapist," Ava said. "Need me to come in with you?"

"Definitely not."

Ava smirked. "All right, then. I'll be back in an hour to pick you up."

"Great." Rae got out and slammed her door shut.

She stomped up to Doctor Anderson's office, letting the door swing closed behind her. Unfortunately, it was one of those doors that automatically measured its pace to close softly and gently. No satisfying door slamming here. The office, too, was all soft and gentle, with a small water fountain burbling in the corner, and lotus-shaped lamps in pale greens, blues, and pinks hung around the room. Behind the desk sat a receptionist, a man with a large nose and skinny eyebrows. He smiled at Rae. "Nice to see you here. Rae Carter, is it?"

Rae nodded.

"Your mom already filled out all the paperwork for you, so you can just have a seat." He indicated a row of wicker basket–looking chairs set against the side wall. "The doctor is finishing up with a client, and then he'll be right with you."

Rae sat down two seats from an older woman wearing very bright pink lipstick and pulled her phone out. Her mom had gotten her one of those child-safe versions, the kind that only allowed her to call and text and take photos. Supposedly when she was thirteen, she'd be allowed to actually download some apps.

She pulled open Vivienne's message again and stared at it. She might be busy tonight, but maybe she should invite Vivienne over tomorrow. She typed: **Want to come to my house tomorrow after school?** and sent it before she could second-guess herself.

Three little dots formed, like Vivienne was typing back a response, and then they vanished. And nothing.

Uh-oh. Rae swallowed. Maybe Vivienne didn't actually want to hang out. Maybe Rae was being too clingy? Maybe—

The door in back opened, and a girl came out. She had long brown hair hanging in a tangle down her back, and a pinched, haunted face. She kept her head down and didn't respond when the receptionist told her goodbye. She just hurried outside and got in a car parked right up front.

"Sad, sad story, that one," the old woman near Rae said suddenly.

"What?" Rae said.

"That's Jasmine Green. You heard of her? Of course you must

have, we all have. It's a terrible thing. Very shocking. Everyone around here has been talking about it."

"Um, I'm new, actually," Rae admitted.

"Oh! Ohh," the woman said, drawing out the second "oh" with her too-bright lips. "A new resident! Well, that *is* exciting. It's a shame that you won't be with us for long."

Goose bumps marched up Rae's back. "Why would you say that?"

"People from outside don't usually stay around here, dear."

Rae hugged herself, still feeling cold all over. "So . . . what's the story with Jasmine Green?" she asked, unable to help herself.

"Have you heard about our town's little serial eye snatcher?"

Rae thought about Brandi staggering out of the woods like some sort of zombie, and the article she'd read earlier this week: the attack on the kids playing hide-and-seek this summer.

The woman leaned closer. "Something," she said in a loud whisper, "is sucking the peepers right out of kids' heads. You'd better keep an eye out." She grinned, obviously very pleased with herself for her terrible pun.

"Thanks for the warning," Rae whispered, feeling sick.

"Doctor Anderson has always been a little, hmm, overly interested in the macabre, if you ask me. Even before his wife died. So of course he's been practically dying to hear little Jasmine Green's story. Too bad the girl's not talking."

"Does Jasmine know who the eye snatcher is?" she asked.

"Oh yes. Six kids have been attacked this year, and so far Jasmine is the only *eyewitness*." The woman waited a beat. "Get it?"

"That's really not funny."

The woman pursed her lips. "Fine. Some people have no sense of humor at all." She sniffed, stood up from her chair, and then glided right through the wall.

Rae gaped.

"Rae Carter?" the receptionist called. "Doctor Anderson is ready for you now."

Rae stood slowly and walked to the desk, feeling like she must be in some sort of dream. "That woman . . . she just . . . she . . . she went through the wall."

"Ah," the receptionist said, not seeming surprised. "Bright pink lipstick? Matching shirt?"

"Yes."

"That's Dorothy Emerson. She had a long-standing appointment here on Wednesday evenings, but she died a few years ago."

"She . . . *what?*"

The receptionist shrugged. "Sometimes she still likes to come out and wait. But don't worry, she's pretty harmless. Most of the time."

"*Most* of the time?"

"Oh yes. Otherwise we'd call in the town exorcists. Although Doctor Anderson isn't on good terms with them these days, so we're lucky that Dorothy isn't a problem."

All of a sudden, Rae remembered where she'd heard Doctor Anderson's name before, and the realization was enough to distract her, even from a resident ghost. "Serial eye snatcher," she whispered.

"What?" the receptionist asked.

Doctor Anderson had been quoted in that article. *Eyes are the windows to the soul, and I'm afraid both of those were taken from them.*

"Nothing," Rae said.

"Well then, you'd better hurry. You really don't want to keep him waiting."

Rae stared at the door standing open at the end of the hall. Eye snatchers, ghosts, soul stealers, and exorcists. Suddenly a man walking a pack of goats didn't seem weird at all.

Maybe a psychologist living in a town like this would actually believe her, if she told him the truth about her dad.

14.
CADEN

Caden's stomach did a slow twist, and he felt suddenly too exposed out here on the porch swing.

I'll be seeing you around . . .

"Are you okay?" his dad asked.

"What? Oh yes. Fine. Definitely." Caden couldn't tell his dad that his brother's ghost had been here. His dad still thought Aiden might be alive somehow, somewhere. He hadn't seen the way those tentacles had torn into Aiden's flesh, hadn't heard him screaming as he fell through the rift.

Caden thought of those creatures lurking behind his brother and the feeling of one of them sliding out past him—something with no eyes and plenty of teeth. He gazed across the street at Rae's house, picturing Brandi with her maimed face, the way she'd pointed at Rae's eyes. And he remembered his dream with cold clarity, the feeling deep in his gut that something terrible was about to happen to Rae.

He wasn't the only one in danger.

"Dad," he said slowly.

"Yes?"

"Do you think things from other dimensions can cross fully over to here?"

"Absolutely," his dad said. "Ghosts. Poltergeists. Demons. All of those things are merely transdimensional beings, after all, trying to force the imprint of their energies onto our plane of existence."

"But they're not corporeal." Caden knew the strongest ghosts could manipulate the energies around them, and sometimes that would be enough for them to injure or kill a person, even without their own physical form. But he didn't believe they could remove a person's eyes.

"Ah, so you're asking if something could physically cross over." His dad rubbed his chin, thinking. "Well, yes, I believe so," he said at last. "Although it would require a sacrifice of some kind, or some sort of major display of power. And a host on this side."

"A host? What kind of host?"

"Well, either someone knowingly inviting the being over and allowing them to use their body—"

"Like a possession," Caden said.

"Exactly. Or an unknowing host who was vulnerable in some fashion. Basically, it would need some sort of physical tie to this dimension. This is why I don't recommend letting kids play with Ouija boards, for instance. Leaves them wide open unless they know how to properly ground themselves first. It's basically an open invitation. And once you invite something to join you, it's much harder to get it to leave. Normal banishing spells and charms won't work."

"What would work?"

"First you sever the physical tie, and then you need to send it back to the place from whence it came. That's really the only way to make sure it's truly gone. Otherwise, you can displace it, but the energies will still be here, waiting for another opportunity." He paused. "Why are you asking?"

"Just curious."

His dad looked hard at him. Caden kept his shields up and his emotions in, and after a long moment his dad nodded. "Okay then. I'm going to head inside, see if your mom is almost done with her appointment, then maybe wrangle us up an early dinner. Sound good?"

"Sounds great, Dad," Caden said. "I'll come inside in a minute."

After his dad left, Caden sat there on the swing alone, his mind racing. If something had gotten out before he'd sealed the rift around his brother, then it was his responsibility to somehow get rid of it. Which meant he had to sever its physical link and then send it back.

Unfortunately, he wasn't even sure where it came from. He didn't know enough about what Aiden had done or where he'd gone. But he knew where he could find out: his mother's Book of Shadows.

The Book of Shadows was his mother's own personal grimoire.

The information in it had been passed down from her mother, and her grandmother before that, and her grandmother's grandmother, and possibly a whole lot further back than that. Caden wasn't sure; his mother always kept it locked up and protected. No one else was allowed to look at it.

Which meant that of course Aiden *had* to read it. Caden remembered how obsessed his brother had been with the idea. It had started just after his thirteenth birthday. He'd gone on an assignment with their mom, and afterward she'd told him how he was already as strong and skilled as any adult practitioner she'd ever met.

Does that mean I'm ready for the book? he'd asked. He didn't have to specify which book; he'd been asking about her Book of Shadows off and on ever since he'd caught her writing in it two years ago. Usually she just brushed him off, but this time she got angry.

No, she'd said. *For the final time, you'll get to read it when you're ready to take over the family business.*

What if I'm ready now?

You are ready only when I say you are ready. And I'll hear no more about this. Her expression had been fierce and furious and a little scary. It was one of the only times Caden had ever seen her yell at his brother.

Aiden had gone sullen for the next few weeks, hiding out in his room, barely talking to any of them. He'd always been moody, so at first it wasn't that unusual. But in the past, he'd sulk for a few days, and then their mom would give in and get him whatever it was he wanted and he'd be all sunshine and rainbows again. This time was different. When he didn't want to leave his room, or talk, she just shrugged and left him alone.

So he stopped coming out for meals. Their mom still didn't budge. *He's not going to starve,* was all she said. Caden had been worried, though, as the first day came and went, and the second. By the third day, he couldn't take it anymore. He loaded up his pockets with food and snuck over to his brother's room.

He'd found Aiden still alive, and still smoldering with resentment. Aiden had devoured all of Caden's granola bars, the banana, and the bag of chips in about two minutes flat. And then he'd started pacing, back and forth and back and forth, the way he did when he was thinking hard about something. *It's not fair,* he'd said. *I'm ready for it, I know I am.*

She said she'll let you read it eventually, Caden had told him.

Yeah, maybe when I'm old and shriveled. I want to read it now. *Somehow or another, I will get ahold of it. And on my own timeline, not hers.*

And Aiden always did what he said. Always.

Their mom kept her book hidden and protected under the strongest spells. Things that would literally peel the skin from your fingertips or make you bleed from your eyes and your nose. And those were just the initial guard spells. If you got past them, there were worse things lurking underneath, and you risked losing more than a little skin and blood. Caden didn't see how even his brother would get past them.

Aiden had eventually come out of his room. He quietly started joining the family for dinners, and he didn't mention the book again. But Caden had sensed a difference in his brother from that day forward. It had felt like a wire pulled taut and vibrating, an undercurrent of tension that was always there.

And three years later, his brother had succeeded. A month before he vanished, he confided in Caden that he'd gotten to read the book.

It's bigger than you could ever imagine, he'd said, his eyes glowing with excitement in a way that Caden had never seen before.

What is? Caden had asked.

The world. The universe. Everything. He'd laughed. *I always knew there was another dimension. It's a place full of power. And now I know how to get to it.*

Caden shifted uneasily on the swing, the memories swirling thick and choking around him. If Aiden had discovered this other dimension through his mom's book, then Caden could find out more about it there too. And then maybe he could send this thing back.

Before it was too late.

15.
RAE

Doctor Anderson's office was more brightly lit than the lobby, and painted a cheerful yellow. The chairs were pine green, the carpet purple. It was too much to take in all at once, and Rae froze in the doorway.

"Go ahead and close the door," Doctor Anderson called from behind his desk. Rae closed it, then took a seat across from him. He looked like someone's grandfather, worn and patched and easy to bully into buying you ice cream. Only his eyes didn't quite fit the rest of his faded appearance. They shone a brilliant blue as bright as this room. He watched her silently, but she was used to this kind of tactic and didn't speak. Finally, after several long moments, he asked, "Did you want to tell me about yourself?"

"Not really."

"Okay. That's fine."

Rae blinked. Was it that easy? It almost made her *want* to tell him about herself . . . which was probably the point. She pressed her lips together firmly.

"We could play a game instead, if you'd prefer?" he said.

"A game?"

"I have several." He indicated a small bookshelf behind him, piled with a variety of board games and stacks of playing cards neatly organized by size. "Choose whatever you'd like."

She shrugged and pulled out some cards.

He didn't ask her anything the whole time she shuffled, which was weird. Was she supposed to crack like an egg under the silence? Spill her guts? Rae clenched her jaw and just dealt the cards. She could handle the quiet.

"I see that you have given me seven cards, and there's the draw stack and our discard pile," Doctor Anderson said. "May I assume we are playing rummy?"

Rae nodded.

Doctor Anderson sorted through his hand. "I have always liked games." He pulled a card from the draw pile and discarded the three of hearts. "But do you know what board game is my favorite?"

Rae shook her head. She drew an ace and tossed out one of her low cards.

"Clue. I love the whole idea of solving those whodunit-type mysteries. It's something that has always fascinated me."

Rae studied the doctor. Maybe . . . maybe he was the kind of person who could understand her obsession, her need for real answers.

His eyes brightened, and he cocked his head to the side, waiting. It was like he could smell her wavering.

Rae clenched her jaw shut and turned her focus back to the game. She'd sworn not to tell anyone else the truth about what happened to her dad—not until she had more proof—and that included therapists. And if she couldn't tell him the truth, she might as well not tell him anything at all.

Doctor Anderson sighed and went quiet the rest of the game. Finally, just before their hour was up, he paused, his long fingers hovering over the cards. "I want you to know, Rae, that you can tell me anything, and I'll believe you." His eyes were fever bright. *"Anything."*

"I've heard that before," Rae muttered.

"I have seen enough oddities in my time here that I don't doubt anything is possible. I actually specialize in the supernatural, the unexplainable, the *extraterrestrial*."

Rae stiffened. But of course her mom would have told him everything.

Doctor Anderson steepled his fingers under his chin, regarding her. "In fact, you might almost say I *collect* such stories. And I would very much like to know yours."

A shiver raced up Rae's spine. She stood up. "Thank you for the game. I'm going to go now."

"Next time, then, perhaps."

"Yeah," she said. "Maybe." And she left his office as quickly as she could. He *might* actually believe her—the man had a literal ghost in his waiting room, after all—but she didn't like the way he'd said "collect," like if she told him her story, it would belong to him.

She paused in the lobby. A familiar-looking boy with curly blond hair and brown eyes sat there, playing on his phone: Jeremy Bentley, Alyssa's on-again-off-again boyfriend. He glanced up at her, then away, not saying anything. Rae took her cue from him, and slipped past as if he were invisible. She wondered what he was seeing Doctor Anderson about, but knew she'd never ask.

While she waited outside the plaza for Ava to pick her up, she glanced at her phone. Vivienne had responded.

VIVI: **Sure, tomorrow sounds great! Got any plans?**

Rae thought of Jasmine Green and her haunted, pinched little face. She pictured Brandi, the first person in this town who had been nice to her. And she thought of Dorothy's warning about keeping an eye out. Rae had sworn to find out who was responsible for attacking Brandi. Maybe it was time for her to stop reading articles in her safe little room and be more proactive.

She typed: **How do you feel about a hike through the woods?**

Her dad would have investigated, after all. He was a big believer in focusing on one thing and then digging from there.

Imagine yourself as a tree root. You need to get nice and deep into that soil, and then you can start putting out your feelers, your little side roots, working all the angles. But that first plunge down is what will determine whether or not your tree survives.

Rae's mom claimed her dad was a little *too* focused. It was one of the last fights Rae remembered hearing them have, a week before he vanished. Her mom practically begging, *Can't you just leave well enough alone? You have a family to think of.*

I am thinking of my family. That's the reason I'm doing this.

And then her dad had opened their bedroom door and caught Rae standing there, and her parents let the argument slide away.

VIVI: I'm game if you're really serious?

Ava honked, her car idling in front. Rae quickly typed a response. Just one simple word: Yes. And then she got in the car.

She would search for the truth, just like her dad. She tried to hold on to her determination and ignore the thought that battered insistently at her mind like tree branches against a window:

But look where that search got him.

16.
CADEN

Caden stumbled through the next day of school, his mind focused on his mother's Book of Shadows. Whenever he pictured himself finding it, a jolt of excitement intermingled with fear shot through him. It was the same feeling he used to have those times when Aiden suggested trying a new spell together: that anticipation of being part of something bigger, something a little dangerous.

Caden hated to admit it, but he'd missed that thrill. And he knew, deep down, that he *wanted* to read his mother's book. He wasn't so different from his brother after all.

That thought terrified him. So after school he hurriedly ate dinner, then headed out to sit on the porch swing and sketch, trying to clear his mind. He'd taken up drawing at recess when his classmates stopped letting him play sports with them in first grade, and it had stuck. Sometimes he tried drawing specific things, but tonight he let his pencil move however it wanted, idly tracing the patterns of trees, snowflakes, a burst of sunflowers.

And a face with no eyes, the mouth hanging open.

Caden dropped his pencil, the lead breaking. "Darn it." As he bent down to retrieve it, he caught movement from across the street. Rae slipped out of her house, accompanied by another girl. He recognized Vivienne—no one else wore a backpack that large— and watched as they headed across the lawn and into the trees, doing that particular kind of walk that people did when they were trying to be sneaky.

Caden straightened, his pencil forgotten. What were they *thinking*? Rae, at least, should know better. She'd seen what happened to Brandi! She *knew* something was out there.

He could report them. The sun would be setting in about thirty minutes, which meant curfew, and the police took that *very* seriously. At least they did during a code yellow.

But Caden knew he wouldn't do that.

He sat there for another minute, and then he stood and walked to the edge of his yard. The ring of salt enveloped their house like a hand cupped protectively around them. As soon as he stepped over that line, the evening air changed, becoming sharper. Wilder. The nearby trees seemed to reach jagged branches toward him hungrily, and he could feel the pull of the moon rising up over the horizon.

Caden glanced once at his house, the windows full of cheerful light. And then he crossed the street and headed into the Watchful Woods.

It only took a few steps before he felt like he was in an entirely different world. The trees closed in behind him, cutting off his view of the street, while in front their branches tangled in walls of greenery, the space beneath them littered by leaves and old pine needles.

He didn't see Rae or Vivienne anywhere.

He hurried deeper into the woods, hunching his shoulders. He'd never liked being in here. There was something a little weird about the space beneath these trees. Cell phones didn't work, and people got lost all the time, even when they were only feet from the edge. Whenever the county tried to map out the forest, they came out with different mileages. And Caden could feel a slight vibration of energy that he couldn't quite read, almost like a sound just a little too low to hear. Maybe it had something to do with the Green On! lab at the northernmost border of the woods.

But Caden also knew that Whispering Pines was a spiritual vortex, attracting all kinds of ghosts and other supernatural energies to the area, and that affected the physical realm more than any science lab. That's why the olden-day witches who had been drawn to the town had built their stone walls in a protective pattern.

But as he walked through these trees, he couldn't help but think about that man from last night. Patrick. And how he hadn't had any kind of psychic footprint at all. Maybe Green On! really *was* up to something, deep in these woods.

Caden shivered and gripped his pendant. The wind whispering through the needles of the old pine trees nearby sounded too much like laughter. And beneath it, the crunch of leaves.

Something was following him, trying to walk silently.

He thought of the thing from the other dimension, with its gaping mouth full of teeth and that blank emptiness where eyes should have been. His mouth went dry, and he slid behind a tall pine tree, pressing as close to the trunk as he could. Pine needles poked at him and sap stuck to his skin, but he didn't dare move.

Crunch. Crunch.

It was moving closer. Closer. It was just on the other side of the tree. Any second, and it would see him. He couldn't stay here, but he also couldn't run. His only option was to fight.

Caden caught his breath, waiting until the last possible moment. And then he lunged forward.

17.
RAE

Rae slid on her running shoes, fear and excitement battling it out in her stomach, threatening to make her sick. She could not believe they were going into the very woods Brandi had staggered out of with her eyes missing.

Had Brandi known how to get home? Did she even realize how close she was?

"Ready?" Vivienne whispered.

Rae glanced up the stairs. Her mom was sleeping in preparation for her night shift at the hospital, and Ava was finally studying in her room. She'd been out in the living room forever after dinner, trapping Rae and Vivienne inside—Rae was pretty sure Ava was purposely keeping an eye on her for their mom. But once her sister hit the books, Rae knew she always put on her sound-canceling headphones. The zombie apocalypse could happen without her knowledge. She definitely wouldn't notice if Rae and Vivienne snuck out into the woods.

"Ready," Rae said.

Vivienne hesitated. "It *is* a little late for a hike, though. Did you still want to go?"

"Yes. But it can be a short hike."

Vivienne nodded and shouldered her huge backpack, then opened the front door.

"Don't you want to leave that here?" Rae asked.

"I don't go anywhere without my bag."

Rae thought that was a little weird, but then so was everything else around here. She quietly closed the door behind them, and they crept across the yard. "So, this isn't just a hike," she told Vivienne as they approached the tree line. "It's also an investigation."

"Oh yeah?"

"I, um . . . I saw Brandi the other night." Rae tried to pretend she was a detective, with no emotional attachment to the case, but it wasn't easy.

Vivienne stopped, her attention sharpening.

Rae swallowed hard. "She was missing her eyes," she finished, trying not to picture it. She waited, but Vivienne didn't say anything. And even though Rae didn't know her well, she did know the look of a person who had a secret and was debating whether to tell it or not. "What?" Rae asked.

"I heard about Brandi already," Vivienne admitted.

"You did? How?" It hadn't been in the papers, and Rae was pretty sure Caden hadn't told anyone. As far as she could tell, he didn't really talk to people. Except her, for some reason.

"I have my sources." Vivienne wiggled her eyebrows.

Rae frowned. "What kind of sources?"

"Oh, you know." Vivienne waved a hand. "It's not called *Whispering* Pines for nothing around here."

"Huh," Rae said, unconvinced. Vivienne still had that squirrelly, not-quite-meeting-your-eyes secretive look. She knew something. But it was obviously something she wasn't ready to talk about.

"So where did you see Brandi?" Vivienne asked.

"She came out of the woods right here." Rae pointed just ahead, and they both fell silent. The trees seemed extra sinister in the early evening light, all those naked branches thrust up toward the gray sky. "You still want to come with me? It might be dangerous."

Vivienne nodded, her mouth a thin, grim line. "It'll be safer for you if I'm there too. I know these woods pretty well."

"Yeah?"

"My mom and I spent this past summer hiking through them."

"That sounds fun."

Vivienne shrugged. "It was, until it wasn't." She glanced at Rae, then away again. "Anyhow. We'd better hurry; it's not a good idea to be out there when the sun sets."

For the next few minutes the only sound was the crunch of leaves under their feet, the whisper of tree branches creaking and swaying, the occasional birdcall. But Rae couldn't shake the feeling that something was watching them. Her back prickled, and she had to resist the urge to keep turning and looking.

Vivienne seemed equally jumpy next to her, her hands wrapped tight around the straps of her backpack. Overhead the sky darkened, the space beneath the trees becoming more shadowy until it felt like anything could be hiding beneath them.

"What's that?" Rae asked, nodding at a moss-covered wall just ahead that weaved through the pines and oaks like some sort of stone serpent. It wasn't nearly tall enough to keep anything in or out, coming up to about her waist, but it looked old, the stone dark and gleaming beneath the greenery.

"It's a New England thing," Vivienne said. "These walls are all over the place, built during the colonial days to separate property. Although the ones here in Whispering Pines are special." Vivienne patted the wall fondly.

"Special how?" Rae asked.

"They form some kind of pattern."

"'Some kind of'? That's a little vague."

Vivienne laughed. "Yeah, well, so is the pattern. Every time someone tries to see what it is, it changes."

"That's not possible."

Vivienne shrugged.

"Walls can't just change," Rae added.

"These ones do." Vivienne climbed onto the wall and leaped down on the other side, nimble as a cat despite the backpack.

Rae wondered if maybe Vivienne was joking. But then, in a town where people walked goats, bunnies showed up with their blood drained, and random sinkholes appeared, maybe stone walls really *could* move. Rae put her hands against the slightly damp surface and hoisted herself up and over.

The woods felt different on the other side. Quieter somehow, the air thicker, like it had been dammed up in this space. Rae's lungs tightened almost immediately, a familiar pressure building like a large rubber band around her chest. "Just a sec," she told Vivienne, digging in her pocket for her inhaler. She took a puff, then silently counted to sixty before taking another dose.

"You okay?" Vivienne asked.

"Yeah. Sorry, I think something in these woods is a trigger for my asthma." Rae slid the inhaler back into her pocket. Her lungs felt better, but now she had the shakes. She hated that her inhaler affected her that way.

They walked more slowly now. Nearby, Rae could hear the burbling sounds of a creek. It was a little creepy, with the sun falling lower in the sky, the trees casting long shadows like fingers clawing at the forest floor. Okay, maybe more than a little creepy.

Vivienne stopped suddenly, and Rae ran into her backpack. Whatever she kept in it was quite hard. "Did you see that?" Vivienne asked.

Rae rubbed her nose. "See what?"

"Something just ran across the path in front of us." Vivienne sounded nervous.

"Was it an animal?" Rae squinted around her friend, but she couldn't see anything except about a million trees. She listened again for the creek, and only then did she notice: no birds were chirping, no squirrels scurrying, not even the caw of a crow could be heard. Nothing.

"I don't think it was," Vivienne whispered. She bit her lip. "Want to go back?"

"No," Rae said immediately. "Not quite yet." Then she felt guilty. "Unless you really want to?"

"No," Vivienne said, but she kept glancing around as they resumed walking, the silence growing thicker around them until even Rae couldn't take it anymore.

"It's too—" Rae began.

Crack!

A dark figure lunged out from behind a large fir tree, crashing into Vivienne.

"Aaah!" Vivienne shrieked, stumbling back into Rae.

Rae tripped over her feet and fell on her butt, but Vivienne kept her own footing. She went all berserk on the figure, landing a real good smack to the side of his head, then whipping out a can of pepper spray.

Rae blinked up at their attacker. "Caden?" Her neighbor stood there, rubbing the side of his head, leaves tangled in his spiky black hair. She pushed herself back to her feet, her jeans slightly damp from the forest floor.

"Stay back, or I'll Mace you," Vivienne told him.

He raised his hands. "It's just me."

"I know." But Vivienne didn't lower the Mace. "Why are you following us?"

"Because you both crept out of Rae's house like a couple of burglars, so I was curious."

"So you were *spying* on us?" Vivienne said.

Caden sighed. "I live across the street. It's not really spying if you're doing it literally in front of me. Now, can you please put the Mace down?"

Vivienne lowered her hand. "It's actually breath freshener," she admitted.

"Really?" Rae asked, trying not to laugh.

"I wanted Mace, but it's harder to get around here than you'd think. So I asked my dad for pepper spray, but he, um, must've gotten mixed up. See?"

Rae read the bottle. "Mint Attack."

"I figure it would still sting a little, if a person got it in the eyes." Vivienne eyed Caden. He shifted back a few inches, and she grinned. "I have an extra, if you want it, Rae-Rae."

"Um, okay," Rae said. "Sure."

Vivienne tossed her the Mint Attack, and Rae pocketed it next to her inhaler.

"So, what *are* you doing out here?" Caden asked.

"Since when do you care what other people are doing?" Vivienne demanded. "You don't even like other people."

"That's not true."

"Isn't it?" She crossed her arms. "Before today, you probably said, like, five words to me the entire time I've known you. But now suddenly you're all interested in what we're doing?"

"Maybe I'm just concerned."

"Why?"

"Because there's something in these woods that doesn't belong here." He said it so matter-of-factly, the same way Vivienne said the stone walls moved, or told her a student or two went missing every year. Just another fact of life here in Whispering Pines. He turned to Rae. "You saw Brandi," he added.

"That's why we're here," Rae said. "We want to find whoever attacked her."

"Now?" Caden said. "Sunset is in about fifteen minutes. You don't want to be here when it gets dark."

"Why not?" Vivienne taunted. "Are you afraid of the dark?"

"Oh yes," Caden said softly. "There are things that can see us, hear us, and sense us much more easily in the darkness."

"Well, that's not creepy at all," Rae muttered, hunching her shoulders. "How about we look just a few minutes longer, and then we'll head back?" It didn't feel right to give up on an investigation so early.

"You don't have to stay with us," Vivienne told Caden. "Rae-Rae and I are just fine on our own." She marched forward, moving easily through the trees. Rae caught Caden's eye, and the two of them followed a little more slowly behind.

"Thanks for coming after us," Rae told him, but quietly. She didn't want Vivienne to hear. Even though she wouldn't admit it, it felt a little safer having a third person along. Especially someone like Caden, who seemed like he knew all about the things that slithered through the night. "And . . . sorry I yelled at you yesterday."

He shrugged.

Rae waited, but he didn't say anything. "That was it?" she demanded. "No response? No 'I accept your apology'? Just a shrug?"

Caden glanced at her. "I'm sorry, I'm a little distracted right now."

"Why?" Rae narrowed her eyes.

"Because . . . I think something is following us."

Immediately her irritation vanished, replaced by cold, hard fear.

"Don't look," he hissed, but it was too late; Rae turned and searched the woods behind them. Nothing. But it was still super quiet out here. Which made her think that whatever had chased off the birds was lurking nearby.

"Guys?" Vivienne called. She'd managed to get several feet ahead. "You should see this."

Rae winced at the volume. It was as if Vivienne were announcing their location to . . . well, to anything. Everything.

When Rae caught up to Vivienne, at first all she saw were more trees. But then she noticed, perched behind the trees like some giant carrion bird, an old wooden cabin lurking, the roof steeply arched and covered in moss, tall grass swallowing up the sagging porch. All of the windows were boarded up, the paint on the sides of the cabin peeling in long strips.

No one had lived there for a very long time. Or at least, it was meant to look that way.

"Perfect hideaway for a serial killer," Vivienne said.

"Want to go check it out?" Rae asked.

Vivienne laughed, then stopped. "Oh, were you serious?"

Rae nodded. "What if whoever attacked Brandi lives there?"

"Then we should tell someone else about it and—whoa!" Vivienne staggered back as something darted past them on the other side of the clearing. "Did you see that?"

"It looked . . . almost like a person?" Rae swallowed, terror clawing up her throat.

Vivienne pulled her pack tight against her back. "Right?"

"Yeah," Rae whispered. "Only . . ."

"Only not," Caden finished.

The shape moved again, slipping out of the trees to appear in front of the house before vanishing behind it. Caden was right; it didn't seem quite *human*, its arms and legs too long, its movements spiderlike.

The three of them instinctively moved closer together until their shoulders brushed.

"Maybe we imagined it—*ah!*" Vivienne yelled.

The thing lurched out from behind the house and rushed toward them, moving too fast for them to see clearly in the growing darkness. They could hear it, though, the leaves crunching under its rapidly churning feet, and something else. Some other sound, almost like a growl.

Caden shoved Vivienne and Rae forward. "Go!" he yelled, and then they were all running, crashing through the trees.

Rae could hear her breath wheezing, despite her inhaler, her pulse pounding way too hard. And beneath that, the sound of footsteps gaining on them.

18.
CADEN

Leaves and branches smacked Caden in the face, but he barely noticed. He just kept his legs moving as quickly as possible. Up ahead he could still make out Rae moving gracefully through the woods. He couldn't see Vivienne anymore.

He was falling behind.

He thought of Brandi and her eyeless, slack-jawed face, and put on a burst of speed. He did *not* want to end up like that. Seconds later and he was at one of the short stone walls. He leaped on top of it, his foot sliding a little on the slick surface, and then he was over on the other side and stumbling on. Another minute and he could see the street up ahead.

He burst out from under the trees, gasping as he joined Rae and Vivienne.

"Is it behind you?" Vivienne asked, her Mint Attack held out protectively.

"I . . . ," Caden panted, trying to catch his breath. "Don't . . ." He leaned forward, his hands on his knees, and took in a gulp of air. "Think so," he finished.

"No?" Rae moved closer, peering into the woods.

"I think it stopped at the stone wall," Caden said, straightening. He put a hand to his aching side.

"Why?" Rae asked.

"I'm not sure." Those stone walls had originally been built by a coven of witches to provide protection against the supernatural. Maybe that protection was still effective? But Caden wasn't ready to share all that. "I think we should keep moving. The sun's about to . . ." He looked past the sky at the house in front of him, sitting at the end of a cul-de-sac, and felt like someone had just punched him in the gut.

It was a very nice house, painted a cheerful blue with rose-bushes in front and a carefully painted fence around the yard. But that didn't matter.

"Are you okay?" Rae asked. "You look like you've seen a ghost."

"I'm sure he sees ghosts all the time," Vivienne said. "It's, like, his job."

"I'm fine," Caden said, not taking his eyes off that house. He remembered the moment he'd first seen it, nine months ago. *This will be a safe, easy job.* He shook off the memory of his mother's words, but he could feel their weight hanging on him, and all the memories that followed. He had to get out of here. "Let's go."

"Wait!" Vivienne grabbed his arm. "There's someone in the woods."

Caden stiffened. "Where?" he asked.

"Right behind that house."

A silhouette moved slowly through the edge of the trees. Rae and Vivienne huddled closer to Caden, the three of them frozen as the shape walked toward them. It resolved slowly into a man, his face shadowed beneath a wide brimmed hat, a camera swinging on a strap around his neck.

He frowned at them. "What are you kids doing out here? It's a code yellow. Curfew sets in any minute."

"We were just leaving," Caden said.

"Caden? Caden Price?" The man took a few steps closer, and Caden recognized the features of Doctor Anderson. "I thought I told you and your family to stay away from here," the doctor said.

Caden didn't mean to open himself up, but he got hit with a wave of the doctor's anger, washing over him like water spilling over a pot to sizzle on the stove. His mind filled with images of red, but underneath, there was something else.

Fear.

Doctor Anderson was afraid of something.

"Because I *will* report this, and—" He stopped, his eyebrows shooting up in surprise, then lowering dramatically. "And Rae Carter," he said slowly, staring hard at her.

Caden felt Rae's anxiety rising like tiny pinpricks against his skin.

"What are *you* doing, running around in the woods after dark, and in such company? Hasn't your family been through enough, without you taking unnecessary risks?"

Rae set her jaw. "It's really none of your business. We're going now." She grabbed Caden and Vivienne and practically pulled them down the street with her.

"What was that about?" Vivienne asked her as they jogged away.

"I'm not sure," Rae said. Caden didn't need any special abilities to tell that she was lying. Just as he could tell she didn't want to talk about it.

"How did he know who you were?" Vivienne persisted.

"He, um, knows my mom." Rae glanced at Caden. "But what was his deal with *you*, Caden?" she asked quickly.

Caden wanted to know more about the doctor's deal with *Rae*, but he let her change the subject. "Let's just say he doesn't like me," he said.

"Okay, that's pretty obvious," Rae said. "Why doesn't he like you?"

"In case you haven't noticed, lots of people don't like me," Caden panted, already out of breath again.

"Truth," Vivienne said. "But only because you ignore everyone. Oh, and you possibly murdered your brother and hid him in the walls of your house."

Caden didn't bother to respond to that. Even if he wanted to, he needed all his breath for the run back home.

By the time he led Rae and Vivienne back to his street, it was almost full dark, and he was sweaty and exhausted. Not that Rae or Vivienne seemed at all tired. They both looked like they were just getting warmed up.

"My mom," Vivienne said when they got back, "is going to kill me." She grabbed her bike. "Let's hope she got stuck late at a meeting so I can sneak in before she sees I missed curfew."

A car door slammed in the street, and all three of them jumped and looked up.

"Is that what you're hoping?" A woman wearing a dark red dress and elegantly twisted hair stepped out from the car, her pale face gleaming and furious.

"M-Mom?" Vivienne's bike crashed to the ground. "What are you doing here?"

"Looking for you," her mom said, her anger so thick now that even through his shielding, Caden could feel it sticking to him like peanut butter thrown at a wall. "You know better than to be out at this time of night. Do you see that?" She jabbed her finger up at the sky where the moon hung fat and swollen and almost full.

"I'm sorry," Vivienne said quickly. "I lost track of time." She crouched and grabbed her bike, hoisting it up in one hand.

"So irresponsible." Her mom shook her head. "Especially now, with the recent string of disappearances."

"Disappearances?" Rae asked. "As in, more than one?"

"Someone else went missing?" Vivienne asked.

"Your friend," her mom said. "Jeremy."

"Jeremy Bentley?" Vivienne gasped. She exchanged a look with Rae. "Does Alyssa know?"

Her mom nodded. "I got the call from Joan."

Caden hung back in the shadows, not sure what to say. He'd never really liked Jeremy, but still, the thought of him being attacked, his eyes removed . . . Or maybe he was fine. Maybe this was unrelated. But Caden didn't believe that.

Vivienne's mom turned and walked down the driveway, her heels clicking sharply against the pavement as she made her way back to her sleek gray car.

"Sorry," Vivienne whispered to Rae. "See you tomorrow. If I live that long."

"Good luck," Rae whispered back.

"Vivienne!" her mom snapped.

"Coming!" Vivienne hurried forward, pushing her bike. She popped off the back tire with quick, practiced movements and crammed it and the rest of the bike into the trunk, then got in the car. A second later it whizzed soundlessly down the street.

And then it was just Caden and Rae standing in front of her door. He felt like he should say something, anything.

"Poor Jeremy," Rae said.

"Poor Jeremy," Caden agreed. Maybe that was all you really could say.

Rae put her hand on the doorknob, then stopped. "I know we shouldn't be exploring the woods by ourselves anymore. Especially not at night. But I don't like not knowing what's out there."

Caden waited. He could feel her watching him, the weight of it pressing down like a gathering storm. This was some sort of test, only he had no idea what answers she was looking for. Just that she was measuring him somehow, deciding if he should pass or fail.

"I'm going to do some research," she said at last. "Want to help me figure out what's going on?"

Research. Caden pictured his mother's Book of Shadows, the book that might have all the answers. "Actually, I might know where to look first," he said slowly. "Want to come over tomorrow after school?"

19.

RAE

Rae lay awake in bed, thinking. Before she'd moved to Whispering Pines, she'd only had one person disappear from her life. Here, it felt like people were disappearing all over the place. First Brandi, and now Jeremy.

Her thoughts kept drifting back to that serial eye snatcher article and the one survivor: Jasmine Green. Jasmine, who was a fifth grader at Dana S. Middle School. The only witness.

Too bad the girl's not talking.

Rae knew how it felt to see something unbelievable, and she understood why Jasmine might not want to talk about it. But maybe she'd be willing to share her story with Rae, even if she didn't want to tell some doctor.

Rae turned over on her side, pulling her blankets tighter around herself. Something weird was up with Doctor Anderson.

He'd totally been lurking in the woods, and there were leaves on his hat and dirt on his coat as if he'd been sprinting. There was no way someone his age could have moved as fast as the thing that had been following them. She *knew* that. Nothing human moved like that.

But maybe Doctor Anderson was more than what he seemed.

The next morning, Rae managed to coerce Ava into giving her a ride to school so she could get there early. "Another student is missing," she told her. "This place you made us all move to is basically a death trap." The guilt trip was effective, and as soon as her sister dropped her off, Rae set out in search of the fifth-grade hallway.

The school kept the fifth graders sequestered on the lower level. Rae walked down the stairs, noticing how the lights seemed dimmer, the walls plain brick, no painted murals. She almost felt like she was wandering down a tunnel.

She made her way to the lockers just as the first fifth graders began trickling in. They eyed her suspiciously.

"Are you lost?" one girl demanded, hands on her hips, all fifth-grader sass. It reminded Rae of how she'd been before her dad disappeared and her friends all turned on her. Back when she felt confident in herself.

"No, I'm just waiting for someone," Rae said.

"You're not supposed to be down here. This is *our* space," the girl said, scowling. But then curiosity took over, and she asked, "Who are you waiting for?"

"Jasmine."

"*Oh*," the girl said, drawing the sound out. "Good luck with that."

Rae frowned. That didn't sound promising.

Jasmine showed up a few minutes later, looking smaller than Rae remembered from Doctor Anderson's office. She walked with her shoulders hunched, her head tucked down low like a turtle's, her long brown hair hanging around her face. Rae waited until Jasmine had crept over to her garishly bright yellow locker and started spinning the dial. And then she made her move.

"Jasmine?" Rae said.

Jasmine squeaked, spinning to face her.

"Sorry, didn't mean to startle you. My name's Rae. Rae Carter."

Jasmine didn't say anything.

"I was hoping I could maybe talk to you?"

Jasmine shook her head.

"No? I just had a few questions."

Another head shake.

"My friend is missing," Rae continued anyhow, "and I think . . . I'm afraid it's the serial eye snatcher again."

Jasmine backed away, her hands clutching the straps of her backpack.

"Wait, please," Rae said quickly. This was not going well at all. "I'm sorry. I understand why you don't want to talk about it. But I have to know what you saw."

Jasmine shook her head a third time. Rae thought she was going to bolt, but instead, she took a small, panicky breath. "I already told the police this summer," she whispered. "And they didn't believe me." She darted a terrified glance around the hall. "No one believed me."

Rae's eyes welled up. "I'm sorry," she said. "I know how that feels. And I promise that *I* would believe you."

Jasmine bit her lip.

"I want to catch the eye snatcher," Rae continued. "If you help me, maybe I can—"

"Stay away," Jasmine warned, and Rae wasn't sure if she meant from the eye snatcher or from *her*. Before Rae could ask, Jasmine turned and melted into the growing crowd of fifth graders, and the moment was gone.

Rae sighed, disappointed, but not really surprised. Most people chose to run away from the truth. It was what her mom and her sister had done, after all.

"Rae Carter," Ms. Lockett barked.

Rae jumped.

The vice principal glared at her, familiar clipboard in hand. "You are not where you're supposed to be."

"I was just leaving now," Rae said, backing away.

"Just a second." Ms. Lockett glanced down at her clipboard, her lips pursing, and Rae could tell she was about to get in trouble.

"I saw someone carrying illicit chalk!" Rae blurted.

Ms. Lockett froze. *"What?"*

"Oh yes. So much chalk."

"Where?"

"Down at the end of the hall," Rae lied. "I think he was selling it to the other fifth graders. For, um, sidewalk art."

"Sidewalk art?" Ms. Lockett looked horrified. She spun on one sensible heel and rushed away.

Rae let out a long breath, then hurried in the other direction. She wanted to be far away before the vice principal figured out she was lying. Ms. Lockett was surprisingly intimidating. It had to be the clipboard. And the aggressively styled hair.

As Rae left the fifth-grade hall behind, she doubted she'd see Jasmine again; the girl was probably going to keep as far away from her as she could. So Rae was shocked when Jasmine approached her at the end of school, just outside the main door.

"Were you waiting for me?" Rae asked.

"Do you really think you can stop it?" Jasmine asked, her bottom lip quivering. She had something clutched in her hands, and she seemed so tiny, half-hidden beneath her tangled hair, deep shadows under her brown eyes.

Rae stepped to the side with her so they wouldn't be trampled by other kids escaping Dana S. Middle School. "I don't know," she admitted. "But I want to try."

Jasmine nodded. "The eye snatcher, it's not human. It had no eyes, only darkness. And teeth. So many teeth. That night . . ." She darted a glance around.

"What?" Rae asked gently.

"The eye snatcher caught me, and then let me go."

"Why?"

"I don't know. It told me it would find me later. I think . . . I think it likes to play games." She held out her hands, revealing a crumpled sheet of paper. "This was in my locker." She thrust it at Rae and backed away again.

"Wait," Rae said. "Jasmine—"

But Jasmine had already turned and sprinted toward her bus.

Frowning, Rae unfolded the wrinkled sheet of paper. It had six words scrawled across it in green ink:

Ready or not, here I come.

20.
CADEN

aden felt oddly jittery as Rae followed him inside his house. It was his first time having a girl over. Okay, so she was just there to do research, but still.

"Hello?" he called. Both his parents' cars were gone, but just in case.

No one answered.

"I think we're safe," he told Rae.

"Safe, huh?" she said. "Why? Would your parents mind me being here?"

"Not at all. But they'd mind what I'm planning on doing."

He felt her curiosity sharpening as she followed his lead, both of them kicking off their shoes and heading into the kitchen. He was suddenly very self-conscious about everything: the cheesy plastic black cat clock with the twitching tail, the overflowing spice rack, the dishes left out in the sink.

"I like your kitchen," Rae said.

"Yeah, right."

"I do. It's very . . . comforting." She sniffed. "Must be all the good spices."

Caden smiled, then glanced down at the note his mom had left on the kitchen table:

Caden —
Gone to Sylvia's for a reading. Will be back late.
Love, Mom
P.S. There's a green bean casserole in the freezer.

He ran a hand over the note, his finger pausing on the word "Love." He swallowed and turned to Rae. "She only makes one dish, you know."

"What?"

"My mom. She's been in some kind of silent war of attrition with my dad—she wants him to cook more, so whenever she cooks, it's green bean casserole."

"Oh. How often does she cook?"

"At least five nights a week."

"And . . . how long has this war been going on?"

"For as long as I can remember."

Rae's eyes widened. "That's a lot of green bean casserole. How have you not died of scurvy yet?"

Caden shrugged. "I eat a lot of oranges for breakfast."

"Good plan." Rae grinned. "I admire your mom's determination and follow-through. Also your dad should take a hint already." Her grin faded. "Speaking of . . . are you going to tell me what we're looking for here?"

Caden cleared his throat. Rae had seen Brandi's missing eyes, and she'd only temporarily freaked out about his dream. Would she believe him now, or run from his house screaming? "Do you know what a Book of Shadows is?" he asked.

"No, but it sounds awesome."

He managed a weak smile. "It's a personalized book of spells. My mom's family has had one going back generations. It gets passed down to the oldest Price in the next generation whenever they prove they're ready."

"How do they prove they're ready?"

"Honestly? I have no idea."

"And isn't Price your dad's name?"

This was why Caden didn't open up to people; every time he explained something about his family, he realized there was more weirdness lurking beneath that he'd have to explain too. "My dad took my mom's last name," he said. "It's tradition in my mom's family—they always keep the Price. I don't know why, but it was one of her stipulations when they got married."

Rae nodded. "Good on your mom."

Caden blinked. "You don't think that's weird?"

She shrugged. "It's probably one of the least weird things I've heard since I moved to this bizarro town. So. You want to look at your mom's spell book. But I'm guessing you're not supposed to?"

"Right. No one is allowed to look at it except her. But I think it can help us. Because I think that whatever chased us through the woods, whatever is taking these eyes, it's not human. Not entirely."

Rae nodded.

"That doesn't surprise you?"

"I talked to Jasmine Green earlier today, the one who saw the eye snatcher without, you know, losing her eyes." She stopped, and Caden knew she was thinking about Brandi. "Anyhow," she continued, her voice a little rough, "she told me the eye snatcher wasn't human. And I know there are things around that don't belong on our world." She looked away, her face impossible to read, her emotions a strange jumble. "So, where do we look for this book?"

Caden took the hint and didn't pry. "This way," he said, leading her down the hall to his mother's study. He opened the door quietly. The air inside felt cool and still, almost like walking inside a crypt. "Bad analogy," he muttered.

"What?" Rae asked.

"Nothing." He took a step over the line of purple chalk his mom had drawn on the floor in front of her door, and immediately the hairs on his arms prickled. Another step, and a creeping sense of dread wrapped around him, the feeling that something nameless and terrible would happen if he didn't turn and run.

Aiden wouldn't have let that stop him, so neither could he.

Caden closed his eyes, clenched his fists, and took several long, slow breaths, counting four in on the inhale, four out on the exhale.

The urge to flee slowly faded into a dull, ignorable ache. Caden opened his eyes and took a third step inside. He turned back to Rae, frozen in the doorway.

"It's not real," he said.

Her teeth were clenched, her body trembling.

"Push through it," he coaxed. "Left foot."

Slowly, like she was fighting gravity, Rae lifted her left foot and stepped inside.

"Right foot," Caden instructed.

Rae eased her other foot in, then took another step on her own to stand next to him. She opened her eyes. "That was awful!"

"That was just a symptom of my mom's binding chalk," he said, impressed that she'd followed him through it.

"Wow...No wonder Ms. Lockett doesn't allow chalk at school."

Caden laughed. "Let's get searching." Rae followed him over to the twin bed tucked in the far corner. The blankets were carefully made, and a small pouch of dried herbs rested on the pillow. Looking at that narrow bed made Caden's heart ache. Ever since Aiden vanished, his mom had started spending more and more time in here, sometimes even staying all night. It was yet more proof that his parents were drifting further apart.

He let his eyes glide over to the nightstand beside it, where his mom kept her tarot deck in a special cedar box next to a single large black candle.

Rae opened the nightstand drawer carefully, like she was afraid something would leap out at her. Inside were a few dried petals, several pages of notes, and a folded pocketknife with a white bone handle. Caden remembered that knife; his mom had used it to cut herself the night she'd cast her summoning spell.

Shuddering, Caden left Rae and moved on to the closet, which was mostly empty. His mom only had her work dresses hung up here, the ones she wore when she really wanted to look the part, all long flowing skirts and bright colors. On the shelf above them was a small stack of folded blankets, but again, no book.

He caught movement out of the corner of his eye. He turned, noticing the tall mirror lurking next to his mother's dresser. It looked innocently clear now, but he remembered the silhouette stretching from it, the sound of Aiden's laughter . . . He heard Rae saying she'd check under the bed, but all of his attention was focused on that length of glass. He walked over and stood in front of it.

At first, he just saw himself, his eyes wide and anxious, lips pressed in a thin line. And then his face wavered, shifting, and it was Aiden smirking back at him.

Caden gasped.

"Look at you. I'm gone for less than a year, and you're already breaking into Mom's private study and sneaking girls into the house." Aiden grinned. *"I've gotta admit, I'm a little impressed. I didn't think you had it in you."* His grin dropped. *"But then again, I didn't think you'd ever betray me, either."*

"Look, Aiden," Caden began. He glanced back at Rae, but she was still half under the bed and didn't seem like she'd notice him talking to a mirror. "I'm really sorry. I didn't want—"

"Oh, stop. Poor sensitive little Caden, wracked with guilt. I don't want your apologies."

"Then what *do* you want?"

"Just one simple favor."

Terror flowed through Caden, black and cold. His brother's "simple favors" were always anything but. "W-what is it?"

"I need you to reopen the rift and let me out."

"Let you . . ." Caden stared into the mirror at his brother's face. He looked different, his cheeks gaunt, hair hanging long and dirty. And his eyes had a wild, half-crazed look to them, darting this way and that, like he couldn't let them rest on any one place for long. "Are you *alive?*"

Aiden laughed, a harsh, awful sound. *"If you can call it that."* He shuddered. *"If you help me escape, I'll forgive your betrayal."*

Aiden had never forgiven anything or anyone in his life. He'd changed in there. "How?" Caden asked.

"The book. Which your pretty little friend is about to discover for you."

Caden turned. Now Rae was kneeling in front of the dresser, checking each of the drawers. "Are you done talking to your reflection over there?" she asked, not looking up.

Caden's cheeks burned. Clearly Rae couldn't see Aiden. "It's not, I mean—" he began.

"Check this out," Rae continued, ignoring his sputtering. "I think there's a hidden compartment in here." She pulled the bottom drawer out of the dresser and set it to the side. "See, this drawer is not as deep as the others. So that means there's probably something . . ." She reached into the space below where the drawer had sat. "Yep, there's—ahh!" She snatched her hand out and fell back, horrified.

"What? Are you okay?" Caden rushed over. Her hand looked okay to him, but she hadn't stopped staring at it. "Rae?"

She finally tore her gaze from her fingers. "Whatever's in there, I'm not touching it again."

Caden crouched down and peered into the dresser. Underneath where the drawer would sit was a small hollowed-out space, hidden in shadow. He reached inside it, brushing against something hard and rectangular.

A jolt ran through his fingertips, and he jerked his hand back. Then he gritted his teeth and made himself reach in again, his hand closing around a book. It vibrated as if it were a box full of scorpions, and his skin crawled. He pulled the book closer as pain shot through his fingertips, his nails peeling back, the skin splitting.

"Ah!" He dropped the book, and the pain slowly ebbed.

"These are just standard revulsion spells. The effects are all in your head."

They felt so *real*. Caden set his jaw and pulled the book out. Blood dripped from his nose, and his ears filled with a horrible dull ache. His teeth loosened in his mouth—he could feel them wiggling—and suddenly they weren't teeth at all, but maggots burrowing into the rotting flesh of his mouth.

Caden sobbed and almost flung the book away.

"Stop being a baby." Aiden's scorn cut through the awful sensations of their mother's spell, and Caden managed to set the book in his lap, but he still couldn't open it. His heart was beating too fast and he had the terrible feeling that if he read past the

cracked leather cover, he would die. His breath came in small, short gasps.

And then slowly the terror faded until it was just background noise. His teeth were just teeth, his fingernails were fine, and he wasn't about to die. He ran his tongue around the inside of his mouth, grimacing. That had to have been one of the worst sensations he'd ever experienced.

"Are you all right?" Rae knelt next to him, her concern wrapping around him like a much-needed hug.

"Never better," he croaked.

"You really scared me! I didn't know what to do."

He let out a short, humorless laugh. "I scared me too. But it worked. Here it is."

"Are you sure that's the right book?" Rae asked.

It *looked* simple enough, with a plain black cover, slightly battered, the pages stuffed full of notes and serrated along the sides, but it *felt* terrible.

People's emotions tended to bleed into the objects they used a lot, especially if they used them while feeling something very strongly. But with his mother's Book of Shadows, it was the other way around. It carried its own energy, and he knew if he held it long enough, it would mix with his own essence like honey in his dad's favorite tea. Only there was nothing sweet about the emotions emanating out of these pages.

"I'm sure," Caden said dryly. He opened the cover, then flipped through the pages, letting intuition guide his fingers. Every available space was taken up by scribbled notes, diagrams, spells, recipes, and stories. There wasn't any kind of organization that he could see. Not at first.

And then he realized that most of the pages referenced something called "the Other Place." He read a description:

The Other Place sits below our dimension, throbbing like a diseased heart. A wrong place, full of the Devourers, the Ravenous, the Unseeing, all feeding on our fears. And because fear is powerful, there is great potential for those who dare to cross its boundary.

But for every crossover, there is a price.

Blood opens and blood closes. A sacrifice given and taken.

"What's 'the Other Place'?" Rae asked, reading over his shoulder.

Caden pictured the world his brother had fallen into. "It's a horrible alternate dimension, full of monsters and tentacles, and this awful light." He waited for Rae's reaction.

"Who named it?"

"I don't know."

"They couldn't have come up with something more imaginative than the Other Place?" Rae shook her head.

"You're not, like, freaked out right now?" Caden asked.

"Oh, I'm totally freaked out." She sat down next to him, and he couldn't help noticing the way her shoulder bumped his.

He tried ignoring it as he turned the page, then stopped, caught by a drawing of a woman with her mouth open in a silent scream, hands pressed to her cheeks, fingernails long and ragged as they raked bloody lines through the skin where her eyes should have been.

"Whoa, what's that?" Rae asked.

"I don't know, but it looks . . . sort of familiar." He looked at the page next to it, where a story had been written in careful handwriting. "'Birth of the Unseeing,'" he read.

"Sounds promising."

"'Long ago,'" Caden continued reading, "'when giants roamed the earth and man knew how to harness the power of starlight, when ice stretched from coast to coast and the warmth of the sun was a distant dream, there lived a man with hair the pale gold of dawn's first light, and eyes the winter blue of the sky. But though he was lovely to look upon, beneath his beauty lay a cold, calculating cruelty, as harsh as the landscape he dwelt upon.'"

"Why is a fairy tale in your mom's spell book?" Rae asked.

"I'm not sure."

"Well, read the rest and see if it says."

Caden skimmed the rest of the story. "The man was eventually cast out of his village, and then he roamed the frozen landscape until he fell in love with a beautiful woman who did not love him back. So he blinded her and abandoned her in the wilderness."

"Sounds like a real charmer," Rae said.

"Don't worry, the girl's aunt gets revenge," Caden said.

"Good. Read me that part."

Caden smiled. "'Her aunt was not an ordinary woman but a

powerful witch, although she had cast no spells in years. In her despair and rage, she tracked down the evil man and cursed him thusly: that he would live out an eternity in darkness, never to see out of his own eyes again.

"'But the aunt had forgotten the first rule of witchcraft: any curse cast upon another will turn upon the caster threefold. The man lost his own eyes, but gained the ability to steal the eyes of others. And so, though he was doomed to wander for eternity in darkness, he never wandered alone.

"'And thus the first Unseeing was born.'"

"Creepy," Rae said. She frowned. "Is that what we're looking for, then? Some kind of cursed person?"

"I don't think so. These stories are probably more like metaphors." Caden flipped through more pages. He saw a drawing of one of the tentacled things that had attacked his brother, and more stories. In fact, it looked like most of his mom's Book of Shadows was about that dimension.

His mom knew about the Other Place this whole time. Which meant she knew exactly where Aiden was. So why hadn't *she* tried to reopen the rift?

"Blood opens and blood closes," Caden recited. "A sacrifice given and taken."

"Um, Caden?" Rae said, her anxiety cutting through his shields.

He blinked, tearing his gaze from the pages of the book in his lap. The room seemed darker and colder, shadows gathering along the edges of the walls and slowly thickening, twining out like the vines of some night-blooming plant.

"The mirror," she gasped. Its surface rippled like a lake on a windy day, flashes of yellow and green swirling up before disappearing into its depths. A shadow grew in the center, elongating, becoming the outline of a person, solidifying into Aiden's familiar face. He seemed somehow more real than his reflection before. And clearly, Rae could see him now too.

"*Stop wasting your time on stories,*" Aiden said. "*You need to find the ritual.*" His eyes lit up with the same eerie yellowish glow as in the Other Place, and the pages of the book began flipping rapidly.

Rae put her hands over her mouth and inched away.

"*We can't reopen the rift here. You need somewhere with lots of negative energy,*" Aiden said, and Caden wondered if Rae could hear him now as well as see him. "*But we can find another place—*" The pages stopped flipping, and Caden stared at the crease in between where a sliver of torn paper poked out.

Something had been ripped out of the book.

"*No,*" Aiden gasped. He looked up from the book, meeting Caden's gaze. "*I'll just have to talk you through it and—*"

Tentacles burst forth from the mirror behind Aiden, cocooning him in their slimy grasp. He flailed against them. "*Not yet! I still need—*"

There was a horrible ripping, sucking sound. Aiden screamed, the veins in his face popping, and then he was gone, and the shadows and weird light with him.

"Who," Rae asked slowly, "was *that*?"

"That," Caden said, "was my brother, Aiden."

21.
RAE

The referee blew one sharp blast on her whistle, and Rae launched herself forward. Her heart thumped in time with her feet as they pounded against the track. She pushed herself, hoping to somehow leave everything she saw the other day behind. She wanted to forget Caden's brother, trapped behind the mirror. She wanted to forget those tentacles that came out and grabbed him. And she wanted to forget Caden's explanation of the Other Place, the dimension that lurked beneath their own.

She rounded the first bend, her eyes on the girl in front of her. She could hear Alyssa practically breathing down her neck, but stayed focused on the lines of the track, on lengthening her stride, on the way her breath hitched inside her tightening lungs.

Eight laps. She just had to make it through eight laps. They'd divided up everyone into two groups; the top five from each group automatically made the team. Rae had done a lot of running with her dad, but never on a track. Still, she knew she was fast, and two miles wasn't that far.

But she should have used her inhaler before this.

By lap seven she was holding on to second place, but just barely. The edges of her vision had gone bright, spots floating in the middle of her eyes. She blinked them away as she started down the eighth lap. Her mouth tasted like blood, and she felt like she was pushing herself through Jell-O, the air growing thicker, holding her back. Alyssa slipped in front of her, her blond ponytail streaming behind her, followed by another girl, Sara, an eighth grader with short brown hair.

Rae tried to speed up as she rounded the next bend. Only one last straight to run, and there was the finish. Her world shrank to the wheezing of her lungs, the slapping of her feet on the track, and one narrow strip of sight. She put on a final burst of speed, passing Sara right before the finish line. Then she bent over and put her hands on her knees, sucking in air in great, wheezing gasps. It felt like she was breathing through a straw that someone had pinched closed.

"Woo-hoo! Way to go, Rae-Rae!" Vivienne ran up to her.

"Third place," Rae wheezed. "I finished third."

"Yeah, but considering you look like death, that isn't bad. Besides, third in any event is high enough to get you on the team." Vivienne beamed. "Welcome to the Dana S. Roadrunners!"

"You sound like a dying goose," Alyssa said, trotting over to them.

Vivienne glared at her.

"What, she does! Also, Coach is looking this way."

Rae straightened up. She didn't think Coach Briggs, a tough woman with a no-nonsense attitude, would approve of her bent over, sucking in air like an amateur. And forgetting to use her inhaler was a rookie mistake. It was just, back home she hadn't needed it so often. Something about this place . . .

"Need your inhaler?" Vivienne asked.

"Vivienne!" Coach Briggs called. "You're up!"

"Rae?" Vivienne said.

"I'm fine." Rae blinked a few times, the world spinning slightly.

Vivienne hesitated, but Rae waved a hand at her, and she jogged toward the start line.

"You use an inhaler?" Alyssa said. "Want me to get it for you?" She actually sounded . . . concerned. Rae waited for some additional comment, something snarky and scornful—something Taylor would say—but there was nothing.

"I can get it." Rae took a careful wheezing breath. "But thanks." She wobbled away from the track, Alyssa walking carefully next to her like she was prepared to carry Rae if needed. It was weird.

"I think that was one of my best times," Alyssa said as they meandered over to the metal bleachers set up on the side of the field. Rae wasn't sure why Alyssa was still talking to her like they were good friends. Maybe she just wanted to rub in her better finish? Rae concentrated on her breathing and didn't say anything back, but that didn't seem to matter to Alyssa. "I actually almost got first," Alyssa continued. "But second is pretty good. I think Mom will be happy."

Rae couldn't help but think that if she hadn't had an asthma attack, that second finish would have been hers. Maybe even first. "I didn't know your mom came out today," she said.

Alyssa looked away. "She didn't."

Guilt punched Rae, hard and strong. She hadn't been trying to be mean. "Oh," she said. "Sorry."

"No, it's okay. She doesn't usually come out to tryouts." Alyssa shrugged. "She'll come out to the meets, though. Sometimes."

Rae glanced up at her own mom. She was sitting at the top of the bleachers furiously typing something into her phone. Rae doubted she'd actually seen any of the race. Still, at least she was here. She tried not to imagine how different it would have been if her dad were here, but it was impossible not to think of how he'd have been cheering louder than anyone. Probably wearing a ridiculous hat and waving a large sign and being super embarrassing in the best way.

Her mom must have felt her staring. She glanced up, gave Rae a small wave and an even smaller smile, and then went back to her phone. Rae sighed.

"My mom's just really busy," Alyssa said as she and Rae sat down next to each other on the lower bench of the bleachers. "I mean, she wants to come out more, but ..."

Rae didn't know what to say, so she busied herself with digging around in her pack. She shoved aside a pair of jeans and a T-shirt, her fingers brushing against Vivienne's Mint Attack before curling around her inhaler.

Vivienne had told her that Alyssa's dad was basically not in the picture. After he and Ms. Lockett got divorced five years ago, he'd moved out of state and barely kept in contact. Rae could tell how much Alyssa wanted her mom's attention, as if it might make up for that loss. Rae knew it wouldn't, but she wasn't sure how to tell Alyssa that. Not without being a lot more open than she wanted to be.

She took a puff of the inhaler.

Another sharp blast of the whistle, and Vivienne and the others took off on the 1,500-meter run. Vivienne effortlessly moved to the front of the pack, holding her lead as they finished the first lap. For someone so short, she sure moved fast. It was the way she loped along so naturally, like a wolf.

Rae released her breath, then pressed on her inhaler for a second puff. It barely seemed to be helping.

"Um, Rae?" Alyssa sounded younger suddenly, her voice high and nervous.

"Yeah?" Rae dropped the inhaler in her bag.

"I'm sorry if I came across as a little harsh before."

Rae stared at Alyssa. "What?"

Alyssa pushed her sweaty bangs back from her forehead, her blue eyes watery. Rae really hoped she wasn't about to start crying again. Alyssa had been crying pretty constantly ever since Jeremy vanished. Not that Rae blamed her, but tears always made Rae uncomfortable. Especially in this case, where she thought she knew what had happened to Jeremy.

"You know," Alyssa said, "not inviting you to the movies and being mad about you taking my seat—you did totally take my seat, though. But I know Vivienne told you to take it, and that's really why I was mad. It wasn't *your* fault."

"Oh." Rae felt like she'd forgotten all of her carefully practiced social skills. She was not equipped for this conversation. "That's okay," she managed. She wasn't sure how she felt about this sadder, nicer, apologetic Alyssa. It was a lot easier before, when she could view her as just another Taylor.

But Taylor had never once apologized.

"It's just, Vivienne." Alyssa sighed. "She's been acting strange all year, even before you got here. Ever since this summer, in fact."

"Strange how?"

"Well, kind of secretive. Like, what is up with that backpack?"

"I thought that was just her thing."

"It didn't use to be." Alyssa stared out at the track. Rae followed her gaze. Vivienne was still well in the lead. Just past the track, Rae could see another field, only it was blocked off with wooden barriers and bright green tape, a large deep shadow darkening the middle of it surrounded by silhouettes. She raised a hand above her eyes and squinted closer, and the silhouettes resolved themselves into a group of Green On! employees in their toxic-colored hazmat suits, all circling the perimeter and jotting down notes.

They were probably just studying the sinkhole.

Just the sinkhole.

Rae frowned. She'd barely lived in Whispering Pines, but already she was getting used to all the oddities. Like Vivienne always carrying around a giant backpack. It seemed strangely . . . normal, at least for here. She hadn't really even questioned it. But now she wondered exactly what kinds of secrets Vivienne was keeping.

"We used to share everything," Alyssa said. "I mean, we've been best friends since kindergarten, you know? But now . . . I don't know. And then here you show up, and suddenly it's like she has this new exciting friend and doesn't need me anymore, and—" Alyssa pressed her lips together, as if she was trying to keep the flood of words back. And then she looked at Rae, obviously waiting for something. Some kind of response. But what was Rae supposed to say to that? Sorry? She didn't arrive in Connecticut with the purpose of stealing Alyssa's friend.

Rae took a deep breath to tell her that, then started coughing. Ugh, that inhaler had been next to useless.

Alyssa frowned and turned away. "Anyhow," she said, her tone colder now. "I just thought I owed you an apology."

"No," Rae gasped. "I mean, I—"

Alyssa stood and flipped her ponytail back over her shoulders. "I'm going to go congratulate Vivi," she announced, and then she marched off, leaving Rae to wheeze in peace.

"Talk about awkward," someone said.

Rae turned. A boy hovered behind her, his blond hair mostly hidden beneath a knit cap. "Rae, right?" he said.

She nodded. "Hey, Ivan."

"Oh good, you remember me." He smiled. "Mind if I sit with you?"

"Um, sure." She couldn't think of a good reason not to let him. But as he climbed forward onto the seat next to her, settling in too close, she began to regret being polite. He seemed like he was a little too interested in her.

She shifted slightly away.

"I make you uncomfortable, don't I?" Ivan said.

Rae admitted, "A little."

Ivan sighed. "I'm sorry. It's just . . . you're the only other new kid at our school. I hoped we'd have things in common." His brown eyes stared very intently into her own. "And I could really use another friend right now."

"Why?" And then Rae could have kicked herself. "Oh. Jeremy."

Ivan looked away, his hand coming up to half hide his face, like he might start crying.

"I'm sorry," Rae said. "I hope he turns up."

"I'm sure he will. Eventually."

But in what condition? Rae kept this thought to herself.

Ivan reached over, and for one panicked moment she thought he might try holding her hand, but he just took hold of the zipper on her bag and closed it.

Rae frowned. "Please don't—" she began.

"Ivan! Hey!" Alyssa bounded over to them. "Have you heard anything yet? Did they find him?"

Ivan shook his head. "Nothing yet."

Alyssa's shoulders slumped.

"You know you'll be the first person I call if I do hear anything," he promised her. He moved over on the bench, leaving space between him and Rae. "Come, sit with us."

Alyssa glanced at Rae and hesitated, like she thought she was trespassing on Rae's turf. It was another way Alyssa was so much different from Taylor. Even back when they were friends, Taylor always wanted whatever Rae had.

Rae wondered if she'd been unfair with Alyssa from the beginning.

"I don't bite." Ivan patted the seat next to him again. "Besides, you must be tired after your race. I watched you out there; you were incredible."

Alyssa's cheeks colored, and with one last sidelong glance at Rae, she stepped over the lip of the bleachers and wedged herself in the open space. "Thank you."

"Rae-Rae!" Vivienne yelled from the edge of the track, waving her over. "Alyssa!"

Rae stood. "Coming?" she asked Alyssa.

"I'm good here," Alyssa said, not looking at her.

Rae shrugged and grabbed her duffel, then headed over to where Vivienne stood with Carly, another girl from their grade.

"You feeling better?" Vivienne asked. "Up for some celebratory ice cream?"

"Ice cream?"

"We always go after tryouts," Carly told her. "All of us who made the team. It's tradition."

Rae glanced up at the bleachers, seeking out her mom, but stopping instead on Ivan, who was staring right at her. He didn't look away now, and as she turned back to Vivienne, she could feel him still watching her. "It's only for people who made the team, right?" Rae asked. "No one else allowed?"

"Only for the team," Vivienne confirmed.

Rae relaxed a little. "Okay, then. Let me go ask my mom."

Rae settled in front of her desk at home, a local newspaper open in front of her. She hummed as she searched through it, feeling content and full of ice cream. She was on the cross-country team now. After only one week at school, she'd managed to find herself a group to belong to. She had figured out how to fit in.

Rae smiled and flipped another page of the paper, skimming the articles. Most of them were small things, local town heroes doing heroic acts, bizarre weather patterns, and the occasional oddity. She stopped at a large photograph of a woman holding a skull in one hand, a proud-looking pit bull sitting at her feet with a femur in his mouth. Next to it was a very weird article:

WERE BODIES LEFT BEHIND?

Whispering Pines, CT. It's a well-known but not-often-talked-about fact that Whispering Pines's brand-new town square used to serve a much darker purpose: a burial ground for the dead. In fact, until about twenty years ago, that whole area was covered in gravestones.

The town paid a large sum to have the graves exhumed and everything moved to Peaceful Pines Cemetery, but recent events have caused citizens to wonder how thoroughly this job was carried out.

"I was just walking Archie—that's my dog, by the way—when we came across a pile of bones! A pile!"

says longtime resident Sylvia Benton. "So now I'm thinking . . . what if they just moved the gravestones, and left the bodies there?"

Whispering Pines has many festivals throughout the year, all of which take place in the town square. Further investigation will be required to determine whether or not citizens of this town have been literally dancing on the dead.

Rae shook her head. It was strange, but not related to her current case. Still, she carefully cut the article out. She unclipped the decoy corkboard and set it to the side, her eyes skimming over the cluttered board behind, searching for a good spot.

She froze.

There was the photograph of her and her dad . . . and next to it, pinned over an article about a possible UFO crash in Texas, was a *new* photograph. One of Caden, and Vivienne, and her. In the woods.

Rae's heart stopped, then started again, racing to make up for missed beats.

Someone had taken a picture of them in the woods. And then somehow snuck into her house, into her *room*, and pinned it here, in the one spot Rae thought was safest of all.

22.
CADEN

Someone was frantically banging on the door. It reminded Caden a little of fall thunderstorms, the sound rising and falling like rain.

He lay in bed, listening. He'd been sluggish all day and didn't feel like getting up. But when a minute passed and no one answered the door, he finally stood and walked slowly down the stairs, his bare feet slapping against the wood. "Mom?" he called. "Dad?" No answer. Just that relentless pounding.

Sighing, Caden threw open the door.

Rae half fell into his house. She caught her balance, then pushed him farther in and pulled his front door shut behind her, locking it.

"Um, nice to see you, too?" Caden said. "Please come in?" Though he was happy to see her. He had wondered if Rae would ever talk to him again after yesterday. She'd seemed super freaked out by the whole his-brother-trapped-in-another-dimension thing. Apparently, witches and spell books were one thing, but the Other Place was something else altogether.

She peered out the small window in his door, then turned around. "Yes, sorry. Thanks for letting me in. I'm really, really glad you're home."

Caden felt strangely pleased, but then he noticed how terrified Rae looked, her skin an ashen gray, her eyes so wide he could see the whites all around. And the fear roiling around her was overpowering. He wasn't sure how he'd missed that initially.

"Tryouts go well?" he said, trying to calm her.

"What?"

He nodded at her new Dana S. Middle School Roadrunners T-shirt.

"Oh. Yeah, I'm on the team. Can we get away from the front door?" Rae glanced back over her shoulder. "I have something to show you."

Caden stepped to the side and waved her through. Rae paused to kick off her shoes, nudging them next to his, and then followed him into the kitchen. She dropped her weight into one of the small wooden chairs and plunked a wrinkled piece of paper on top of the table, then waited.

Caden sank slowly into the chair next to her and leaned over to look.

It was a photograph: there was Caden, his hands raised slightly, and Vivienne, her Mint Attack aimed right at his face, both of them just slightly out of focus. And Rae centered in sharp relief, sitting on her butt in the leaves and staring openmouthed up at him.

Caden caught his breath. No wonder Rae was terrified. "Where did you get this?" he asked.

Rae's lips trembled. "I found it," she whispered. "In my room."

"Your room?"

She nodded. "Someone was in there, Caden. Someone got in while I was gone, and I've been closing and locking all the windows and doors since the night Brandi turned up." She shuddered, and Caden wondered if she would ever feel secure enough to sleep again. "How could someone possibly sneak in without breaking any of the locks and manage to get into my second-story bedroom? Unless you're right, and it's not some*one* at all, but some*thing*." She took a deep breath. "So. How do we get rid of it?"

We. It filled him with warmth, before the reality of what she was asking him sank in. His dad had told him how: they needed to send it back "from whence it came." Which meant . . . "We need to reopen the rift," he said.

"Do you know how?"

Caden hesitated. The honest answer was "no." After Rae left last night, he'd gone through the rest of his mother's Book of Shadows. There were a few mentions of the Other Place, alluding to a ritual, but the description of the ritual itself was missing. Without the torn pages, Caden had no idea what to do. And he hadn't felt a hint of Aiden since his brother had been pulled away, back into the mirror.

But Rae was staring at him like he might actually have the

answers. Like he knew what he was doing. It wasn't a look he was used to, but he liked it. So he lied. "Yes," he said, even though his stomach wriggled. He'd just have to figure it out somehow.

Rae smiled. "Good. So we just have to find out where it's hiding." She fiddled with the photograph on the table.

"According to my dad, creatures like the Unseeing can cross over from other dimensions as long as they find a host on this side." At Rae's blank look, he clarified, "A possession."

"Like *The Exorcist*?"

Caden winced. That was always the first thing people thought of when they found out what his family did. "Sort of," he admitted reluctantly. "Anyhow, that means this Unseeing is probably hiding among us, pretending to be fully human."

Rae nodded. "Creepy, but okay. That makes sense." She tapped her chin. "Actually, it makes a *lot* of sense. I think I might know who it is."

"Me too," Caden said. "I think it's—"

"Doctor Anderson," Rae said, at the same time that Caden said "Patrick."

They both stared at each other. "The Green On! guy?" Rae said at last, wrinkling her nose. "Why him?"

Caden paused. He may have told her what happened to his brother, but he wasn't ready to share his ability to feel others' emotions. He got the sense that might be the thing that finally scared her off. "He just seems suspicious," he said. "I mean, he already knew who I was, and I'd never met him before."

"Hmm," Rae said, but she sounded unconvinced.

"Plus he's personally collecting all the victims and taking them off to some secret lab? If that doesn't scream suspicious, then I don't know what does."

"Okay," Rae said slowly. "While I will agree he may be a *little* suspicious, I think we need a bit more to go on before shoving him into another dimension. Plus I don't think he should be our prime suspect."

"Prime suspect?" Caden laughed. "What are we, detectives now?"

"Laugh away, *Detective Price*, but I think Doctor Anderson seems like a much more likely candidate. Here's why." She ticked off reasons on her fingers. "First of all, he's creepy. There's no denying that."

"No denial here."

She smiled. "Second of all, he was there when we came out of the woods. Like, standing right there. *And* he had a camera on him. He could easily have been the one stalking us through the trees, taking our picture . . ." She shivered. "Third of all . . . I saw him on Wednesday. Before the woods. In his office."

"Oh," Caden said. He thought of how anxious she'd been when Doctor Anderson recognized her outside his house. Now he understood: for some reason, she didn't want anyone to know she'd been seeing the doctor. "Okay," he said. When he didn't ask her anything else about it, some of the tension seemed to slide out of her.

"Anyhow," she continued, "when I left, I saw that Jeremy Bentley was waiting to see him too. And then Jeremy vanished."

Caden fiddled with his pendant, debating. Then he sighed. "I actually have a fourth reason to add to your list. You know I said Aiden vanished during an exorcism?"

"Yeah?"

"Well, it was at Doctor Anderson's house."

Rae gasped. "And you're just *now* telling me that? Well, that settles it!" She leaned forward, putting her elbows on the table. "He's got to be our guy."

"Maybe."

"Maybe? Come on, Caden. You told me this creature can possess people—"

"I said it *might* be like a possession."

"—and here it came out of the wall in Doctor Anderson's house?"

"It was actually a doorway."

"Whatever. It's gotta be him. I'm sure of it."

"To quote a wise person I know, I still think we need a bit more to go on before shoving him into another dimension."

Rae grinned. "Okay. That's fair." She leaned back in her chair and looked around his kitchen, radiating purpose and contentment. She liked doing this kind of research and discussion, Caden realized. And even more surprising, he kind of liked it too.

"I guess we'd better investigate the good doctor, then," Rae decided. "I mean, if we're detectives now, and everything. We can break into his house on Monday when he's working, and see if we can find anything."

Caden stared at her. "Break into his house? Are you serious?"

Immediately her good mood vanished. "Look, Caden, in case

you haven't noticed, all of the victims of this Unseeing have been students from our school, aged twelve to fourteen. And as far as I can tell, I'm the next target." She jabbed the photograph on the table. "So yeah, I'm very serious."

Caden couldn't argue with that. "How are we going to break in?"

"I have no idea," Rae admitted. "But I'll think of something, then text you."

"You don't have my number."

"No, but I will before leaving here." She smiled sweetly and held her phone up to him. Caden took it. His face felt too warm as he punched in his number, and when he passed the phone back, he had a hard time meeting Rae's eyes.

"Your brother disappeared in late December, right? Nine months ago?"

Caden studied the rings on his fingers. "Yeah. Why?"

"Well, I looked up missing people in Whispering Pines, and it looks like another kid went missing around that same time. A thirteen-year-old boy."

"Peter McCurley." At Rae's look, he explained, "His parents asked my mom to try to find out what happened to him."

"And did she?"

"I don't know. She hasn't said."

Rae nodded. "After Peter, then, there was nothing for three months. And then after that, three kids from our school vanished in March, and then were found with their eyes removed, and again, nothing for three more months. Then those three kids playing hide-and-seek this summer. Late June."

"And nothing again," Caden said slowly, "until this past week. With Brandi. And then Jeremy. So he's looking for his final victim."

"At least for this round," Rae said. "It's like that story said. Threefold. Right?"

Caden hadn't considered that. "Possibly. But what about Peter? He doesn't really fit the pattern."

"Maybe Peter's disappearance is unrelated."

"The timing seems rather coincidental."

"Hmm . . ." Rae tapped her lip in thought. "Well, I've read that often a serial killer's first kill is different from the rest. It takes one victim before they establish a trend."

"Been doing some light reading, huh?"

Rae smiled. "I know, it's a little weird."

"My family hunts ghosts," Caden pointed out. "I'm not about to accuse you of weirdness."

"That's true," Rae laughed. She stood up, grabbing her photograph and stuffing it in her back pocket without looking at it.

Outside came the rumble of a car up the driveway. "Want me to walk you home?" Caden asked quickly.

"That would be nice," she said.

Caden grabbed his jacket off a hook by the door and slipped outside just as his dad got out of the car. "Did I beat your mom home?" he asked. Then he noticed Rae, and his eyebrows shot up. "Oh! Why, hello there!"

"Hi," Rae said shyly.

Caden knew he was stuck. Better to get it over with quickly and hope his dad waited to be embarrassing. "Dad, this is Rae.

She lives across the street. Rae, my dad. And we'd better go," he added, before his dad could say anything, "because it's almost curfew."

"Wait just a second," his dad said. "I want to know more about this mysterious beauty you're trying to hustle out of here."

Caden's cheeks burned so hot, he thought his hair must be smoldering. "Dad. Seriously."

"What's your name?" his dad asked Rae.

"Rae."

"A drop of golden sun, eh?"

Caden winced. This was so, so awful. But to his surprise, Rae actually laughed at that. "My dad used to make jokes just like that," she said.

"He sounds like a man of good taste."

Rae's smile faltered. "Yeah," she said.

"We really have to go," Caden cut in.

"Where are *you* going?" his dad asked him.

"I'm just walking her home." Caden nudged Rae forward.

"Oh you are, are you? How gallant."

Caden winced. "Hurry," he whispered at Rae.

"That's not very gallant," she whispered back, grinning. They crossed the street, stopping outside her door. "I'll text you tomorrow so we can plan."

"Sure." Caden shoved his hands in his jacket pockets and shifted his weight. Should he say something else?

"I might invite Vivienne, too."

"Okay. It'll be nice to share a jail cell with more people."

"We're not going to get caught," Rae said. "Worst case? We get grounded for skipping school."

"You remember Vivienne's mom, right? She might literally murder us."

"Then we'll be very careful." Rae unlocked her door. "Thanks for walking me home."

"You bet."

Rae glanced once more at the trees looming over them. "Good night, Caden." She closed her door, and he heard the sound of the lock and the deadbolt turning.

"Good night, Rae," he whispered. He headed back to his house, his skin prickling like he was being watched. The feeling grew stronger, and by the time he was back in his driveway, he was almost running. He stepped over his dad's salt line, then turned and studied the woods. Nothing. Then he looked at Rae's house.

Something moved on the roof. A shadow, darker than the rest. It dropped from the roof and scuttled down the side of the house like some sort of enormous spider before slipping away into the woods.

23.
RAE

Rae wasn't used to breaking rules. She didn't like to get in trouble, and tried hard not to do anything that would upset her mom. Skipping school and breaking into someone's house? Definitely not her usual style. But if she was going to do it, she was going to do it *right*. So she spent her whole Sunday planning and watching how-to-break-into-houses videos online. And then she very carefully deleted her browsing history.

When she woke up Monday morning, she knew she was really going to go through with it. Someone was targeting her. Or some-*thing*. She could tell her mom about it . . . but would her mom even belicve her? Doubtful.

She got dressed and headed down to the kitchen, trying to act as casual as possible. Her mom was still up from her night shift at the hospital, drinking coffee and chatting with Ava. Both of them looked up as Rae entered.

"Top of the morning to you both," Rae said cheerfully in her best I'm-not-planning-on-skipping-school voice.

"Top of the morning?" Ava blinked. "What's wrong with you?"

Rae frowned. Maybe she'd overdone it? "Nothing. What's wrong with your face?"

Ava scowled and went back to her coffee.

"Rae," their mom said.

"Sorry," Rae said. She resisted looking at the kitchen clock, ticking away all her minutes, and instead made herself pour a bowl of cereal and sit down. Nice and casual. Then she realized that usually her sister would be heading out the door by now. "Don't you have class to get to?" she asked Ava.

"I have study hall first period, so I'm going in late." Ava took a sip of coffee. "Why?"

"No reason. Nope. None at all." Rae slurped a spoonful of cereal. Man, she was really terrible at this. Time for plan B: get out of here quick.

She ate the rest of her cereal as fast as she could, then stood, dumped her bowl in the sink, and started for the door. "See you both later!"

"Wait, Rae?" her mom called.

Rae stiffened, her hand on the doorknob. "Y-yes?"

"You know how I feel about dishes left in the sink."

Rae relaxed. "Oh yeah. Sorry." She went back in, rinsed her bowl, even gave it a cursory wipe with a sponge, and stuck it in the dishwasher. The whole time she could feel Ava staring at her with her beady eyes.

"Why are you leaving so early?" Ava asked. "Your bus won't be here for another ten minutes."

"Why are you policing my time?" Rae said.

"You started it."

"Why *are* you leaving so early?" their mom asked. Of all the days for her to be sharp and present.

"I, um, thought I'd enjoy the sunshine before school."

"It looks like rain," her mom said.

"Even better," Rae said quickly. "I love the rain."

"No you don't." Ava frowned. "Why are you being so weird?"

"Why are *you* being weird?" Rae shot back, sweating. This was so not going well.

Her mom cleared her throat. "Speaking of weird, I caught our neighbor's kid pouring salt around our house yesterday."

"What?" Ava and Rae both said. "Why?" Ava added.

Their mom shrugged. "No idea."

"Is this the neighbor across the street?" Ava asked. "Because I heard he murdered his brother and stuffed him in the walls."

"That's not true," Rae said immediately.

"If you say so." Ava gave her a *look*, one that made Rae's cheeks go pink. It was a smug I-know-something-about-you look, the kind that only an obnoxious older sibling could give. It made Rae wonder if Ava had seen her hanging out with Caden. She remembered Ava's comments about Ivan being cute and she scowled. Her sister always got the wrong idea.

Rae grabbed her backpack. "I'm going to enjoy the rain. See you later." And she stomped out of the house before her mom or sister could stop her.

As soon as the door shut behind her, she got that feeling again. That eerie, shoulder-blade-prickly feeling of eyes on her back. She glanced at the trees around the house. They seemed dark and forbidding. Or maybe that was the gray clouds roiling overhead. Hunching her shoulders, she hurried over to the spot where the bus usually stopped, but the feeling of being watched didn't go away.

She glanced over her shoulder, then ducked into the nearby woods, walking slowly, cringing at the snap of twigs under her feet. Something darted across her path, and she froze, her heart beating too fast.

Just a squirrel.

She relaxed.

"It's about time," Caden said from behind her.

Rae shrieked and spun around.

Caden put up his hands. "It's just me."

Rae put a hand to her chest, gasping. "Sorry. I've been a little jumpy lately."

"Understandable. I guess I'm just lucky I didn't get Mint Attacked in the eyes." Caden smiled. "Speaking of, is Vivienne joining us?"

Rae shook her head. "Since she got caught out past curfew on Thursday, she's basically under extreme surveillance now."

Caden nodded. "I told you her mom is scary. She's one of the senior project managers at Green On!, and I've heard everyone in her department is terrified of her."

Rae pictured Vivienne's mom, the way she'd been so furious the night they got back from the woods, and could believe it. *Rae* was a little terrified of her. It was hard to believe she and easygoing Vivienne were related.

Rae followed Caden over to the little camouflaged lean-to they'd made yesterday out of an old tarp covered in leaves and branches. "Anyhow," she said, wedging herself inside next to their bikes, "I promised I'd text her when we got to the house, and then when we got out again. She said it was one of the first rules of back-packing: to have a designated safety person."

"We're not backpacking." Caden shifted into the space next to her.

"No, but we are going into unknown territory."

"Not entirely," he muttered, and Rae remembered that Caden had been to Doctor Anderson's house before. Nine months ago. When his brother disappeared.

Would it be hard on him to go back to the place where it happened? Guilt swam up in her chest. She hadn't even thought of that. "Did you want to stay here?"

"No, I'm fine."

They heard the bus rumbling up, and both went quiet, waiting. A minute later and it drove on past.

"So, I hear you've been pouring salt around my house?" Rae whispered.

Caden's cheeks went pink. "I was hoping you wouldn't notice. I know it's kind of strange."

"Is it?" Rae asked dryly.

He laughed uncomfortably. "It's for a protection spell. I thought it couldn't hurt."

That was pretty weird, but at this point, really any protection was probably good. Even if it came in the form of a pourable spice. "Thanks," she said.

He smiled. "I've got your back."

Rae grinned, then pushed herself to her feet. "Let's do this." She rolled her bike out of its hiding place and onto the street, Caden right behind her. This was the most vulnerable part of their plan, because if anyone looked at the road right now, they were both in plain sight. Rae and Caden hopped on their bikes as soon as their tires hit the pavement, and started pedaling as fast as they could.

They reached the end of the street in record time and turned left, still pedaling hard. Rae didn't relax until after the next turn.

And then a familiar car pulled up right in front of her.

Rae skidded to a stop, almost falling over her handlebars.

Ava rolled down the driver's side window. "You are so busted." She looked past Rae at Caden and smirked. "I knew you were up to something."

Rae didn't realize there was a shade more painful than red, but her cheeks felt like they'd gone right past it into fluorescent territory. "It's not what you think."

"I'm sure it isn't." Ava's smirk grew larger and more irritating. "Skipping school to go off somewhere with the neighbor boy? Of *course* there's a perfectly innocent explanation." She leaned on her elbows out her window. "And I can't *wait* to hear it."

Rae glanced at the woods to her left. She could ditch her bike and run. Ava wouldn't be able to follow . . . but then she'd absolutely tell their mom, who might be worried enough to call the police, and then people would be looking for her, and it would be a whole mess. She looked over at Caden. He could go on without her, but that idea was almost as bad. She wanted to be in on the investigation.

"Well?" Ava demanded.

Rae decided on the truth, something she hadn't shared with her sister in a long time. "Several kids from my school have been attacked lately, and Caden and I are looking into it."

Ava frowned. "You mean that whole serial eye snatcher thing?"

"Yes."

"I'm pretty sure the police are handling it."

"I'm pretty sure they're not doing a good job of it," Rae countered.

Ava sighed and rubbed her temple. "This is so like you, Rae. Sticking your nose in things that you should leave alone. Let the authorities handle this, okay?"

Rae scowled. "Is this about Dad? Because I know what happened, even if you don't believe me. And I'm not going to sit on the side and do nothing. Unlike certain sisters of mine."

Ava flinched. "I'm not doing nothing."

Rac snorted.

"I'm *not*!"

"You're right. You're doing worse than nothing. You're running away. And you dragged us all out here with you."

Ava pressed her lips together, her nostrils flaring.

Rae could feel Caden watching this whole exchange, but she didn't care. She was just so, so angry. It felt like all the hurt and frustration she'd ever felt about her dad, and his disappearance, and how no one believed her, was about to come pouring out of her mouth, and she couldn't stop it. "You want to pretend we don't even have a dad. That he just left us, and it's totally normal, and we can move on and live our ordinary lives without him. Well, I'm not going to do that."

"Why," Ava said quietly, her teeth clenched, "do you think I applied to WestConn in the first place?"

"To get as far away from Sunnyside as possible."

"Because they offer an astrobiology major," Ava said, still in that tight, gritted voice. "And why do you think I want to major in that?"

"I don't know. You've never told me."

"So I can try to find Dad, okay?"

Rae blinked. "R-really?"

"Yes, really!" Ava exploded. "God, Rae, sometimes you're so selfish! You think that the rest of us have just moved on? Maybe some of us are still looking, we're just doing it in a smarter, subtler fashion than you are."

Astrobiology, to find Dad. Did that mean . . . "So, you believe me?" Rae whispered. "About Dad?"

Ava sighed. "I'm not sure *what* I believe. But I know something weird happened with him." She drummed her fingers on the door of her car. "And I'm doing what I can to find out what."

"Then why didn't you tell me?" Rae asked. "This whole time, why did you pretend that I was making stuff up?"

Ava stopped drumming. "I guess I just didn't want you involved. It's dangerous."

"He's my dad too."

"I know." Ava went quiet. A few raindrops splattered across her windshield, and Rae felt them drip down her face like tears. Or maybe she *was* crying. She couldn't tell. "I'm sorry," Ava said at last. "I should have been more honest."

Rae sniffed. "Yes, you should have." She sniffed again. "Does Mom know I'm skipping school?"

"Not yet," Ava said.

"Are you going to tell her?"

Ava hesitated. "Where *are* you going?"

"Just . . . to look around a little. Not far."

"Is it somewhere dangerous?"

"No," Rae lied.

"Will you be back soon?"

"Yes."

Ava studied her for a long minute. "Tell you what. You text me as soon as you're done, and that better be within an hour. And I won't tell Mom."

It felt like an apology. Ava was telling her she trusted her, at least a little. Rae knew this was the best chance she'd have, but still, she needed to negotiate. "Two hours," she said.

"An hour and a half. And I'll want details."

"Deal." Rae and Ava shook hands, and then with one last look back at her, Ava drove off.

"What was that all about?" Caden asked.

Rae wiped at her eyes. The rain had picked up, and so had the wind, flinging cold drops down the neck of her sweater. "That was my sister."

"Yeah, I kind of figured that out. I mean . . . what was that about your dad?"

Rae started pedaling, but slowly enough for Caden to bike next to her. The last person she'd told about her dad had turned on her.

You are so, so weird. I can't believe we were ever friends.

Rae pedaled a little harder, wanting to leave that memory behind, but she could still see Taylor's face, her blue eyes narrowed, her lips pursed, the way she had flipped her hair and turned away.

But Caden wasn't Taylor. He'd said he had her back. And he'd told her the truth about his brother.

"Would you believe me . . . ?" Rae swallowed hard. "Would you believe me if I told you that my dad was abducted by the government?"

"What did he find?"

It was the right question. "Aliens," Rae said. "He found proof of aliens." She waited, but Caden didn't scoff at her, or laugh, or anything. He just nodded. She let out her breath, her limbs shaking with relief.

"So," he said. "How did it happen?"

Rae took a deep breath and launched into her story. . . .

Her dad had been working on Operation Gray Bird for almost a year. At first, he'd been very excited about the project. He'd tell Rae little hints, mentioning that it was *something special*, that he was doing work on *never-before-seen technology*, that it was a huge honor to be picked for this team. *It's top secret, so I can't tell you much more about it*, he'd say.

What if I guess? Rae had asked. *Can you tell me if I'm right?* And she'd thrown out bigger and wilder possibilities, until finally she'd come to, *Is it a spaceship?*

I can neither confirm, nor deny, her dad had said, laughing. *And I think our game is done, kiddo.* And that was how Rae knew.

And then her dad started working longer hours, coming home stressed and tired. He lost weight, lost hair, lost his easy smile. The light in his eyes when he talked about work turned to cold dread, and his face developed more hard lines than a city road map.

It's not going well, he confided in their mom one night when Rae was supposed to be asleep. *Our progress is extremely slow. And frankly, I'm beginning to think that's a good thing. We don't really know what this craft is capable of. We shouldn't be messing with it.*

I'm sure they wouldn't have you doing something dangerous, Rae's mom had said. *They have safety nets in place, I'd imagine.*

Rae remembered how her dad had laughed, because it had been a terrible sound. Not at all amused. *They don't really know what we're messing with either. Or maybe they do know, and they're not telling us.*

What are you thinking, Chris?

I'm thinking I'm getting tired of being kept in the dark.

That conversation had happened a month before Rae's dad disappeared. Three weeks later, her dad had come home early from work, extremely upset. This time he didn't even seem to notice or care that Rae was listening.

It exploded. Exploded! he said. Rae remembered how he'd paced, his hair as wild as his eyes. *I'm not the first one to work on this project. Oh no, there was another team assigned to it before.*

Chris, calm down.

Only that time, the whole experiment ended like . . . like . . . well, in a blasted explosion!

How did you find out about this? Rae's mom asked, worried. *What have you been doing?*

Her dad ran his hands through his rapidly thinning hair. *Not everyone who worked on the last project died in the explosion. One of the engineers tracked me down.* He dropped his hands. *The things he told me . . .* But then he'd finally noticed Rae, standing quietly in the doorway, and he'd stopped talking.

Rae had heard enough to scare her, though, and that night her dreams had been full of explosions and spaceships and her dad's frantic voice. So a few days later, when her dad told her he'd decided to quit his job, she had been so relieved.

I just need to work through the end of the week, he'd told her. *And then I'll have more time. In fact, I'll come home early on Friday, okay? I'll be here when you get home from school, and we'll go for ice cream, like we used to. Just you and me, kiddo.*

"Only when I got home that day, he wasn't there," Rae finished, pedaling slowly.

"He was just . . . gone?"

"Yes. Him, and another engineer on his team. A woman." Rae sighed. "Most people think they just ran off together, but I know that's not it."

"And why do you think it was the government?"

"Because . . . when I got home that day, my dad wasn't there, but a bunch of men in suits were. They ransacked our house, and they took everything my dad owned. And I mean *everything*. Like, we got him this cheap ceramic Grinch mug for Christmas one year, just as a joke, and they took that, too. They were very thorough."

"Sounds like the government."

Rae was silent, thinking of the only things they hadn't taken: her dad's calendar, and the picture she'd found, the one hidden behind the photo in her desk. Her biggest secret. "Anyhow," she continued, "the night before he disappeared, my dad told my mom about something they were keeping in the lab. Something he wasn't supposed to see, but it was alive, and not of Earth origin. Plus, you know, he was working on a spaceship. And . . . he wanted to quit. I don't think they could allow him to leave, knowing what he knew."

She wondered if anyone else was aware of how much he'd told *her*. For the first time, she felt a tiny sliver of fear for herself. Maybe she was in danger too. Maybe their whole family was. But then, why hadn't anyone come after them yet? Unless the government was still watching them, waiting for something.

Maybe Ava's college wasn't the only reason her mom had moved them all across the country.

Caden turned onto another street, and Rae followed him, recognizing the cul-de-sac and the blue house up ahead. He stopped a few houses away from their target and got off his bike, and Rae copied him. "I . . . don't really have any experience with aliens," he admitted. "But I've seen enough strange things in this world to believe that anything is possible."

"That sounds like something my dad would say." Rae's dad believed you couldn't prove a negative, which meant there were no limits on possibility.

They walked their bikes behind Doctor Anderson's house. It didn't look like he was around, and none of the neighbors appeared to be out and about either.

"I'll help you," Caden said abruptly.

"What?" Rae said.

"After all of this." He waved at the house. "When it's done, I'll help you look for your dad. If you want."

Rae stared at him, at his black hair, flattened by the rain, and his dark eyes, too intense. And she knew he was being honest. He would help her.

Gratitude swelled up in her chest, enveloping her. She wasn't alone anymore. She hadn't realized how much that would mean to her, but the emotion was so strong she was afraid if she opened her mouth, she'd start bawling. So she just nodded and hoped Caden understood.

He smiled. "Let's get this over with quickly, then."

Rae leaned her bike against the wall and pulled her cell phone out of her backpack to text Vivienne, then paused.

She had a text message from an unknown number.

Frowning, she tapped it open.

And all those warm feelings vanished immediately when she saw the words on her screen.

UNKNOWN: Did you like the picture I left you? I could send you more; I have several in my collection.

24.

CADEN

Caden had never seen the blood literally drain from a person's face before. Until now. Rae went from pink to gray in a matter of seconds. It was like watching a photograph fade in sped-up time, and the fear rolled off her like a tsunami, threatening to take him under too. "What's wrong?" he asked.

She tore her gaze away from her phone and whipped around, scanning the trees nearby, the other houses, the street.

"What?" Caden asked again, doing his own quick search. Nothing was there, only the other quiet houses and the silently watching woods.

"I just . . . Someone texted me." Rae showed him her phone.

The words were chilling, the kind of thing a serial killer would do when playing with a future victim . . .

"Do you think he's here now?" Rae whispered. "Watching us?"

"No," Caden said, more confidently than he felt.

"Are you sure? Because it's awfully coincidental, him texting me like that right before we break into his house."

"You think Doctor Anderson sent that text?"

Rae nodded. "He made a creepy comment about collections when I met with him before. And look at that punctuation. Who uses a semicolon in a text message?"

"Some kind of psycho," Caden said.

"Exactly. But a well-educated psycho." Rae took one last look around at the trees, her face still too pale.

The woods didn't feel like they had the night Brandi stumbled out of them. They felt quiet, the sound of the rain trickling off the branches almost soothing. Unlike the house, which seemed restless, like it had been patient for too long and wasn't going to wait much longer.

"We can come back later," Caden said.

Rae shook her head. "I'm not sure I'll have that chance." She shoved her phone into her back pocket and turned to the window, running her fingers along the edge and pressing up. The window slid open half an inch. "I guess he doesn't lock his windows. Lucky us."

Was it lucky? Caden's stomach clenched uneasily. Doctor Anderson had been a very private and careful person. Why would he leave his windows unlocked?

Rae worked her fingers into the gap and pushed. The window slid another few centimeters before it stuck again, the wood warped from all the humid East Coast summers. Caden moved to the other side and helped her. Slowly, the window squeaking and sticking and fighting them for every inch, they got it open almost a whole foot.

"Good enough?" Caden panted.

"I can fit through that." Rae looked him over. "You probably won't have a problem either. You're pretty scrawny."

"I think you mean 'lean-muscled,'" Caden said.

Rae laughed. "Sure. Why not?" She tucked her backpack against the side of the house, out of the rain, hauled herself up on the window ledge in one smooth motion, and vanished inside.

Caden blinked, surprised. Apparently, when Rae decided to do something, she didn't waste a lot of time. He supposed he should have realized that by the way she plunged into the woods the other day, not to mention their lack of a real plan now. He hoisted himself up and stuck his head and shoulders in, doing a quick scan of the inside. All he could make out in the gloom was a dining room table and chairs. He wriggled forward on his belly, then lowered himself down the wall in an awkward roll, pulling his legs in after him and managing to land on his head.

"Interesting choice," Rae said.

"Sorry, I don't have a lot of experience breaking into houses," Caden grumbled. He clambered to his feet and shoved the window closed, blocking out the sound of the rain. Immediately the house felt too quiet and still. He could feel it pressing in on him, full of the memories of the last time he was here. His mom had set her supplies up on that dining room table, and for a second he almost saw them: her candles, the abalone shell, the smudge sticks, and her three singing bowls.

Caden shook the memory off, along with rain droplets that dripped from his hair to the wood floor.

"You okay?" Rae asked.

"I'm fine," he said firmly.

Aiden hadn't haunted him since the Friday night Book of Shadows incident, but as Caden followed Rae through the house, it felt as if his brother were walking next to him again, like he had that evening nine months ago. Memories of that visit overlapped everything he saw now.

"Here is where we lit our smudge sticks," Aiden seemed to whisper. Caden paused and looked at the fireplace. *"And there's the photograph Mom wanted to move out of the house. But the doctor refused, remember?"*

Caden turned and looked at the slightly saggy brown suede couch, and above it, the large framed photo of a striking woman in her mid-fifties, her chin gently resting against her hands. He remembered that argument.

Doctor Anderson had been furious at the suggestion, claiming it would be a dishonor to his late wife's memory to remove that photo. Their mom had insisted, explaining that there was a lot of negative energy attached to it. The two of them had gone back and forth, until finally Caden's dad had set up a small incense stand of sage and sandalwood below the photo, letting the smoke cleanse the energy from it.

"It didn't work," Aiden said. *"Every time he looks at it, he thinks of her death. He stares at it for hours sometimes, and his despair and anger grow and become tangible things. I've watched him."*

Caden started. This wasn't his memory after all; Aiden was back. He'd survived. "I'm so glad," Caden whispered, relieved.

"What?" Rae said.

"Nothing," Caden said quickly, turning away from the photo. He didn't want to tell Rae that his brother was talking to him again.

I get lost here, in the Other Place. Everything moves strangely, and that light—that constantly pulsing light—changes things, makes distances impossible to judge. But I could always find my way back to this house. It was the only place I could find, at first. I needed another anchor."

Caden thought of his mother's sloppy summoning spell from last week.

"Now you're getting it. She gave me something to focus on."

A hand on his shoulder. Caden jumped, but it was only Rae, peering up at him. "Are you sure you're okay?" she asked.

He glanced at her hand, his cheeks reddening. "I'm fine." He walked out of the living room, past the neatly organized bookshelves and the landscape oil painting, and paused in the painfully clean kitchen. Just beyond it the hall extended, long and empty and very dark.

Caden hesitated. He knew what lay at the end of this hall. That sense of restlessness built, like a boiling pot with a too-tight lid.

Rae glanced at him again. He wished she'd stop. "You're sweating," she said.

He wiped a hand across his forehead, and it came away damp. "It's just from the rain outside," he lied.

"You should go. You're not safe here. And neither is your little girlfriend."

Rae started down the hall, flinching at every creak in the floor-boards beneath her. Caden followed, trying to ignore Aiden's voice. Shadows seemed to drip from the corners of the hallway, making it darker than it should have been, and the sense of disquiet grew stronger until it felt like the house was squeezing him in one anxious fist.

Whatever Aiden had started that night nine months ago hadn't ended when Caden closed the rift into the Other Place. Maybe Rae was right, and Doctor Anderson had been possessed by the Unseeing. And maybe he'd been working on reopening the portal ever since.

Aiden had told him that all major spells required several layers of energy. First, the foundation—for dark spells, that usually meant some kind of horrifying ritual. And then that energy needed to be stoked and banked like a well-tended fire, eventually serving as fuel for the spell itself.

Could that be the purpose behind the eye snatching? Was Doctor Anderson using that ritualistic destruction to build a foundation of dark energy so he could rip another hole in the fabric between their dimensions?

Threefold . . . The eye snatcher had taken three and then three. If Brandi and Jeremy were both victims as well, then the next victim would be the third of three.

Caden glanced at Rae's back and shivered. Maybe Aiden was right. They really shouldn't be here.

The text message, the building sense of anticipation in the house, it all felt . . .

Like a trap.

He realized Rae was already at the cellar door, her hand on the doorknob. "Wait, Rae," he called.

She glanced at him, then pushed the door open. For a second, Caden saw his brother outlined in that all-too-familiar rectangle of inky darkness, the way he'd been that night. Laughing and excited. *Mom and Dad are wasting their time with the other rooms of the house. This is where the magic happens.*

Caden squeezed his eyes closed. He'd said they should go back for their parents, but Aiden hadn't wanted to. And Caden had known it was a mistake to follow him down. But when his brother was like that, all eagerness and enthusiasm, it was like being swept up in a windstorm, impossible to stop.

"Can you feel it?"

Caden opened his eyes. Rae had already vanished down the stairs.

"Better hurry, brother. Clearly she's not the kind of person who waits for help."

Caden hurried to the cellar doorway, then paused. The dim light of the hall filtered down several feet, illuminating a few narrow stairs before they vanished in the pitch black below. He really, really didn't want to go down there.

"Any light switch up there?" Rae called. "Because it's like a cave down here. I can't see a thing."

Caden took a deep, calming breath, but it didn't help. Panic tightened his chest, and he kept imagining tentacles made of shadow lurking there in the depths. He fumbled along the wall at the top of the stairs until he found the switch, and flipped it.

Yellowish light bloomed and flickered ominously, then held.

"Thanks," Rae said from the bottom of the stairs.

Caden left the door of the cellar open and walked down after her, blinking against the brightness.

The cellar looked exactly the way he remembered it. Mostly empty. In one corner was a bookshelf full of the doctor's secret obsession: books on the occult. A large fancy camera rested on top of them. "This looks like the camera he was wearing that day in the woods," Rae said, taking it down and flipping through the photos on it.

"Any luck?" Caden tried peering over her shoulder, but for such an expensive-looking camera, it had the world's saddest display screen.

"Not really," Rae said. "A couple of trees, a bird, and then a bunch of pictures of some huge ugly building in the woods." She frowned. "It has a tall electric fence around it and a bunch of guards."

"Maybe the Green On! lab?"

"Maybe," Rae said. "But why would he have pictures of that?"

Caden shrugged.

"He must have deleted the picture of us after delivering it to me." She sighed and put the camera back on the shelf.

In the opposite corner of the room sat a small wooden shrine. Doctor Anderson kept another picture of his dead wife above it, and below were dried flower petals, a few charms, and a candle burned down almost to the nub. And next to the shrine . . . a door.

Rae reached for the doorknob.

"Don't!" Caden lunged forward, grabbing her wrist and pulling her back.

"What?" Rae twisted, searching the room.

"Just . . . stop rushing forward, would you?"

Rae looked down at his hand on her wrist, frowning.

Caden let her go. "It's dangerous to open doors like that," he said. "Especially *that* door."

"Why? What's in there?"

"It doesn't matter what's in the room," Caden said. "It's the doorway itself." He pressed his lips together to stop them from trembling. He could still see that door opening, the yellow light throbbing, his brother screaming . . . "Aiden used that doorway as his anchor when he created a portal into the Other Place."

"Why?" Rae asked.

"Because this cellar was full of negative energy, and using a physical door helped strengthen the structural integrity of his spell."

"But the portal is gone now, right?"

Caden hesitated. It still felt wrong, with that same fear-smell as the Other Place, almost like an oily taste on the back of his tongue. But he remembered the swell of power when Aiden performed his spell, like a wave building and building and then crashing on the shore. This didn't feel strong like that. More like a ripple. "I don't know," he admitted finally.

"Well, isn't that what we came here to find out?"

"Yes, but—"

Creak. Creak. Creeeeaaaak.

They both froze. "Did you hear that?" Rae whispered.

"Someone is upstairs," Caden breathed. He looked around the cellar, but there was nowhere to hide, especially with that light spilling into every inch of space. And it was too late to run.

He heard a doorknob rattling and turned in time to see Rae opening the furnace room door. That feeling of wrongness increased, and he knew with deadly certainty that something was in there that shouldn't be. "Wait," he hissed, but it was too late. She'd already gone inside.

25.

RAE

R ae thought of that creepy text message, and Brandi's maimed face, and knew they needed to hide. Now.

There was only one place. No matter how much Caden might not like it, there wasn't a choice. She yanked open the door.

"Wait," Caden hissed.

Rae stepped inside the room. The darkness of it enveloped her, crashing over her head like a solid thing, almost suffocating. And it smelled strange, a mixture of musty and too-sweet, and over that, a fake flowery scent like the room had been doused with bathroom spray. Rae wrinkled her nose and tried to breathe shallowly as she walked farther in. She could barely make out shapes ahead of her: boxes, a very full shelf pushed against the wall, some dusty books stacked in a haphazard pile.

"Wait, Rae," Caden whispered again.

"Close the door," Rae said.

He glanced back like he might make a run for it. But then he pulled the door shut, plunging them into total darkness. Rae closed her eyes, then opened them. It didn't make a difference. It was that awful type of darkness where you think you see shapes that aren't really there. She pulled her cell phone out of her back pocket, the screen's glow shedding a tiny bit of light around them. The room extended farther than she'd thought, and she slowly, carefully waded around boxes toward the back.

"Where are you going?" Caden whispered.

"If Doctor Anderson sees the light on in the cellar, he's probably going to look in here," she said softly. "We need to hide deeper."

Caden grimaced, the blue glow of her screen casting weird shadows across his face. "Okay," he said. "But let me go first."

"Why? Is this some weird chivalry issue? Coming here was *my* idea, so I should take the lead."

"It's not a 'chivalry issue.' I just have more experience with this kind of thing."

"With what kind of thing? Hiding in a storage room?"

"With . . . there's something in here, okay? There's something *wrong* in here. Something supernatural."

A shiver ran down Rae's back. "Are you sure?"

"Don't you hear it?"

Rae went quiet. She could hear her breathing, and Caden's, and the beating of her heart. And . . . rustling noises from the back of the room, like something large was rifling through boxes. "Maybe it's just rats?" She really hoped she was sharing a room with rats, which made her wonder about her life choices.

"Too big," Caden whispered.

The rustling got louder, and now Rae could hear other noises. A low moaning sound, like an injured cow, and the scraping of feet against the concrete floor. She inched back toward Caden, still clutching her phone. Only now it seemed like a signal flare, advertising their presence to anything in the room. Rae hurriedly thumbed the screen off and shoved it back in her pocket.

Immediately the room felt too dark and too close. And without any light, her imagination painted a whole sea of monsters shuffling forward, arms extended, teeth bared, eyes giant hungry pits. That sickly sweet smell grew stronger, filling her nostrils and making her gag.

Thump-thump-thump.

Someone was coming slowly down the stairs.

Rae shivered, terror roaring in her ears, freezing her body. For one second she was eleven years old again and waiting for her missing dad to come home.

But she wasn't eleven anymore.

Maybe Caden was right, and she did rush forward into things, but she'd sworn that she would never again hang back and do nothing. Even if she was scared. *Especially* if she was scared. They had come here to find out what Doctor Anderson was hiding, and that was precisely what she was going to do. She owed it to Brandi.

Rae pulled her phone back out of her pocket and punched open the flashlight app. She held it up, the light highlighting more boxes, gleaming off plastic bins full of clothes, and disappearing into the darkness. She carefully picked her path toward the thing hidden at the back before she could lose her nerve again, Caden's breathing loud and harsh behind her.

Rae turned a corner, her flashlight glinting on a metal surface at the back of the room. The furnace, tall and cylindrical, the space around it clear. And empty.

Rae moved closer, her steps slowing. There was something else crossing that space, a line of some sort. She crouched down, studying it. Rope, one end tied loosely around the base of the furnace. And the other end—

"Hello?" a man called from the cellar. It definitely sounded like Doctor Anderson, home from work early.

She caught Caden's eye. He looked surprisingly calm, like he was resigned to whatever happened next.

But Rae wasn't. She refused to be caught here, now, in this creepy place. She swept her flashlight quickly around the furnace, noticing boxes stacked in a row to the side, rising up practically to her waist. She pulled Caden behind them. There was a surprising amount of space, almost like the boxes were there to form a little den. Plenty of room for Rae and Caden to hunker down.

The darkness in the room shifted, grew lighter. Someone had opened the door.

She ducked and shut her flashlight off.

Rae could hear Doctor Anderson's breathing as he moved closer, his footsteps loud. She tried to breathe as shallowly as possible, her fingers gripping the hard plastic of her phone case, Caden going still next to her.

"Where are you hiding?" Doctor Anderson asked.

Rae bit her lip, willing her heart to beat quieter. She felt way too exposed crouching here, practically in the open.

"Come out, come out, wherever you are," the doctor sing-songed.

Caden gripped Rae's arm. Doctor Anderson was mere feet away. All he had to do was look over the boxes.

She pictured Brandi, how she'd been the first night, vibrant and friendly. And then the thing she'd become later, her eyes removed, her mouth slack-jawed. How had he done that to her? Would it hurt? Rae squeezed her eyes shut, blocking out the dim light, and praying this darkness wouldn't be permanent.

Go away, she thought. But she could hear the doctor walking closer, the scuffle of his shoes, the brush of his clothing against the boxes. And beneath that, something else.

Someone else. Breathing. Right *behind* her.

Rae's eyes shot open, and she turned. But too slowly.

26.
CADEN

Something crashed into Rae, something long-limbed and pale and hungry, knocking her back into Caden. Both of them tumbled to the ground, boxes falling around them, Rae's phone skittering across the floor.

Caden struggled to get up, but he was pinned beneath Rae and her attacker, and a heavy box of books, his mind swirling with images of his brother wrapped in tentacles, screaming.

Rae put her hands up to protect her face, but her attacker didn't do anything, just crouched over her, his own arms hanging limply at his sides, knuckles dragging on the ground.

"Eyes," he moaned.

Rae stopped struggling. "Jeremy?" she said.

Light flared through the small room, chasing away the

shadows and illuminating the figure of Jeremy Bentley. He lifted his head, his curly blond hair hanging in dirty clumps around his face, framing the dark pits where his eyes should have been.

Caden felt Rae's horror stab him in the gut. He shoved the box of books away and scrambled up, pulling Rae back with him, leaving Jeremy hunched alone.

"What are you—" Doctor Anderson stopped, staring down at them. "Why are you in my house?"

"Why is *he*?" Caden demanded, pointing at Jeremy's trembling form. "What did you do to him?"

"Me? I didn't do anything." But Doctor Anderson's face had gone nearly as pale as his hair, and he took a small step back.

"Lovely eyes." Jeremy twisted his face up as if he was trying to see them. He raised his arms, and Caden noticed the frayed length of rope knotted around his left wrist.

"You tied him to your furnace?" Rae whispered, horrified.

"It was just temporary," Doctor Anderson said. "Just so he couldn't hurt himself."

"You mean, so he couldn't escape." Caden glanced around the room, looking for a weapon. The box he'd shoved away had opened, heavy leather-bound books spilling across the floor. He scooped up the largest, then immediately dropped it again, his hand tingling like he'd just shoved it in a stinging nettle bush.

The gold-embossed title caught the light: *Blood Magicks and Sacrifices for Greater Power.*

Caden looked up, meeting Doctor Anderson's eyes. His fever-bright blue eyes. Eyes the winter blue of the sky . . .

Doctor Anderson's mouth opened, his lips trembling. "I . . . I was just trying to help."

"Help who?" Rae asked, moving closer to Caden.

"Isn't this a sight for sore eyes?" a new voice said, cool and calm.

Doctor Anderson whirled just as Patrick strolled over to their corner of the cramped room. He wore his same immaculate black suit with his same carefully styled hair, and he was flanked by four large men in bright green one-piece outfits.

"I'm sorry, that was a bit insensitive, given the circumstances," Patrick said.

"What are you doing here?" Doctor Anderson demanded. "What are *all* of you doing here? This is my house!"

"This *was* your house," Patrick said. "But we're taking charge of it. And of you."

"What?" Doctor Anderson looked completely bewildered.

"We've been watching you for a while, William. Monitoring your energy usage. You've been experimenting again, haven't you?"

"I have done nothing wrong," Doctor Anderson insisted.

"This"—Patrick waved a hand at Jeremy—"looks very wrong to me."

"I'm *helping* him," Doctor Anderson hissed. "Saving him from *you*."

Patrick stepped to the side. The men behind him moved forward, two of them grabbing Doctor Anderson by the arms and hauling him back. It happened so fast, Caden almost missed it.

"Wait! You can't do this!" Doctor Anderson yelled, struggling, but it didn't have any effect. "This is just a cover-up! I know what you did to Helen! I'll prove it!" And then they were out of the cellar, his voice fading.

The other two men followed behind with Jeremy, who had gone limp and quiet in their arms.

Caden and Rae exchanged glances.

"Thank you for your help," Patrick said. "We've been hoping to catch the person responsible for these atrocities for months. I'm just glad we got here in time before he was able to claim any other victims."

Rae hugged herself. "So you really think Doctor Anderson is the serial eye snatcher?"

"I think . . . Doctor Anderson has not been entirely himself ever since his wife died. You can ask your friend here about that." Patrick nodded at Caden. "I'm sure he has more insight."

Caden didn't say anything. He knew Doctor Anderson had been trying to contact his wife after her death. Messing with the afterlife was tricky, especially if you didn't know what you were doing. It was too easy to put out a call for a departed loved one, only to accidentally issue an open invitation to anything out there.

And there were a lot of bad things out there.

That was why Doctor Anderson had needed the Price family to cleanse his house in the first place. But Caden wasn't sure how Patrick knew about any of that. If Doctor Anderson was the serial eye snatcher, that cleared Patrick. But it still didn't mean Caden had to trust him.

"Who's Helen?" Rae asked.

"His wife," Patrick said.

"How did she die?"

Patrick sighed. "It's a sad story, really. She worked for Green On! for a number of years, but there was a tragic accident."

Rae tensed. "What kind of accident?"

"It happened a year before I joined the company, so unfortunately, I'm not really clear on the details. All I know is that William has blamed us ever since." Patrick's features were molded into the perfect mask of regret and pity, but Caden could feel nothing from him. No emotions whatsoever. Even people who were good at masking their feelings still gave off an impression. It was like dropping a rock into a quiet pond; there would still be ripples after that rock had vanished from view. But with Patrick, it was as if that rock had never existed. Standing next to him felt like standing next to a void.

Rae's emotions, on the other hand, were all over the place. Relief and confusion and the lingering echo of fear. "Why did you suspect Doctor Anderson?" she asked.

"Let's get out of this depressing space," Patrick suggested, turning and walking out of the furnace room. Rae followed him, leaving Caden to trail a little behind. "There were a number of reasons we suspected the good doctor. Especially after we detected an unusual energy spike here this past December. We have been keeping a close eye on him ever since."

Caden stepped out of the doorway his brother had fallen through nine months ago. Was that the December energy spike Green On! had noticed?

"Energy spike?" Rae asked.

"Green On! monitors energy usage for most of the houses in Whispering Pines," Caden said.

Rae frowned. "I didn't know that."

"It's actually a great deal for you folks." Patrick closed the furnace room door behind them. "You don't have to pay for your energy as long as you're willing to be hooked up to Green On!'s Energy-Efficiency Program. We monitor energy usage and use that data to help with our research into better renewable options."

"Seems almost like an invasion of privacy," Rae said.

Patrick smiled. "I think you'll find, Ms. Carter, that most people are more than happy to trade away a little privacy in exchange for convenience and cost savings. It's a very human trait." He glanced at Caden. "Although there is the occasional hold-out."

Caden shrugged. His family had opted out of the Green On! system, but he didn't know anyone else who had. His mom had always valued her privacy much more highly than saving money. And after what Caden had discovered in her Book of Shadows, he could understand why she'd want to keep her habits secret. Who knew what Green On! could figure out if they had access to the Price family's energy levels?

"Shall we?" Patrick waved a hand at the stairs, and Rae headed up.

Caden paused by the shrine, studying the picture of Helen, the dried flowers underneath, the used-up candle. He could feel the echo of energy pulsating here, something beyond grief and rage. A quiet determination weighted down beneath deep feelings of despair.

It made sense that Doctor Anderson was possessed by the

Unseeing. He had been so desperate to make contact with his wife, and Caden knew how desperation could lead to vulnerability. His mom's increasingly frantic attempts to find Aiden had led her to do sloppy summoning spells, and she *knew* what she was doing. Doctor Anderson was a dabbler in the Arts at best, so it was all too easy to imagine him leaving himself wide open.

But now that Jeremy had been taken from the house, Caden had no sense of the Other Place at all. As far as he could tell, Doctor Anderson had been experimenting again, just as Patrick said. But he'd been experimenting on reaching the dead, not on reopening a portal to another dimension.

This whole thing was beginning to feel more and more like a setup.

"Are you coming, Mr. Price?" Patrick stood at the top of the stairs, a dark silhouette in his dark suit. And as Caden stared up at him, he couldn't shake the feeling that they'd caught the wrong person.

27.
RAE

So then Patrick insisted on following us home," Rae told Vivienne as they wound their way through the crowded hallway the next day at school. "And of course my mom was there, and he told her where I'd been, and now I'm grounded for life." Rae had only managed to respond to one of Vivienne's increasingly frantic text messages yesterday, letting her know they'd caught Doctor Anderson and she was okay, before her mom took her phone away.

"That's a long time," Vivienne said.

"Hopefully," Rae said.

"That's the spirit." Vivienne grinned. "You caught the guy, right?"

"We did. Thanks to Patrick." Rae frowned. "I still don't understand how he knew we'd be at the house then. But he wasn't surprised to see Caden or me there at all."

"Hmm." Vivienne looked away and adjusted her heavy back-pack.

"I mean, Green On! monitors energy usage, but it's not like they have cameras pointed at the houses. Do they?"

"I don't think so," Vivienne said. "But maybe?"

"We don't have cameras pointed at the houses," Patrick said.

Rae and Vivienne whirled. Patrick was leaning against the wall a few feet behind them, typing something into his phone. He glanced up at them and smiled. "Sorry for eavesdropping."

"Is everything okay?" Rae's heart was still beating too fast. Had Doctor Anderson escaped?

"Everything is fine," Patrick assured her. "I'm just tying up some loose ends." He straightened, tucking his phone away and pulling out a small cloth sack about the size of a deck of cards from his inner suit-jacket pocket. "For you, Ms. Matsuoka." He tossed it to Vivienne, who caught it easily.

"What's that?" Rae asked.

"It's, um, for my mom," Vivienne said, unslinging her backpack and tucking the sack away into its mysterious depths. "Thank you," she told Patrick.

He nodded.

"What are you doing at our school, though?" Vivienne asked.

"I'm here to meet with your charming vice principal."

"We have a charming vice principal?" Rae said.

Vivienne giggled.

Someone coughed loudly, and Rae turned. Ms. Lockett glared at her, fingers clenched around her clipboard.

"Whoops," Vivienne whispered.

"Shouldn't you girls be heading to class?" Ms. Lockett said.

"We were just going," Vivienne said. "Bye, Patrick," she called, pulling Rae along with her. Once they were out of earshot, they both burst out laughing.

"Talk about bad timing." Rae shook her head. "Ah well. I don't think she liked me before, and she definitely won't now."

"Don't worry about it. She doesn't like anyone." Vivienne sighed. "Poor Alyssa, having that for a mother. I mean, my mom is scary, don't get me wrong. But she's not, like, a rule-obsessed robot."

Rae's smile faded as she thought of Alyssa. "Do you think we should tell her about Jeremy?"

Vivienne nodded. "We can tell her together. At lunch, okay?"

"Okay," Rae said.

First bell rang, a lingering banshee call that echoed off the walls. Rae and Vivienne picked up their pace, hurrying up the stairs to the seventh and eighth grade hallway.

"Is Caden in trouble too?" Vivienne asked.

Rae shrugged.

"You didn't talk to him last night?"

"I couldn't," Rae said. "Grounded, remember?" She sighed. "Besides, he was being kind of weird on the way home."

"I hate to break it to you, my friend, but he's kind of a weird guy." Vivienne stopped at her locker.

Rae laughed. "Yeah, true." She moved to her own locker a few feet away, twirled the combination, then popped open the door.

And froze.

A note was taped inside. It read, in large green letters: *You're not the only one I'm keeping an eye on.*

The noise in the hall fell away. Rae felt as if she were standing in a tunnel, everything distant and distorted. Her hand shook as she reached up slowly and pulled off the note, flipping it around to reveal another photograph. This one was of her and Alyssa after the cross-country tryouts, sitting in the booth together at Kathy Jones, a fancy little diner tucked away at a gas station.

Rae tried remembering who else had been around. She pictured the diner, with its gift shop full of knickknacks, things like rubber stamps, New Age books, and funny magnets. There had been a couple of people wandering through, but no one who stuck out in her mind. Past the gift shop, all the seats were set up in giant booths, and the newly formed cross-country team had a section to themselves. No one else was there.

She looked harder at the picture. She and Alyssa both had half-eaten ice creams on the table in front of them. Alyssa was laughing, probably at something Vivienne had said. Rae was looking away, her face slightly blurry.

They'd been facing the window, Rae realized. So whoever took this picture must have been creeping around outside.

The second bell rang.

"Rae? Earth to Rae." Vivienne waved a hand in front of her face. "You probably don't want to get detention on top of grounding, so we'd better book it."

Rae nodded but didn't move. She kept seeing Doctor Anderson the way she'd seen him that night in the woods, his shadow long and twisted, the camera glinting around his neck. Had he been following her after cross-country tryouts?

But then, how did he get the picture into her school? Into her *locker?* It didn't make sense.

Unless . . . she'd been wrong about Doctor Anderson, and the Unseeing was someone else. Someone with access to this school.

"You okay?" Vivienne asked. She leaned in closer. "What's that? Did someone leave you a note?" She grinned. "Is it a love letter?"

Rae turned to her. "I—" She stopped as Patrick walked by with Ms. Lockett. He glanced up, his eyes locking on hers briefly. And maybe it was a trick of the bad hallway lighting, or the angle, or something, but in that second, Rae felt like she'd been transported back a year, back to the afternoon when she'd come home to find those men in their nice suits cornering her mom in the kitchen.

Mrs. Carter? We just have a few questions. About your husband.

Did he ever discuss work with you? With your children? Do you know where he is? Do you know what he was doing?

And her mom, frantically answering, again and again, *I don't know. I don't know anything.* The fear in her eyes when she noticed Rae standing there. *Go to your room, Rae. . . .*

Rae shook her head, the memory gone, just like her father. But as Patrick and Ms. Lockett disappeared around the corner, the suspicion remained. Patrick could have been one of those men, with his carefully tailored suit and his emotionless speech. The kind of person who could blend in anywhere, do anything, and then slip away again afterward.

He hadn't been surprised to see her and Caden at Doctor

Anderson's house, or Jeremy, either. He definitely had access to this school, and probably to her house, too, if her family was on the Green On! energy plan.

"Well?" Vivienne asked.

"It's nothing," Rae said, stuffing the picture into her backpack and grabbing her books. Obviously Patrick was friends with Vivienne's mom if he was bringing stuff for her to school; Rae doubted her friend would believe her without some kind of proof.

"If you say so," Vivienne said, eyeing her.

"Let's get to homeroom." Rae closed her locker. She needed to talk to Caden. He had never trusted Patrick.

But when she got to homeroom, Caden wasn't there. Rae sat down at her normal desk and waited, drumming anxiously until the announcements ended and the final bell rang. And still he didn't show up.

And neither, she realized, did Alyssa.

You're not the only one I'm keeping an eye on.

Dread expanded in Rae's stomach, that horrible sensation that something terrible was about to happen. And she wouldn't be able to stop it.

28.
CADEN

Caden watched from his bedroom window as the bus came and went. Then he sat down at his desk and turned on his laptop, trying not to feel guilty about skipping school for the second day in a row. But he doubted his parents would even notice, and anyhow, this was too important to wait.

He spent the day researching Green On!, looking for information about Patrick. First he had to wade through the Green On! origin story, how fifty years ago Frank Thompson had been hiking through the Watchful Woods with his dog when he discovered a pond that stank of sulfur and brimstone. The trees nearby, all pines, were discolored and hazy from the steam rising along the edge of the water.

It was the first geothermal vent discovered in Connecticut, and was unusual enough that soon geologists and other scientists began flocking to the area. From there, it was just a matter of time before someone realized this could be a good business opportunity. An unknown investor donated a large sum of money to build the first Green On! factory specializing in geothermal energy. Eventually, the company expanded into other areas of renewable energy: solar, wind, nuclear, hydro, basically anything that wasn't fossil-fuel related.

Caden tried to look up more specifics about the "unknown investor," but couldn't find anything concrete. One article quoted an anonymous source who insisted the CIA was funding Green On!, but that same article also claimed there was an abandoned military base nearby, and Caden highly doubted that. He'd have heard of it. Or someone would have.

He moved on, scrolling through pages and pages of articles about how great Green On! was: the jobs! the salaries! the benefits! And how it revitalized their small town. And then finally, he found what he was looking for:

GREEN ON! MOVING IN EXCITING DIRECTION, THANKS TO NEW LEADERSHIP FOCUS

Whispering Pines, CT. Green On! has been on the cutting edge of renewable energy technology for the past thirty years, but recently sources within the company have admitted that they have reached a plateau, thanks in large part to in-fighting amongst the various project heads. "Each department believes their work is the most essential, and that all scientific funding should be focused on their chosen energy field," an executive administrative assistant stated, asking that she not be directly identified. "Battles have been raging between the wind and solar people, and the nuclear and hydropower. You wouldn't believe the memos flying back and forth. All-staff meetings are a nightmare."

But all of that changed recently with the arrival of one man: Patrick Smith. A former CIA agent working in northern California, Smith moved to Whispering Pines after accepting a position as senior consultant to Green On! in late December. His goal is to advance Green On!'s mission by looking at "alternative" renewable energy sources, devoting most of the company's resources to E & R (Experimental and Research Department).

"He's amazing," says Phillip Harding, department head of Solar. "I've never met anyone so innovative. So daring. So willing to look at options outside the norm."

"I still believe the future is nuclear," claims Audrey Matsuoka, senior project manager of the Nuclear Energy Department. "But I recognize that we have a sadly ignorant population who views *nuclear* as a scary word. I respect Patrick for the work he is doing to counteract that ignorance, and look forward to working with him to find a viable alternative."

"If even Audrey is willing to work with this guy, then he must be good," an anonymous source stated, in a sentiment that was echoed several times over.

No one from E & R was willing to discuss their current project, only that they are on the verge of a breakthrough that will forever change the way energy is harnessed in our world.

Caden stopped reading, his mind whirling. That article told him almost nothing about what Patrick was up to. "Alternative renewable energy sources" and "options outside the norm" were very vague terms. But the fact that Patrick was new to Whispering Pines? That he'd moved here around the same time Aiden vanished? That seemed very coincidental.

And then there was the feeling Caden got from Patrick, the sense of wrongness. Like he wasn't fully human.

Caden glanced at his window again. He'd have to tell Rae. But she might not believe him. She'd been so sure it was Doctor Anderson, and after finding Jeremy there . . .

Caden sighed and ran his fingers through his hair, frustrated. He didn't know what the truth was. He needed more information about the Unseeing. And he knew he wouldn't be able to find it online.

He needed to do something extreme. Something desperate, and foolish.

He needed to talk to his mom.

Caden paused outside his mother's study. He'd avoided this part of the house ever since the Book of Shadows incident. Even standing here, on the other side of the door, he thought he could hear the echo of Aiden screaming.

Caden clenched his fists, then made himself relax, and knocked once. He waited a beat, then knocked again. Part of him hoped his mom wouldn't answer, and he could go back upstairs and—

The door opened. "Caden," his mom said. "Come in." She pulled her door open all the way and stepped aside. Two cushions sat side by side in the middle of her floor.

Caden stared at them, surprised. "Are you waiting for someone?"

"I was waiting for you." She sat down on a cushion and waited for Caden to settle himself next to her. He automatically sat in the same posture as she did, his legs crossed and hands resting lightly on his knees.

"How did you know I'd be here?" he asked.

"Call it mother's intuition." She smiled. "Plus I noticed you skipped school this morning."

Caden blinked.

"Don't give me that look," she said. "I pay attention."

"Not to me you don't." Caden didn't mean to say it, but the words slipped right out.

She frowned. "What do you mean?"

He should be quiet, but now that the words had started, he couldn't stop them, or the tide of anger that carried them forth. "You only ever cared about Aiden. Now that he's gone, you've been acting like I don't exist. Like you wish we'd switched places." Caden hadn't realized he'd felt that way until he said it.

His mom flinched. "Is that really what you believe?"

Caden nodded, not trusting his voice.

"I'm really sorry you feel that way. I never meant . . ." She took a deep breath. "I've been preoccupied, trying to find Aiden. But I love you, Caden, and I'm glad you're here with me; I wouldn't trade you for anyone." She put a hand on his.

Caden's eyes burned, and he looked away. He wanted to believe her so much, it hurt. "You've always spent more time with him, though," he said, hating how sulky he sounded. Like a little kid.

"Aiden . . . is very different from you. I knew he was experimenting with things beyond his capabilities." She pressed her lips together, a thin hard line. Only now Caden noticed how they trembled. "You, on the other hand . . . You're careful, and sensible, and maybe a little *too* cautious. So it's not that I don't care about you the same as I care about your brother. It's that I never had to worry about you the same."

Caden blinked rapidly, his vision blurring. "What if . . . ?" He swallowed, tried again. "What if I told you that it was *my* fault? I pushed him into the Other Place." He waited for her to scream at him, tell him what a terrible brother and son he was. He'd deserve it.

She exhaled. Not a sigh, but a release. "Oh, Caden. I already knew."

"You . . . what?"

"Blood opens and blood closes," she said sadly. "A sacrifice given and taken. This is what the Other Place requires. Since Aiden opened the rift, it could only be closed again behind him. And"—she sighed—"I knew your brother wouldn't have gone in willingly. Not after he saw what it was like in there."

"I didn't want to." Water dripped along his nose and off his chin. He touched his face and realized he was crying. His mother had known this whole time, and she'd never said a thing. He wanted to be angry about it, but there was so much guilt pressing down on him, he didn't have room for any other emotions. "I didn't know what else to do."

An arm dropped around his shoulders, warm and comforting, and his mom pulled him in for a hug. He couldn't remember the last time she'd hugged him. He sank into it, breathing in the soothing scent of lavender and vanilla while she rocked him.

"I'm sorry, Caden. You did what you had to do." She stroked his hair. "Did you know the very first Price was given that name back in the 1650s? It was just after the Hartford Witch Trials."

"Hartford Witch Trials?" Caden pulled away.

"The very first of the witch trials. They happened about thirty years before the more famous Salem Witch Trials. One of our ancestors escaped the night before her execution and came here to Whispering Pines. I won't bore you with the details, but she made a deal in order to escape, and part of that included a sacred duty: she was in charge of overseeing that the line between our dimension and the Other Place would remain unbroken. She accepted the surname of Price, because if the rift opened, she had to be prepared to pay the cost to close it again. And we have been Prices ever since."

"What is the cost?" Caden asked. He wondered why his mom had never shared this family history with him before. Maybe she'd told Aiden all of this. Aiden, who had always been next in line to take over the business from her.

"The cost is everything. The cost is your life." She looked away, her eyes unfocusing. "I didn't want Aiden to look at my Book of Shadows because I knew he would see the possibility, but not the price he'd have to pay. Once the rift is open, it is our job to close it, even if it means going into the Other Place ourselves."

Caden recalled those missing pages from her book. "You tore out the description of the ritual," he said.

She nodded. "I should have ripped those pages out sooner, before your brother . . ." She shook her head. "But yes. I thought you might eventually seek out the book, too, and I didn't want you to be tempted into trying to open the rift on your own."

"I thought you didn't worry about me."

She managed a small smile. "I might not be *as* worried for you, but I still worry. And I know how much you love your brother."

Caden swallowed hard. He *did* love his brother, almost as much as he feared him. He thought of Aiden talking to him through the mirror, begging for his help. "Will Aiden be trapped over there forever?" he asked softly.

"At first, I was afraid he would be. But I think I might have found a way to free him."

"Really?"

"Do you remember the McCurleys? They wanted me to find their son?"

Caden nodded.

"Well . . . I found him." Her lips curved down. "Poor boy. He was attacked by something called an Unseeing—"

Caden gasped.

"You've heard of it. I thought you might have." She fiddled with one of her rings, twisting it back and forth on her finger. "Unfortunately, it killed him. But . . . it did a sloppy job. Their first kills usually are."

"Usually?" Caden said. "What, are they regular occurrences?"

"They can be, if our family doesn't stay vigilant. And I . . . I've been lax. I was too distracted by my own grief to notice that one of those creatures was in our town. And then it figured out how to disguise its psychic footprint from me. But I have Peter's hat, which links me to him, and from there to the Unseeing. And I have a theory that if the rift is reopened near that creature, the Other Place will attract it like a magnet, pulling it inside and sealing up afterward."

"So . . . Aiden might be able to get out before it closes?"

"Maybe," his mom said. "But in order to make all of this happen, I'll need your help."

"*My* help?"

"No one senses energies as well as you do."

His mom had never complimented him on his supernatural abilities before. And coming from her, there was no higher praise. He thought of all the times he'd longed to hear her say something like that to him. Only now, he knew it was just a lead-up to a question he was afraid to hear.

"Will you help me reopen the rift?"

And there it was.

Caden pictured the Other Place, full of tentacles and teeth and that horrible pulsing light. If he opened it, would he get trapped in there too? But if he didn't, then the Unseeing would continue hunting. And Rae was obviously its next target.

Very slowly he nodded.

29.
RAE

For the first time since she'd transferred to Dana S. Middle School, Rae actually wanted to see Alyssa. She searched for her in the halls, kept glancing up in each of their shared classes, and hurried to her first cross-country practice of the year, hoping Alyssa would at least turn up for that. According to Vivienne, Alyssa never missed a practice.

Except this time, apparently.

Rae waved goodbye to Vivienne and climbed into her mom's car, her stomach queasy with dread.

Her mom drove her home in stony silence, but Rae was so preoccupied, she didn't notice. Until they pulled up the driveway to her house, and her mom turned to her. "Remember, you're still grounded. So go straight in and do your homework, and then get to bed. Understood?"

Rae scowled. She'd forgotten she was grounded. "Does that mean no dinner, then?" she said, trying her best to keep her voice even. "Next are you going to have me sleep in the closet?"

"After dinner," her mom snapped, "*then* you go to bed."

"Fine. Whatever."

"Don't give me that attitude. You skipped school and broke into someone's house. These are serious things, Rae. And not like you at all!"

"I told you, I was investigating. It was important."

Her mom took a deep breath through her nose, then let it out. "Obviously," she said, "this transition has been difficult for you. And since Doctor Anderson is no longer an option—"

"What, because he was stealing kids' eyeballs?"

"—I'm looking for a new counselor for you. In fact, I have an appointment with one right now, before I head to work."

"I don't need one."

"That's not your call."

"What about you?" Rae demanded. "Why am I the only one going to counseling?"

"Because I don't have time."

"Yeah, right. Maybe you should make some time." Rae kicked her door open, grabbed her backpack, and stormed into the house. Not for the first time, she wished it had been her mom who was abducted and not her dad. And then, like every other time she had that thought, she immediately felt guilty for it.

But her mom never got her the same way her dad did. Whenever she was upset, he'd ask, *What's wrong, sugar cube?* Rae always used to scowl at him when he called her that. *What?* he'd say. *They're sweet, and so are you. Now spill.* And then he would listen to her, something her mom no longer even pretended to do.

Rae slammed the front door, kicked off her shoes, and dropped her backpack on top of them.

"What was all the shouting about?" Ava asked. She had papers spread out all over the dining room table.

"It's impolite to eavesdrop," Rae huffed.

"It's hardly eavesdropping if all the neighbors can hear you."

Rae looked around and saw that Ava had opened most of the windows. She always did that, opening the windows in whatever room she was working in before putting on her sound-canceling headphones. It made Rae uneasy. Anyone could sneak in here.

"I'm supposed to be your jailer tonight," Ava said.

Rae threw a Hot Pocket into the microwave. "That's nice. You'll have a boring job of it."

"You are really in a mood today, aren't you?"

Rae shrugged.

"Maybe this will cheer you up." Ava held something out. Something small and metallic and rectangular.

"My phone?" Rae took it.

"Just don't tell Mom."

Rae struggled between irritation and gratitude. "Thanks," she said finally.

"You're welcome. Try not to get into any trouble on my watch, would you?"

Ding!

Rae grabbed her Hot Pocket and sat at the kitchen table across from Ava and her mess. She took a careful bite. Scalding. But she knew from experience the middle would still be frozen.

"I don't know how you eat those." Ava wrinkled her nose.

"Aren't you supposed to be studying?"

"Aren't you supposed to be upstairs, doing your homework?"

Knock-knock-knock!

"Rae?" A boy called from the front door, his voice carrying through the open windows. "Rae, are you there?"

Rae hesitated. She was sure her mom didn't want her to have friends over. She glanced at Ava.

Ava deliberately put her headphones on and turned away. "Plausible deniability," she said. "Just don't be out there long."

"Thanks," Rae said.

Ava shrugged and went back to her work.

Rae opened the front door, expecting Caden, but instead getting—

"Ivan?"

"Oh, I'm so glad you're here!" His eyes were wide, his blond hair sticking out in all directions. "I need your help."

"My help? Why?"

"It's Alyssa," Ivan said. "I think she's in trouble."

Immediately Rae felt a burst of adrenaline, like she'd just taken a dose of her inhaler. Her whole body shook. "Is she . . . was she taken?"

Ivan nodded, his hands twisting together miserably. "But it's not too late to save her. I think I know where she's being held. Will you come with me?"

Rae hesitated. She glanced back at her sister sitting there, working. "Just a second," she whispered. She jammed her sneakers back on and grabbed her inhaler out of her backpack, thrusting it into her coat pocket. And then she slipped out the front door, closing it silently behind her.

Even before Ivan led the way, Rae knew they were heading back into the Watchful Woods.

"We need to hurry," Ivan said, leading her beneath the trees. The sky had begun to darken around the edges as evening crept in, the forest growing cold and dark. Up ahead, Rae could see the outline of the stone wall. Everything felt even quieter than it had the night she'd explored here with Vivienne and Caden. That night, she'd felt like something was watching her the whole time. Now it was a stronger sensation. No longer watching, but waiting. As if the forest knew what was about to happen.

Rae knew she was just imagining things. The trees were just trees, and the forest was just a forest. But as her lungs tightened up, her breath wheezing with every step, she couldn't shake the sense that there was something more here. Something aware, and eager, and not very nice.

She shivered and hunched deeper into her jacket.

Ivan paused at the stone wall, his hands hovering an inch from the moss-covered surface. His nose wrinkled in disgust. Then he took a few steps back, charged forward, and leaped the wall without touching it.

Rae blinked. "You should be on the track team."

"Maybe I'll try out in the spring."

Rae climbed over the wall and dropped down on the other side. Her breathing was getting worse, but Ivan had already started moving again. Rae hesitated, then slipped her hand into her coat pocket for her inhaler. She pulled it out.

"Mint Attack" was printed in bold letters on the metal cylinder.

Rae groaned. In her haste to rescue Alyssa, she had grabbed Vivienne's breath freshener instead of her albuterol.

She slipped the Mint Attack back into her coat pocket and glanced down at her phone. No new messages, and not a single bar of reception. She tucked her phone away and hurried to keep up with Ivan, concentrating on taking shallow, even breaths, like little sips of oxygen.

Ivan led her down a very familiar deer trail, the forest silent around them. The only noise Rae could hear above her own ragged breaths and the leaves crunching under her feet was the soft whispering sound of a nearby brook.

She knew exactly where he was leading her. "Wait, Ivan," she called, but he didn't turn around, and he didn't slow down.

Fear swam through her head and made her dizzy. She should never have come out here. What had she been *thinking*? Why hadn't she called the police?

She looked around at the trees hovering over her, their branches bare and skeletal. She could always go back. But the thought of Alyssa maimed like Jeremy and Brandi, her eyes missing, her mouth slack, all the things that made her Alyssa taken away . . . it was too horrible. Rae couldn't turn around now, not if she could help save her. So she picked up her pace, catching up with Ivan just as he reached the crest of a small hill.

"Did you call the police before coming to me?" Rae asked.

"Of course," Ivan said.

Rae breathed a small sigh of relief. Then she wondered why he *did* come to her. Trust? He barely knew her. "Shouldn't we wait for them?" she asked.

"Can't. No time."

Ahead, the rundown cabin peered through the trees like a wild creature. Rae followed Ivan closer, unable to look away from the ruin. The best anyone could say about it was that it had personality—just not the warm and fuzzy type. It had a slanted roof that had probably seen better days, and a sagging porch that definitely had. All of the windows were boarded up like the house was trying to either keep something out or trapped inside, and paint peeled from the walls in long, curling strips.

"How do you know she's here?" Rae asked Ivan.

He stared up at the house and didn't answer. Rae didn't know if it was the darkening sky, but an alien shadow seemed to pass over his face, his features shifting, the hollows around his eyes deepening, mouth stretching, until he looked something other than human. He stepped onto the porch, the wood groaning under his feet like an agonized living thing. And when he opened the front door, the dark rectangle hung there like the gaping maw of a large beast.

He disappeared inside without a word.

Rae's heart hammered painfully, her pulse filling her ears. Spots flickered at the edges of her vision, threatening to engulf her.

This didn't feel right. Not at all.

She wondered if her dad had felt like this when he'd come face-to-face with something that did not belong in their world. If he'd still confronted it anyhow. She pictured him standing tall and brave, even as he was taken.

Rae swallowed hard and stepped onto the porch, the wood shaking beneath her feet. Each step felt harder than the last, until she reached that doorway. She flicked the flashlight on her phone, and looked back at the silent wood. Then she turned, and walked through into the dark, dark house.

30.
CADEN

What do we have to do?" Caden asked his mom.

She rubbed her temples, suddenly looking exhausted. "I have some supplies to gather first."

"Like what?"

She dropped her hands. "Just . . . supplies."

Caden frowned. "If you want me to help, I need to know what we're doing."

"And I'll explain everything eventually, I promise."

Caden wasn't sure he believed that.

"We'll also need to find a place where the barrier between dimensions is already thin," she continued. "Somewhere with a lot of negative energy."

"Somewhere like Doctor Anderson's house?" Caden guessed.

"Yes."

Caden pictured the house, the way the cellar had looked the night Aiden had used it as his portal to the Other Place.

She walked toward Caden, the lines on the sides of her mouth etched in too deep. "When this is over, you and I will need to sit down and have a much longer chat." She put a hand on his shoulder. "I've always thought it would be your brother . . . but maybe you, Caden, will be the one to take over from me."

Caden squirmed uncomfortably beneath the weight of her hand. Ever since Aiden had performed his own version of justice against Zachary Mitchell, Caden had decided he wanted nothing to do with the supernatural. All he wanted was to graduate and leave Whispering Pines, and his family's business, behind. But he hadn't told his parents that yet, and this didn't really seem like the time. "This Unseeing," he said instead. "Is it Doctor Anderson?"

"What?"

"Is he the host?"

His mom frowned. "It doesn't work that way. The Other Place isn't like the spirit realm. The things that exist there have corporeal bodies—they are physically present. So if one were to cross over, it could perhaps shape itself to *look* human, but it wouldn't be able to take over a human body. It wouldn't be a possession."

Caden's heart sank as he thought of the doctor being hauled away to Green On!, the place where his wife had died. Maybe he really had been keeping Jeremy at his house to save him from those secret labs.

"What would the Unseeing look like?" Caden asked, trying not to think too hard about Doctor Anderson. There wasn't much he could do for the doctor right now. Not until he found the real Unseeing.

"Oh, I don't know. A normal person, probably. More or less. It would need some sort of physical tie to this dimension in order to stay here."

"Like . . . a human's eyes?"

His mom gave him a tight-lipped smile. "Exactly. And I would guess it would model itself to look very similar to its chosen prey."

Caden thought of Patrick and his carefully handsome face and carefully handsome attire. He had supposedly been living in northern California before he moved to Whispering Pines, but maybe that was all made up.

"I'll meet you at the doctor's house in, say, an hour?" his mom said, already walking to the door.

"Wait, we're going to do this now?"

"Of course. Once a decision is made, there's no sense in waiting."

"What about Dad? Shouldn't we tell him?"

Her mouth twisted. "Let's leave your father out of this one." Which meant she didn't think he would approve.

Which *really* meant this was a terrible, dangerous idea.

Caden's mouth was too dry as he followed his mom out of her study and watched her leave the house. In an hour, he'd be opening a rift between dimensions. A rift that could only be closed by going into the Other Place.

His mom said she thought they could send the Unseeing back instead, and that would be enough of a sacrifice. But what if she was lying? What if she planned to trade herself for Aiden? Or what if she planned to trade *him*?

I love you, Caden. . . . I wouldn't trade you for anyone.

He wanted to believe her. But he'd spent his life in the shade, watching the light of his mother's attention shine on Aiden.

Someone knocked on the front door.

Caden opened it, half expecting his mom, but instead finding . . .

"Vivienne?"

"Hey," Vivienne said. "Is Rae here?"

"What? No. Should she be?"

Vivienne frowned and glanced over her shoulder. Outside, the sky had already begun to darken, night hanging in the air. "I tried calling her, and no answer. So I biked to her house, and her sister told me she was with a boy." Vivienne's frown deepened. "I figured that would be you."

"Sorry to disappoint, but I haven't seen Rae since last night." Dread unfurled in Caden's stomach. "Why are you looking for her?"

Vivienne adjusted her heavy backpack. "I just . . . I don't know. She seemed worried about Alyssa today at school."

"Why?" Caden had gotten the impression Rae didn't really like Alyssa.

"I'm not sure. Maybe because Alyssa wasn't there? And she skipped cross-country practice; Alyssa never skips practice. So I called her when I got home, and she told me her mom actually let her take a sick day from school because she couldn't stop crying about Jeremy—so maybe Ms. Lockett isn't a complete monster?" Vivienne tilted her head, considering. "Anyhow, Alyssa said she had still been planning on coming in for practice, but then Ivan called her, said he had more information about Jeremy. About how to help him."

Caden had a weird sensation of déja vù. It was like one of his prophetic dreams, like he could see everything falling into place and was powerless to stop it.

"Alyssa was supposed to meet him, and she said she waited, but he never showed up. And now Rae is missing . . . I don't like it."

Caden gripped the doorway, his fingernails digging into the wood. "And she's with a boy," he said. "Someone who isn't me."

Vivienne nodded.

"So you think *she's* with Ivan?" Caden asked. He'd seen Ivan around, but always from a distance. He didn't really know him at all.

"Maybe?"

"But why would he call Alyssa, then meet with Rae inst—" Caden stopped, a sudden thought striking him.

And I would guess it would model itself to look very similar to its chosen prey.

He gasped. He'd been thinking about this all wrong. The Unseeing only took the eyes from *kids*. Which meant . . .

"Rae is in trouble." Caden turned and darted into his kitchen, grabbing the flashlight his dad kept plugged in there. He left Vivienne alone on the doorstep while he sprinted into his mother's study, grabbing her folded bone-handled knife and jamming it into the back pocket of his jeans. Then he hurried out the front door. "I think she's in the woods," he told Vivienne. That creature had chased them off for a reason, and if his prophetic dream was about to come true, then Rae would be going into some sort of building . . . "At the cabin."

"The . . . oh." Vivienne's eyes got very round. "Oh no."

"I'm going after her."

"I'll get help," Vivienne said, "and then I'll meet you there."

As Caden ran for the trees, he could feel the weight of his mother's knife pressing against him like a promise.

31.
RAE

The gloom of the house pressed against Rae in all directions, swallowing up the timid glow of her phone and turning the evening light that dared to trickle inside into a sluggish ooze. The cabin itself felt strangely hot and way too stuffy, the air thick and musty-smelling.

The landing in front of the door opened up into a small sitting room, where a moth-eaten couch faced a large old-fashioned fireplace, the coals inside long dead. Past the couch, a doorway opened into a shadowy hallway. There was no sign of Ivan or Alyssa.

"Alyssa?" Rae called, stepping deeper into the stomach of the house. She turned slowly, noticing a second doorway across the room, and through it, stairs leading down into pitch black.

Bam!

The front door slammed shut, cutting off the main source of

light. Rae whirled, her phone's flashlight beam landing on Ivan's pale face. He leaned against the door, his eyes shadowed, almost resembling the hollows of the eyes in the victims of the Unseeing.

"Ivan?" Rae hated how her voice trembled, fear shivering through her whole body. But this didn't feel right. And as she looked at his strangely distorted face, she realized that every instinct in her body was telling her to run, and had *been* telling her to run every time she saw him.

He'd been at cross-country tryouts and could have overheard where they were going afterward. He obviously knew where she lived, and where her locker was. And he'd moved to the area in the last nine months . . .

I'm pretty new too. Got here last year.

Rae couldn't believe it had taken her this long to think of him, even though she'd known deep down that there was something wrong there. But since no one else had seen it, she'd doubted her own instincts.

She never used to doubt her instincts. But after Taylor turned on her, she'd become unsure of herself. How could she trust her judgment when she'd been so positive Taylor was her best friend? If she was wrong about that, what else would she be wrong about? Humiliation had frozen Rae in that moment when Taylor had told all the others in her class about her "conspiracy freakiness." And maybe part of her had remained frozen there still.

But not anymore.

Ivan was the Unseeing. Rae was sure of it, the same way she was sure about what had happened to her dad.

"It was you," Rae whispered. "The whole time."

Ivan grinned, his mouth stretching until the corners brushed the base of his ears. "Very good. I was wondering if you'd figure it out. You never did seem to trust me." The proportions of his body were all wrong now too, his arms and legs stretching too long and thin, his torso thickening.

There was no way Rae was imagining it. "W-what do you want?" She backed away, her cell phone light wobbling in her trembling hand.

"Ahh, Rae." Ivan shook his head. "I think you and I both know the answer to that."

Her eyes. She felt sick, thinking of Brandi, of Jeremy, of what she would look like after this. Doctor Anderson had said the eyes were the windows to the soul. Was that what Ivan would take from her?

He glided toward her. Rae almost stumbled over her feet as she tried to keep some distance between them, the back of her foot bumping into the couch. Ivan stopped in front of the fireplace. He lifted his arm, his long fingers curling outward, bending in the wrong direction toward the back of his hand. The skin on his palm tightened, then ripped with a sound like splitting wood, the gap widening until the center of his hand was nothing but a giant gaping hole.

He brought his hand up to his left eye, covering it. All Rae could see were those twisted fingers, the dirty nails brushing against the back of his wrist, but she could hear the most horrible squelching noise, followed by a quiet *pop*. He lowered his hand, turning it so Rae's light fell on his palm. So she could see the eye cradled inside it.

The blood roared through her ears. She clutched the back of the couch, her mind whirling. She'd never make it past him to the door.

Ivan lifted a jar from the mantel of the fireplace. "When I first arrived here, I was blind and hungry." He held his mangled hand over the top of the jar, his fingers slowly uncurling, releasing the eye to drop into the goo inside. "So I took my first pair of eyes quickly and messily. Desperation drove me, and unfortunately, the boy did not survive the procedure."

Rae remembered Peter McCurley, the boy who had disappeared around the same time as Caden's brother, the one who was never found. She had a sick feeling she knew what had happened to him now.

"There are those who seek to destroy my kind, but if my victims remain alive, it masks my presence here. Anyone who looks at me will see nothing but a simple, charming human." He grinned. "*You* suspected something, but even you didn't see the truth." He set the jar back down. "I had to lay low for three months while I burned through the energy of my first host. I learned from my mistake: my next hunting trip, I sought three, so I could spread out my hunger." He raised his other hand toward his right eye. "But it was over so fast. Very unsatisfying."

Rae cringed, but couldn't look away as those fingers curled, the palm splitting.

"And then three months ago I came across a most delightful game of hide-and-seek. I took it upon myself to join in and had quite a good time." He pressed his hand to his face, and popped out his remaining eye.

When he moved his hand away, the loose skin that had been his eyelids shriveled and sloughed off like a snake's skin, leaving smooth, polished hollows behind.

"I realized I didn't have to rush my hunt. I could spread out my next three victims. The first was the quickest: she was already intrigued with the human she thought I was, so I simply invited her out for an evening walk. The second I strung along all year, pretending to be a friend, until I got tired of him. And the third? Well . . ."

Rae swallowed hard.

"Originally I'd actually planned on inviting little Jasmine to play." He uncurled his fingers, his eye popping free to quiver on his palm. "I so hate loose ends, you know. And I thought it would be very enjoyable to take the eyes from someone already so terrified of me. But then *you* came to town. You with your mistrust and your nosing about my woods."

Rae thought of Jasmine, and what she'd told her about the eye snatcher. *I thinks it likes to play games.* The first seeds of a desperate plan blossomed in Rae's mind. "You said you joined in Jasmine's game of hide-and-seek," she said. "But that's not really true, is it?"

Ivan cocked his head to the side, those awful gaping hollows somehow sharpening on her face.

"They were playing by themselves, and you just crashed their game. That's not the same."

"I suppose not."

"But we could play now," Rae continued. "For real."

"Interesting idea." He picked up the jar again and dropped his second eye inside. "You came here to find your friend, right? Well, how about these rules: if you find her before I find *you*, you are both free to go home."

It was a chance, however slim. Rae nodded, throat dry.

Ivan shook the jar gently, then set it on the mantel, the goo inside oozing. And suddenly Rae was staring at not two eyes, but a half dozen, all different shades of brown, all looking back at her. Pleading. Warning.

She gasped and put a hand to her mouth.

"Oh, and Rae?" Ivan said. "If you try to leave before finding her, I will make sure you never see the outside world again." He smiled, his eye sockets as deep and bottomless as the school's sinkhole, all of his humanity gone like the illusion it always was.

"I will give you a thirty-second head start. Beginning . . . *now*."

Rae turned and sprinted from the room, Ivan's laughter chasing her deeper into the house.

32.
CADEN

Caden raced the night falling thick and fast over the treetops. The air flowed around him, the wind rustling the leaves and filling the woods with the whispers that gave the town its name.

As he ran, he tried picturing himself surrounded in white light, but all he could see were his jumbled emotions: the throbbing red of anger at his brother for setting all of this in motion; the poisonous green of guilt that he could have done something sooner, and he hadn't; and the fear, a black so deep and dark he couldn't look at it, because to stare too long was to be lost.

What if he got to Rae in time but then froze up like he had the night his brother vanished?

He didn't know what to do. He didn't know how to open a portal, or fight a supernatural creature, or save anyone.

Caden hadn't always been so uncertain. When he was younger, he'd known exactly who he wanted to be: someone just like his brother. Powerful and confident and able to do anything. So he'd practiced on his own, doing exercises to increase his awareness and studying books of spells.

But after the Zachary Mitchell incident, Caden kept seeing Aiden's face the way he'd looked that day in the hall, so cold and detached, his smile small and as secretive as a knife to the back. And whenever Caden tried practicing one of his brother's spells, he'd hear Zachary's broken voice sobbing and begging. Even after Zachary moved away the next year, Caden couldn't shake the memory.

The worst thing was, there was a part of Caden that believed Zachary deserved it, a part that had thrilled at the sight of him slapping himself bloody. That part of Caden longed for the power to do the same thing.

Caden was terrified of that side of himself, dark and unexplored and ravenous. So he'd run the other way, focusing instead on spells of protection and learning how to control his empathy while avoiding anything dangerous. And not just magic. He'd avoided people, too, keeping himself closed off from his classmates.

Until Rae came to town.

Caden wasn't sure if they were friends, exactly. But he felt like they understood each other. Both of them had lost someone in an unexplainable way. Both of them had been isolated by it. And both of them knew what it was like to pretend to be someone else. And Caden *wanted* to be her friend, which was a strange new thing for him. Before he met her, he hadn't realized how tired he was of being alone all the time.

And now she might be gone from his life forever.

He put on a burst of speed, trying to leave his fear and his memories in the past where they belonged.

Caden reached the overgrown trail Vivienne had noticed and slowed his steps. Just ahead lurked the rundown cabin. As he moved closer, he could feel the way it hummed and throbbed with that same unnatural energy as the Other Place, all sickly sweet rot and a sense of things out of place. This was definitely the den of the Unseeing. Closer still, and he realized there was something more going on here. Evil rolled from this place like nothing Caden had ever felt before. Whatever event had tainted this house had happened well before Ivan crawled into this world.

Caden left the safety of the trees and crossed the weed-choked lawn. Overhead, a whippoorwill cried, the drawn-out sound eerie and lonesome. It felt like a bad omen to hear birds singing at night, and he hesitated in front of the sagging porch.

Why had Rae been so willing to come with Ivan *here*, of all places? It seemed very like her, though. He remembered how she'd practically thrown herself inside Doctor Anderson's house with little to no planning. Maybe he *was* too cautious, but she was definitely too impulsive.

He stepped up onto the porch, ignoring the way it groaned and shifted beneath him, and suddenly he wasn't alone anymore. "Aiden?" He couldn't see his brother, but he felt him standing there beside him.

"I'm glad I found you again."

Caden smiled. "I'm glad you did too." And he meant it; if he was going to save Rae from the Unseeing, he'd have to embrace the part of himself that scared him most. He would have to open himself up and draw on every ounce of his own power.

He would have to become like his brother.

33.
RAE

Rae sprinted down the hall, shining her cell phone's flashlight ahead of her. She saw a door to the left and yanked it open, revealing a storage closet full of old cleaning supplies and rusting shelving units, but no Alyssa.

"Twenty-four, twenty-three," Ivan's voice boomed down the hall.

Rae left the door to the closet open and hurried down the hall and into the kitchen at the end. Every breath was a wheeze, loud and painful. She pressed a hand to her lungs and kept moving through the kitchen, her light bouncing off the old-fashioned stove and illuminating the rotting wooden cabinets. A short counter separated the cooking side of the kitchen from a small breakfast alcove with a round table and three chairs.

"Eighteen, seventeen, sixteen . . . Half your time is up, and you've only made it to the kitchen?"

Rae leaped forward, her mind a blank sheet of terror, and her foot caught on the fourth chair, the one she hadn't noticed, lying broken-legged to the side. She stumbled and went down, skidding across the floor on her stomach. She was up again in seconds, but she had precious few of them left.

Half sobbing, she sprinted out of the kitchen and down the next hallway, past a bathroom with nothing in it but a cracked toilet, a claw-foot tub, and a mason jar sitting on the sink counter, the whole room stinking of mold. No Alyssa. She hurried to the next room, a small bedroom, the bed carefully made, the desk tidy.

"Ten, nine, eight," Ivan chanted.

Rae bolted into the next room—the last room of the house. Another bedroom, this one a little larger and a lot messier, full of the stench of rotting wood and dirt.

"Five . . . four . . ."

Think, Rae, think! she told herself, fighting down the rush of panic. Obviously Alyssa wasn't on this floor, so that left the basement. But she'd never make it there before Ivan caught up with her. Which meant she needed to hide. But how did you hide from something that didn't need eyes to see?

She opened the closet door. It was full of jackets and clothing and stacks of old paper. It would also be the first place he'd look. She closed it, but not quite all the way, and turned to the bed. It didn't look promising, just a lumpy old mattress, a rumpled comforter lying half on the floor, and three large pillows.

"Ready or not, here I come!"

Rae tugged the mattress away from the headboard a little and squeezed into the gap left behind, pulling the pillows on top of her and flicking off her cell phone flashlight. Mold and dust filled her nostrils, and all the things that had been hiding under the mattress and burrowing into the soft wood of the bedframe began crawling over her, slithering up her shirt, wriggling through her hair. She didn't move, even as she imagined spiders, beetles, and more.

If she miraculously survived this, she was going to take the world's longest, hottest shower.

Creak!

Rae caught her breath. That creak had come from right outside the bedroom door. She held herself as flat as she could, the headboard pressing into her back while certain doom loomed from the other side. She squeezed her eyes shut, tears spilling from the corners.

She couldn't die here; she had to keep looking for her dad.

"Rae," Ivan's voice sang out. He was close. Too close. She could picture him standing right over the bed. "I know you're in here."

She dug her fingernails into the palms of her hands, expecting the pillows to be removed any moment.

"Got you!"

Rae flinched, then forced herself to be still. She could hear Ivan rustling around. He must be in the closet, barely a foot from her head. She waited for him to grab her, but apparently he hadn't heard her movement.

"Pretty good, Rae. Pretty good."

Rae kept her eyes closed and held her breath. Even without the wheeze, she knew breathing would make the pillows move. Finally she heard Ivan's footsteps moving back toward the door, and then out into the hall again.

The breath exploded from Rae's lungs in a painful wheeze, and she clawed her way out from behind the pillows, gasping as silently as she could. She listened hard for Ivan, but in such an old wooden house there were plenty of groans from all directions, and she couldn't be sure where he had gone.

She had to get to the basement, and fast.

Rae slipped her hand into her pocket and pulled out Vivienne's Mint Attack. It wasn't much as far as a weapon went, but she felt better holding something in her hand, at least. Then she eased her way out of the room, leaving her phone off. The shadows were so dark, Ivan could be hiding anywhere, and she wouldn't be able to see him until it was too late. But her flashlight would just make *her* easier to see.

Rae retraced her steps, creeping to the end of the hallway. She peered out at the dark kitchen.

Still no sign of Ivan.

It was somehow worse. She kept imagining him leaping out at her, or waiting around the next corner, or sneaking along just behind her . . .

She swallowed down the fear and inched through the kitchen, keeping close to the wall. She made it to the next hall, and then into the sitting room. Now that her eyes had adjusted, she could see a little bit of light filtering through the cracked wooden boards over the windows, enough to show her that Ivan wasn't there.

Maybe he'd gone outside to see if she'd made a run for it?

Rae hesitated near the couch. She looked at that front door, so inviting, and then she turned away from it and over to the stairs heading to the basement. She kept one hand on the wall, her feet feeling the way down one step, two, eight, a dozen. She had to be near the bottom now.

Creak!

Rae froze.

Something large scurried behind her, long nails clicking against wood like an insect's legs.

Her shoulder blades prickled, and she *knew* it was right behind her. She could feel it watching her, waiting for her to notice. She didn't want to look, but haltingly, the world moving in slow motion, she turned.

A trickle of dim light filtered in through the upstairs, gently outlining the top steps, and nothing else. No one was there.

Until a large dark shape dropped from the ceiling.

Rae bit her lip so hard to keep from screaming that she tasted blood, metallic and sharp, as Ivan landed at the top of the stairs like a humanoid spider. He lurched upright, his silhouette framed in the stairway, too-long arms hanging loosely at his sides.

She crouched low, pressing herself against the wall and hoping the shadows were thick enough down here to cover her. *Please, please,* she thought, *just walk by. Don't come down here...*

"I know you're there." Ivan seemed to grow larger until he blocked the whole top of the stairwell. "You can't hide from me any longer, Rae."

She was trembling, her lungs burning with the effort of keeping her breathing quiet. If he knew she was there, her only hope was to get down to the basement, find Alyssa before he caught her, and pray he kept his word and let them both go.

She straightened, slowly and carefully, and inched her foot down another step.

Ivan leaped abruptly down the stairs, so fast Rae didn't have time to react before he crashed into her.

She fell backward, tumbling the last few steps and landing awkwardly on the cement basement floor. Her vision filled with sparks, everything going too bright, and then dark. She knew she needed to get up and run, but her body wasn't listening very well. She blinked, her vision clearing, but all she could see was Ivan's monstrous face looming over her. His skin throbbed with a sickly yellowish light, flickering like a bad fluorescent lamp, giving her flashes of that wide mouth full of jagged teeth, the tiny sliver of nose, and the swirling pits of deepest pitch where his eyes had once been.

34.
CADEN

aden opened the front door. It swung wide silently, the house beyond dark and disturbingly still. The flashlight was a comforting weight in his hand, but he didn't want to turn it on yet. It would feel too much like a beacon announcing his presence to whatever lurked inside. Instead, he waited a few seconds for his eyes to adjust to the gloom.

The inside looked innocent enough, just a small sitting room with a couch and a bulky mantel, and no people.

Caden knelt and pulled off his shoes, wedging them under the door to keep it open, then continued on in his socks. As he moved deeper into the house, he could feel pressure building like a large unnatural storm. And beneath that, Rae's fear vibrated from the walls, as if the house itself was feasting on it.

"You know what you have to do, right?" Aiden whispered.

Caden swallowed hard. He did know. The only way to truly defeat the Unseeing would be to send it back to its own dimension. Which meant he'd have to somehow reopen the rift here.

"Don't worry, I'll help you."

But after he opened it, he'd have to close it again. And there was only one way he knew to do that.

Blood opens and blood closes. A sacrifice given and taken.

Caden tried not to think that far ahead. He didn't want to remember the way the Other Place looked or imagine what it would be like to be trapped in there forever. If he spent too long thinking about it, he'd never get up the nerve to do what he had to do, so for now he just focused on each step at a time, starting with number one: find Rae.

Caden squinted in the dim lighting, studying the couch, the doorway behind it, and—

Thump! Thump!

He spun, accidentally knocking a jar off the mantel of the fireplace. The glass shattered on the ground. Caden winced, looking down at the mess.

At first he wasn't sure what he was looking at. Marbles? Balls of goo? And then he realized: they were *eyes*. A dozen of them sliding around in some weird jelly solution, oozing slowly across the floor. They all rolled around until they were staring right at him.

Caden put a hand over his mouth and backed away. He couldn't do this. He couldn't—

Somewhere deeper in the house, Rae screamed.

And Caden ran without thinking, leaping over the eyes and sprinting toward the sound.

35.
RAE

Rae struggled back, managing to half sit before Ivan dug his long, sharp fingers into her shoulders and shoved her down again. He shifted his weight, one spindly leg curling beneath him and then dropping down onto her chest like an anvil, crushing the breath out of her. Pain burst in her lungs, spots exploding around the edges of her vision. She was suffocating, drowning on land.

Ivan let go of her shoulders and raised his hands toward her face, his fingers curling backward once more, the skin on his palms splitting open. The gaps inside looked just like the hollows of his eyes, bottomless and hungry.

Rae screamed as Ivan slowly lowered his palms toward her face, those gaping holes pulling at her like a low energy vacuum, threatening to suck the eyes right out of her head. She couldn't blink or look away as her vision filled with darkness. And she knew this would be the last thing she ever saw.

And then suddenly Ivan sat up and turned away from her, growling. Rae wasn't sure why, but she knew she wouldn't get another chance. She thrust herself up and shoved Ivan's chest as hard as she could to knock him away from her. When he spun back, she whipped up the Mint Attack still clutched in her right hand and emptied the entire canister in his face.

Ivan shrieked and fell back, dragging his hands like claws down his face. The metallic smell of his blood mingled with the overpowering minty goodness in the air.

Rae stumbled to her feet and staggered away from Ivan, but she'd only taken a few steps when she tripped over something. It shattered under her, the broken pieces moist and slimy like moss, her fingers sliding over them when she tried to push herself back up. And it *stank*.

She wrinkled her nose and glanced down.

For a second, in the dim basement light she couldn't understand what she was looking at. Horror cushioned her mind, softening the image, allowing her the chance to let it go, to pretend it was furniture clutching at her skin and clothing.

But Rae had always believed in chasing the truth, no matter how horrible it might be. She blinked and made herself see the reality: she was tangled up in a rib cage—a *human* rib cage—splinters of bone jabbing into her clothing, snagging her in place. There was no moss, just the decayed remains of clothing left to rot. And of the rest of the body, now almost completely decomposed.

Immediately the smell seemed to double, and Rae gagged. She thrust herself to her feet, pieces of rib clinging to her, the damp of the body soaking into her pants and sweatshirt. Frantic, she batted at her clothing, stumbling over the leg bones, desperate to get away.

The skeleton wasn't that big, only a little bigger than her. A kid. Alyssa.

No, Rae told herself, panic twisting in her mind. No, Alyssa wouldn't be so decomposed. This had to be someone else, someone who'd been dead almost a year. Ivan's first victim.

Rae realized this must be what happened to poor missing Peter McCurley.

Peter McCurley. Ivan must've killed him when he'd arrived in their dimension. Alyssa still had to be alive somewhere in—

Rae stopped and looked at Ivan. He no longer clawed at his face. He could have passed for one of the basement's many shadows as he stood between her and her one way out.

"You told me Alyssa was here," Rae whispered.

Other than a boarded-up window, a drain in the middle of the cement floor, and the body of Peter, there was nothing in the basement, and nowhere else Alyssa could be.

"And you foolishly believed me." Ivan laughed, showing off all his rows of teeth.

Rae backed away, her mind a whirl as she tried to think of a way out. She kept picturing that jar of eyes, and how hers would be joining them. All brown eyes . . . It made sense. Ivan wouldn't want to attract attention by changing eye colors, and his first victim had brown eyes. Which meant Alyssa had never been in danger, not with her blue eyes. This whole thing had been a trap for Rae from the start.

Rae's back hit the cracked brick walls. She looked past Ivan at the stairs, but they seemed so far away. She would never make it to them.

Ivan advanced on her, his hands raised, showing off the gaps in his palms that were waiting to be filled with her eyes. "And now," he said, "you have nowhere left to go. Game over."

36.
CADEN

Caden got to the top of a dark stairwell and clicked his flashlight on.

"Are you trying to get yourself noticed?" Aiden demanded.

Caden flinched and immediately turned off the flashlight again. He kept one hand on the railing while he hurried down the steps, trying not to trip in the darkness. As he got closer to the bottom, he realized there actually was some light coming from the basement, just not much of it.

"Rifts are unstable by nature, so you need something to give it shape. Like this stairway."

"Here?" Caden whispered.

"Here and now, if you want to save your friend."

Caden's eyes adjusted to the dim lighting, the gloom of the basement lifting enough that he could see two shadows in the far corner. Rae . . . and the Unseeing. He started forward.

"The rift!" his brother shrieked. *"You need to open it now! It's her best chance."*

Caden knew Aiden was right. He wouldn't be able to beat the Unseeing in a fight; he needed to send it back into the Other Place. He just didn't know how.

"Immerse yourself in the energies of the house, and . . ."

"Aiden?"

"Something's happening. Someone is here who . . . no, stop! Cad—"

His brother's voice abruptly cut out. Caden couldn't feel his presence at all.

Caden's mouth went dry, his hands trembling. He needed to save Rae from the Unseeing and rescue his brother from the Other Place. And there was only one way he could truly help both of them now.

Somehow he had to reopen the rift by himself.

Caden took a deep, cleansing breath and closed his eyes. He'd watched his brother do this. He *could* do it too. He pictured his usual protective white bubble surrounding him, and then he imagined that bubble popping, opening him up to all the negative energies of the house.

Death, despair, hopelessness. Blood, fear, hunger.

He felt it all scraping and crawling over him like rats in a nest, digging claws into his very self. Dimly he was aware of the flashlight clattering from his hand, of Rae screaming, of the Unseeing saying something, but he was frozen on that bottom step as images of the victims the Unseeing had targeted flashed through his mind in quick succession. He felt their terror as the creature pulled their eyes from them. And not just their eyes. He fed on *them*, on their internal essence, burning through it the way a fire burned through wood.

Caden didn't want to know this, didn't want to feel this. He tried pulling away, but the more he struggled, the more it sucked him down. He fell below the victims' emotions, and toppled into the memories of the Unseeing.

Caden saw his brother through its eyes. Aiden stood frozen with his arms outstretched, blood trickling down his arms. Behind him the blue light of another dimension pulsed with energy. Caden felt the Unseeing's interest, its hunger for this new place. And he was with it when it stepped through the rift and suddenly found itself plunged into complete and all-encompassing darkness.

It reacted instinctively, like a spider suddenly thrust into light, scuttling from the house and into the woods. It crashed through the trees, confused and disoriented, until it stumbled upon its first victim: a boy camping alone in the woods.

The boy barely put up a fight as the Unseeing fell on him, yanking the boy's eyes out and feeding on his soul. Afterward, the Unseeing slid the new eyes into the hollows in its face, and the darkness lifted until it could see the world around it. A world full of possibilities. It could do very well here.

The eyes were an anchor. With them, the Unseeing could look at this world the way the humans looked at it, understand things the way they understood. It could blend in among them. But it knew there were those nearby who would be able to sense the truth of its nature. It had to protect itself.

It looked down at the body of its first unwilling host, and knew it would have to do things differently the next time. If it spread out its feeding over three, it could leave just enough of their own essence to mask its presence here in this dimension.

The Unseeing scooped up the body of Peter and carried him deeper into the woods. The cabin called to it, the energies of the place welcoming it. And as it stepped through the creaking doorway, Caden slid out of its mind and sank beneath the memories tied to the house.

These memories were several hundred years old and had fragmented into broken pieces of emotion. Caden caught the overwhelming feeling that something terrible had happened here, followed by a glimpse of a woman doing some kind of summoning spell. A ripple of negative energies cascaded out in one violent wave as the spell fell apart. Caden saw the woman's face clearly, her mouth open, eyes wide and terrified, and then his vision went crimson with blood—*her* blood—while the fabric of her reality tore open.

There were other people with her, helping her with her spell. Caden sensed the wave from that tear crashing against them, too, and was part of their group as they all died, crushed beneath that tide. He felt himself getting washed away with them—

Focus, Caden, he thought. *Don't lose yourself to the past.* Aiden wouldn't.

Aiden. Caden concentrated on his brother, using that as an

anchor to the present reality. He had to rescue Aiden and save Rae.

He kept that thought firmly in mind and pulled back from the energies of the house. He could still sense them, but he wasn't entangled within them anymore. Now he was able to use them, binding them together and weaving them into a net across the doorframe at the bottom of the stairwell, his own essence the glue holding them in place.

The pressure in the stairwell changed, the air growing colder.

Caden opened his eyes. Everything glowed a soft, pale yellow, the stairs flickering in the light, the air hazy, like he was dreaming.

But the Other Place still required blood.

He pulled the knife from his back pocket and slid it open. The blade seemed longer and skinnier than he remembered, the edge gleaming unnaturally in that strange light. He pushed up his right sleeve. Then he took a deep breath and carefully sliced a thin, shallow line on the underside of his arm.

It burned as the blood bubbled out. And just like he'd seen Aiden do all those months ago, Caden scraped the flat of the blade along the cut and then flicked the bloody knife at the doorway and the invisible net of negative energies woven there.

Drops of blood hit the doorway, and it began pulsing a vivid red, like an angry wound.

Caden gasped. Each pulse felt like it was pulling more blood from him, more power, the color in the doorway deepening from bright red to brown, back to its sickly yellow-green as it grew larger and larger.

He'd done something wrong. The rift was supposed to stay

contained in the stairway, but it kept expanding. The whole thing wobbled at the edge of the stairs, and then spilled out into the basement.

Caden's legs trembled and he collapsed to his knees, the knife clattering from his numb fingers.

He was unraveling, spinning himself out, stretching across the doorway and beyond.

37.

RAE

Ivan took a deliberate step forward. Rae moved to the left, but he moved faster, blocking her. She tried darting to the right, but he was already there, shoving her back against the wall. She wheezed, panic choking her. There was no escape.

"I told you," he said. "I've already won. You—"

Crack!

Both Rae and Ivan turned toward the stairs and the source of the noise. In the dim light filtering in from the basement window, Rae made out a dark cylinder rolling across the floor. It stopped on top of the rusty old drain.

The room blurred, filling with a strange greenish light. Something about that glow scared Rae almost as much as the Unseeing. Maybe it was the way it pulsed, shifting from green to yellow to green. It made her think of toxic animals, diseased flesh, decay.

And then she noticed the figure framed in the bottom of the stairs, his silhouette obscured by the light. It was like staring at someone lying on the bottom of a swimming pool, a person with spiky black hair. Caden.

Rae's heart lurched. She was both terrified for him and relieved she wasn't alone here anymore.

Caden made an abrupt slashing motion, and the pulsating light around him slowly shifted from green to a reddish brown, like old blood. The air pressure changed. Rae clapped her hands over her popping ears as a strange wind picked up, whipping her ponytail in her face.

Ivan toppled over with a guttural cry and began sliding toward the stairs as some invisible force pulled him. His long fingers dug into the cement, leaving gouges. "No!" he screamed. "You won't send me back!"

Too fast for Rae to react, his hand lashed out and caught one of her ankles.

Rae fell on her butt, the cement scraping against her back as she was dragged with Ivan toward the rift.

"Caden!" she screamed, kicking out at Ivan with her free foot and trying to grab at anything to slow her progress. But Ivan's fingers were strong as bone, and the opening to the Other Place was practically on them.

Through the light Rae could see a mass of tentacles swirling, waiting hungrily for their prey.

38.
CADEN

Caden's vision went blurry. He blinked and realized it wasn't him; the basement was full of a strange greenish fog. Flashes of sickly yellow light illuminated the twisted things lurking within, creatures with tentacles, beasts that walked like humans, and others that crawled like worms. They didn't seem to notice the opening torn behind them, but Caden knew that they would soon.

Blood opens and blood closes. But how much more did Caden have left to give?

Caden put a hand against the wall, fighting a wave of dizziness. He was losing too much blood too fast, the portal pulling it right out of him. He closed his eyes and tried to rebuild the mental image of a bubble of white light surrounding him. Then he clenched his hand hard around his protective talisman, using that pain to ground himself.

He felt a jolt inside, almost like he was on an elevator that stopped too suddenly, and the sense that he was bleeding out faded as the portal stabilized.

Caden slowly opened his eyes.

One of the creatures in the Other Place looked up, its tongue extending out, tasting the air like a snake. It made a strange clicking sound, and the thing next to it straightened, staring out at the opening. It shifted closer, curious. Another came, and another, until the rift was surrounded by ravenous faces.

A tentacle slid out into Caden's world, seeking the blood on his arm.

He knew what would happen next. He'd seen it. The creatures would pull him into their world and the portal would close behind him. He wasn't as strong as Aiden, and wouldn't be able to fight off the things in the Other Place. They would slowly devour him.

"Aiden," he gasped as another tentacle caressed the side of his face. He tried feeling for Aiden's presence, but there was still nothing. His brother wasn't waiting on the other side of the rift. He wasn't anywhere. All Caden could sense was the mindless hunger of the creatures in front of him.

"—den! Caden!"

Caden squinted, searching past the tentacles and the mist.

He saw the thing that had been Ivan sliding toward him, its

limbs contorting as it struggled against the pull of the Other Place. And held in its grip . . .

"Rae!" Caden cried.

She met his gaze through the barrier, the pulsing light reflecting in her terrified eyes as she slid closer and closer to the rift. And there was nothing Caden could do to stop it.

39.
RAE

Rae tried to pull her leg free, but Ivan's grasp was too tight, and digging her other foot and her hands into the cement barely did anything to slow them down. It was like trying to stop on a steep water slide.

They were almost at the rift. A tentacle crept out, hovering above their heads, almost like it could sense them.

Time seemed to slow down for Rae. Caden had told her that the portal needed a sacrifice to close, so Rae knew what she had to do. She only hoped she had the strength to pull it off, because she would only get one shot.

Ivan twisted to look at her, the empty hollows of his face seeming to stare right through her. And then he grinned, like he knew what she was planning and was daring her to try.

Maybe this was all just another game to him.

A blur of speed, and the tentacle whipped toward them. Rae choked back a scream, but the tentacle slid over her and wrapped instead around Ivan's leg, yanking him halfway into the rift. He shrieked as another tentacle joined the first, both of them making horrible slurping noises like they were eating Ivan alive.

Rae knew this was a preview of what would happen to her if she failed.

Ivan slashed at the tentacles with his long, sharp fingers, and gnashed them with his teeth. They let go, and he started dragging himself out, away from the rift.

Rae raised her free leg up. "This is for Brandi!" And she kicked him, driving her sneaker into his eyeless face and yanking her ankle right out of her shoe and his grasp.

Ivan staggered, then fell back into the Other Place, where he was engulfed in the waiting horde of monsters. His scream only lasted a second before the horrifying grunting, suckling sounds of creatures eating filled the glowing green air.

40.

CADEN

Caden felt the energies of the rift unraveling. He tried to hold it together longer, searching for his brother.

"Aiden!" He felt for him, but there was no sense of human emotion anywhere inside the portal. His brother wasn't there. Caden's mental control began slipping from his grasp like sand through a clenched fist. The only way to stop the slide would be to give the rift everything. Already he could feel its eagerness to devour him as well, to take his power and consume it.

"Blood opens and closes. A sacrifice given and taken," Caden said, his voice weak, and barely audible above the sounds of the monsters feasting.

The rift had gotten his blood, and it had gotten Ivan. *You don't get anymore*, he thought, letting go.

The energies holding the rift open unwound faster and faster.

The pressure in the stairwell shifted, building like a terrible storm about to crash down on them all. Caden's ears popped, and he braced himself for the worst, and then abruptly, it was gone.

Caden opened his eyes. The stairwell was dark and quiet, the portal gone, the storm passed. "It worked," he murmured. "I really didn't think it would." He sank back onto the step behind him. He was so tired. The burning in his arm had become a dull ache, and when he put a hand to the wound, he realized it wasn't bleeding anymore.

". . . den. Caden."

He blinked. Rae was crouched in front of him, holding the flashlight he'd dropped.

"Are you okay?"

"I don't know," he mumbled.

"Can you stand?"

He tried, but his legs were like sticks of burning incense, crumbling to ash beneath him. Dimly he was aware of Rae dragging his good arm over her shoulders and sliding her arm around his waist. "Step left foot," she ordered.

It seemed easier to listen, so he did.

"Right foot."

Another step. And another. What seemed like a year later, they reached the top of the stairs. No light filtered in through the cracked boards over the windows, and when the front door banged open, all Caden could see was the inky black of night. He closed his eyes and felt as if he were floating through it, bouncing off stars.

The energy of the cabin had changed. He could still feel an

echo of the terrible things that had happened here, but it was like the park after a hard rain, everything fresh and clean, the darkness burned away.

From somewhere far away he could hear Patrick's voice and the voices of other adults. Something about surrounding the house. Rae was speaking too, but Caden couldn't focus on any of that. And then Vivienne's voice cut through the others, close to his head. "I got Patrick and led him and his team here as fast as I could. How did you get away from Ivan?"

"Mint Attack," Rae told her. "Emptied the whole canister in his eyeless face."

"Mint Attack, huh?" she said. "I told you it could be useful." That was the last thing Caden heard before everything faded away, and he was left to drift silently in peace.

He jolted awake, flailing.

"Shh, Caden," his mom whispered, putting a hand to his forehead and gently pressing him back down. "You're okay."

"Mom?"

"I'm here."

He blinked, his eyes adjusting. He was in his room, in his own bed, the shades drawn, a lamp glowing softly in the corner. His mom knelt next to him, smoothing back his hair. "I'm sorry I didn't meet you at Doctor Anderson's house," he whispered.

"That's okay. I heard what happened."

"You did?"

"Patrick brought you home."

Caden frowned. Patrick obviously hadn't been the Unseeing, but there was still something off about that guy. He didn't like the idea of him being in his house.

His mom must have recognized his look. "I stopped him at the front door," she said. "I don't trust him, either. He seemed a little too interested in hearing your side of tonight's events. Specifically, how you were able to open and close the rift to the Other Place." She dropped her hand, her eyes narrowing.

Caden looked away, staring up at his ceiling. "Aiden started to help me open it," he said. "And then . . . and then he was gone." He made himself look at his mother. "I don't know what happened to him. I'm sorry."

A tear leaked silently down her cheek. "It's not your fault," she whispered.

"We can try again."

She shook her head. "He's not there anymore. I've been able to sense him off and on these past few days, but then this evening that connection snapped." She sniffed and wiped at her face. "I'm afraid he's really gone now. Truly and completely." She sniffed again, but the tears kept coming, and she gave up and just cried.

Caden sat up awkwardly, the wound on his arm pulling with the movement. He put his arms around his mom and held her as she cried.

Goodbye, Aiden, he thought. *I'm sorry. I tried.* Part of him wanted to cry too. But mostly all he felt was relief that it was finally over.

41.

RAE

Rae cautiously peeked into the kitchen the next morning.

"It's just me," Ava said. "Mom's upstairs sleeping. You don't need to lurk."

Rae crept inside.

"What did I say about lurking?" Ava asked, annoyed.

"Sorry," Rae mumbled. She got out a bowl, spoon, and cereal. At the last minute, she remembered to grab the milk, too. She carried them all over to the table and sat across from her sister, then waited.

"You don't need to stare at me either." Ava sighed. She put down her book and her coffee cup. "I've decided I'm not going to say anything to Mom about last night."

"R-really?" When Patrick had brought Rae home last night, her mom had been at work. But Ava had been there, and while

Patrick didn't really know all the details, he'd told her sister enough. Rae had carefully avoided her ever since.

"Yes." Ava ran a finger along the rim of her mug. "In exchange for a promise from you."

"What kind of promise?" Rae asked suspiciously.

Ava looked up, meeting her gaze. "You need to keep me in the loop. No more getting yourself in trouble, running off to investigate things, sneaking into houses, and literally following a monster into an abandoned cabin in the middle of the woods." She shook her head. "I can't even believe I have to tell you that last bit. Haven't you seen any horror movie ever?"

"I was trying to save Alyssa," Rae said.

"And that's all well and good, but not if you get yourself killed doing it. Besides, wasn't Alyssa totally fine?"

Rae looked away, her cheeks burning. That had been one of the worst parts; Vivienne had filled her in on the ride back that Alyssa had been home the whole time.

"Look, you just need to tell me what you're up to, okay? That's it. Tell me what you are doing so I can help you. If you promise to do that, then I won't tell Mom you snuck out last night and tried to get yourself killed."

"You just don't want Mom to know what a terrible jailer you were," Rae said.

A small smile slipped through Ava's very serious expression. "Fine. That's part of it." But then her smile fell. "I was really worried, Rae."

"I didn't think you cared."

Ava's eyebrows drew together. "Of *course* I care, Rae. I love you and I don't want anything to happen to you."

Rae wanted to make some flippant remark, but she couldn't. She and Ava never said the *L*-word to each other, even before their father disappeared. To their parents, sure. But not to each other. Hearing it now healed something deep inside Rae, some jagged broken edge she hadn't known was there. "I love you too, Ava," she sniffed. Then she pulled herself together. "And we have a deal—*if* you agree to let me know what *you* find too." She held out her hand.

Ava hesitated. "I don't want you involved."

"He's my dad too, Ava. I'm never going to stop looking for him. Don't you think that if you're looking too, we'll have more luck working together?"

Ava sighed. "Fine. Deal."

They shook on it.

"I'll make you a second deal," Ava said after she released Rae's hand. "You put in a good word for me the next time you see that Patrick guy, and I'll give you a ride to school today."

"What? Why?" Rae suddenly realized. "You *like* him!"

"Well, he is pretty handsome. Great hair." Ava shrugged.

"But . . . he's old."

"Not that old. I'm guessing mid-to-late twenties, maybe?"

Rae knew her sister had had boyfriends in the past, and she was almost eighteen, but the idea of her being interested in Patrick of Green On! was just . . . *weird.* "I might never see him again," she said.

"Oh, I don't know about that." Ava grinned, a sneaky little smile like she knew something.

"What?" Rae asked.

"Do we have a second deal, or no?"

"Can we stop for bagels on the way? I'm tired of cereal."

"Okay."

"Then sure," Rae said, grinning back. And for the first time since her dad had vanished, she felt like she had her real sister back.

Rae slipped into homeroom early, taking her now-normal seat in the back. It felt surreal to be sitting here, when last night she thought she might never see this school again. A few minutes later, and Vivienne stepped inside.

"Got a ride to school?" Vivienne asked, taking her seat next to Rae.

Rae nodded.

"Me too." Vivienne was quiet for a minute. A couple other kids came in and took their seats. In the front, Russell and Gary started up a loud, obnoxious conversation, and Vivienne leaned in closer. "Hey," she whispered. "Are we good?"

"Why wouldn't we be?" Rae fiddled with a pencil.

"You've been a little weird since last night. And I know it was probably a pretty traumatic thing with that whole creepy cabin and Ivan and the *eyes*." Vivienne shuddered. She'd accidentally stepped on one of the eyes when she'd burst into the cabin last night. Honestly, Rae thought that was just about as traumatic as everything she went through herself. "But I also kind of feel like you're maybe mad at me too? You know, for not telling you?"

"You mean that you've been secretly working for Patrick and Green On! this whole time?" Rae turned and looked at her friend.

Vivienne bit her lip. "It's . . . I mean, I started there this summer, so before you were even here."

"You still could have told me."

"Part of the deal was I couldn't say anything about it, since the internship program hadn't officially begun yet. My mom helped set it up, and she didn't want anyone to accuse Patrick of favoritism."

"Why *are* you working for him?"

"Scholarship opportunities."

"You're twelve."

"It's never too soon to think about the future," Vivienne deadpanned. She managed to keep her face serious for a full second, and then she cracked up. "Sorry. Okay, yeah, that's a bunch of hooey. The honest reason? I think Patrick can help me find something."

Rae frowned. "What are you looking for?"

Vivienne's lips quirked in a challenge. "What are *you* looking for?"

Rae hesitated. She'd told Caden about her dad, and he'd believed her. Maybe Vivienne would too. She opened her mouth, then shut it. She wasn't ready to trust someone else with her secret. Not yet.

She had thought Vivienne was a different person. Someone uncomplicated, but now she realized Vivienne had her own hidden agenda, and it changed the way Rae saw her.

But maybe that was okay.

"Perhaps I'll tell you later," Rae said. "If you tell me what you carry in that ridiculously oversize backpack of yours."

Vivienne laughed. "All right, we'll have an exchange of secrets. Later."

"Then I guess we're good," Rae decided. "And Vivienne—thanks for coming through last night."

"Of course. What are friends for?" Vivienne nudged Rae with her shoulder. "If you need me, Rae-Rae, I'm there."

Rae's eyes prickled slightly. After what Taylor did, she hadn't known if she'd ever have a friend she could trust again.

"Hey," Caden said. Rae and Vivienne looked up.

He stood in front of them, his face grayish and drawn, his movements stiff like he was still in pain. "What are you doing in school today?" Rae demanded. "You should be home resting!"

"I missed two days this week. If I missed today, Ms. Lockett would probably hunt me down personally."

"Truth," Vivienne said. She patted the desk in front of her, the one Alyssa had been using ever since Rae stole her old desk. "Sit with us today. If you want."

Caden looked at that desk, then at her, and finally at Rae.

Rae gave him a small shrug and a smile.

"Just today," he said, carefully sitting down.

As if on cue, Alyssa walked into the room, spotted Caden in her seat, and went pink. "Seriously?" She stalked toward them. "That's *my* seat."

"Relax, Alyssa. You can sit next to Caden," Vivienne said.

"Why is *Caden* allowed to sit by you?" Alyssa demanded.

The room went quiet, and Rae could feel all the other kids listening hard while pretending not to. The pressure of all that scrutiny reminded her too much of her old school, and she dug her hands into her seat, resisting the urge to run. Instead, she made herself speak. "Because Caden is my friend," she said.

Vivienne nodded. "Mine too."

Alyssa scowled. For a second, Rae thought she might start flipping over desks. But then her shoulders sagged. "Fine." She dropped into the seat next to him. "Do me a favor and don't murder any of us," she told him.

"I make no guarantees," Caden said dryly.

Rae hid a grin behind her hand as the loudspeaker crackled on, shouting out the morning's announcements. She listened for anything about Ivan, but of course it was all boring stuff, like that day's lunch menu, a reminder to sign up for after-school art lessons by next week, a plea from the Latin teacher to return her missing textbook. And then a new message at the end.

"A reminder to all students: anyone caught throwing their garbage into the sinkhole will be given an automatic detention. Second infractions will result in suspension."

Vivienne raised her eyebrows at Rae. Rae shook her head. It was nice to have a reminder that normal here was still anything but.

"And . . . would Rae Carter and Caden Price please report to the front office? Rae Carter and Caden Price, front office please." The speaker went silent.

Rae could feel her heart beating too fast, her face red. Had Ms. Lockett found out she and Caden had skipped school on Monday? Was she in trouble? She gathered her stuff and followed Caden into the hall, both of them quiet as they walked to the office. They stopped outside the door and looked at each other.

"After you," Rae said.

"No, no, after you." Caden waved a hand. "I insist."

"Don't tell me you're scared."

"Of course not! I mean, we faced the Unseeing. We can handle Ms. Lockett, right?"

"I don't know," Rae said. "I might prefer to take my chances with the Unseeing." She grinned and pulled open the door. But when she stepped inside, it wasn't their vice principal waiting for them.

It was Patrick.

"Nice seeing you both again. Come in back with me, please." He led them to Ms. Lockett's empty office, gesturing that they should each take a seat and then closing the door behind them. Rae sat, but Caden stayed by the door, his arms folded across his chest.

"Yesterday was a bit of a whirlwind. I trust you're both recovered?"

Rae nodded. Caden shrugged.

"And . . . were there any details of the night you'd like to add? For instance, where, exactly, Ivan disappeared to? Or how?"

Rae glanced at Caden. He looked straight ahead. "No," he said simply. Last night, Rae had told Patrick that Ivan had vanished somehow, but she'd left out all the details because only Caden really knew what the Other Place was or how he'd sent Ivan back to it. And obviously Caden wasn't talking.

"Well." Patrick steepled his fingers. "If you think of anything you'd like to add, I would be very interested in learning more. Regardless, we were able to clean up yesterday's events smoothly and keep your names out of any *public* reports."

"Should we thank you for that?" Caden said.

"If you'd like. But it's really not your thanks I'm interested in." He turned to Rae. "Ms. Carter. I have to admit, you have impressed me with your willingness to investigate, your sharp instincts, and your survival abilities. I believe you may have exactly the right combination of talents that would make you invaluable as part of my internship program."

Rae wasn't sure what to say. What kind of internship required those types of talents? "Thank you," she said slowly.

Patrick flashed her one of his wide smiles, and now he turned to Caden as well. "Mr. Price. You strike me as someone who would be very difficult to work with. But with the right motivation, I believe you could be exactly the right fit for our team."

"The right motivation?" Caden frowned. "That sounds almost threatening."

"Oh, nothing like that." Again with the wide smile. "I just believe we can help each other, you and I. I know there is a lot we could learn from you, and even more we can teach—"

"No thanks," Caden said.

Patrick dropped the smile. "Are you sure?"

"Definitely. I don't want to get involved in . . . whatever it is you're really involved in."

Patrick turned to Rae. "And you?"

Rae glanced at Caden. She might not know him that well yet, but she trusted him. And it had been a long time since she'd trusted anyone. If he didn't want to work with Patrick, then neither did she. "Thank you for the opportunity, but I'm with Caden on this one." She stood up.

Patrick sighed and stood as well. He opened the door to let them out, but after Caden stepped outside, Patrick stopped Rae in the doorway. "What if I could help *you*?" he asked.

"Help me how?"

"I might have information that could lead you to your father."

Rae froze. It was like she was standing on that darkened stairwell all over again. She could race up it, into the light, and follow Caden out. Or she could go back down and see what else was in the basement. She turned slowly back to Patrick. "What could you possibly know about my dad?"

"I know he was assigned to Operation Gray Bird."

"A Google search could tell you that."

"True. But I also know he found something. Something he wasn't supposed to see." Patrick leaned closer, and whispered, "An extraterrestrial."

Rae bit her lip to keep from gasping.

"Just as I know who assigned him the contract in the first place," Patrick continued softly.

"Who?"

"He was working on a new energy source." Patrick watched her intently. "Who do you think would be interested in something like that?"

It felt like too big a coincidence. "Green On!?" Rae said. For the second time, she wondered if maybe her mother had more than one reason for moving them out here. Before, she'd thought her mother might be trying to get away from something—but now, she considered that her mother might be conducting her own investigation, and what better place to be than Green On! headquarters?

"Exactly so. I don't have all the details . . . yet. But if you help me?" He shrugged. "I can certainly find them out."

Rae hesitated a moment longer. She could feel Caden watching her. He had promised to help her find her dad too. But if her dad really had taken a Green On! contract, then Patrick might be her best lead.

She couldn't trust Patrick—not if Caden didn't, and *especially* not if Patrick was working for the very company that might be involved in her father's abduction. But she also couldn't walk away now.

Rae turned to Caden. "I'm sorry," she said. "But I have to do this."

Caden didn't say anything, just shook his head and walked away. Rae's stomach sank. She'd have to make him understand later.

Patrick's smile was wide and triumphant as he ushered her back into the office, closing the door behind her. "Okay, Ms. Carter. Let's talk."

EPILOGUE
{ THREE DAYS LATER }

Audrey Matsuoka detested this part of the lab. They were nearly a mile underground, the walls, floors, and ceilings all made of concrete, and everything illuminated by those horrid, headache-inducing fluorescent lights that constantly buzzed and flickered.

Despite the chill—they always kept these tunnels at a brisk fifty-seven degrees—Audrey's face felt flushed. "Look, Patrick," she said. "You *must* see that this is not science. This is kidnapping."

"I *don't* see that, Audrey, I really don't," Patrick said, not taking his eyes off the cell in front of him. "Thanks to our rift experimental team, we were able to recreate the rift opening and save this poor teenager. You have to admit, that is quite a scientific accomplishment."

Audrey hadn't been on the rift experimental team, but she had heard about it. They'd reopened the rift, all right, for about thirty seconds—and three people on their team had died. And people thought nuclear was dangerous!

"And now, we are merely keeping him safely contained for observational purposes," Patrick finished.

"To what end?" Audrey glanced inside the cell where a teenage boy slept on a long narrow bed, his body twitching every few minutes almost like he was trying to run from something in his sleep. And no wonder. She had heard from one of the lab techs that the boy had screamed for an hour straight when they first pulled him out until they'd finally been forced to tranquilize him. He'd been asleep ever since.

They'd buzzed his head, clipped his nails, bathed him, and stuck him in a set of loose cotton pajamas the same bright green as the company's hazmat uniforms. It made him look far too young and very innocent.

"Here's a question for you," Patrick said. "What do you think would happen to a town like Whispering Pines if we released Mr. Price, and he turned out to be contaminated?"

"Contaminated?" Audrey said, thinking of Vivienne and her unusual . . . affliction. An affliction that only Patrick knew about, since he made sure she got the medicine she needed to slow down its effects until a cure could hopefully be found.

"Yes. Contaminated, diseased, plagued . . ." Patrick paused, obviously waiting for his words to soak in. "The Other Place could be crawling with all sorts of contagious things. You know, much like that cave you and your daughter explored."

Audrey winced, but refused to allow herself to be swayed.

Patrick really just wanted a chance to study the boy more thoroughly, to run his little tests without oversight or disturbance. And this boy was a minor, with a family who missed him and deserved to know where he was.

But what if he *was* contaminated somehow?

"Just think of the nightmare we would have to deal with if we were to accidentally release a plague on our good citizens," Patrick said, still in that reasonable voice he always used. "It certainly would interfere with our efforts to find your daughter's cure."

Audrey couldn't help picturing her Vivienne trapped in one of these cells, which would be her daughter's fate if they never found a cure. Quickly, Audrey shoved that image from her mind. She was too practical to imagine such things. But being practical, she had to admit that Patrick made a point.

Audrey risked one more glance in the cell. Really, it wasn't *that* bad, she tried to reason. More of a bedroom, actually, than a cell at all. Except for the instruments beeping in the corner, taking constant measurements, and the walls made of shatterproof glass so Patrick and the others in his carefully selected department could observe.

"I suppose we really don't know enough about this Other Place," Audrey hedged, already feeling her resolve crumbling.

"Precisely. Which is why, for the time being, it is best that we keep this boy in our custody. Not just for his safety, but for everyone's."

Audrey nodded. "Fine," she sighed, knowing she'd lost this one and hating herself a little for it. "But you will send someone to his family's house soon, letting them know that their son is safe?"

Patrick smiled. "Of course, Audrey. You know how much I like things to be done thoroughly."

Running footsteps echoed loudly down the tunnel behind them as a woman rushed over, her black hair coming loose from its tight bun and her green lab coat flapping around her simple business attire. "Patrick!" she called.

"Yes, Doctor Nguyen?"

"There's something you should see. We've finally reached the bottom of the sinkhole. And . . . we found something there."

"Well?" Patrick said.

"You won't believe it. We almost didn't believe it ourselves."

"There is no need for dramatics," Audrey said, annoyed. "Stop drawing it out."

"A spacecraft," Dr. Nguyen said. "We found a spacecraft."

Audrey gaped, then managed to recover herself.

Patrick's smile was wide and satisfied. "Excellent."

"You're not surprised?"

"No, Doctor Nguyen. I'm not surprised. In fact, I've been expecting this for quite some time now."

Audrey took the back roads carefully. There was very little light in these parts, which made the turns quite treacherous. And it was only too easy to sneak up on a herd of deer, or worse.

Audrey turned down Silence Lane. She didn't normally like coming this way because of the rumors of a nineteenth-century ghost haunting these parts, but she had promised Vivienne that she would be home a half hour ago for their weekly family movie night, and this road was the shortest route.

She tried focusing on the road, but her thoughts kept drifting back to the mysterious spacecraft. The one that Patrick had, apparently, been expecting . . .

Her high beams illuminated something on the road directly in front of her: a tall boy with buzzed-short black hair wearing a green cotton pajama set.

Shock hit Audrey like a bucket of ice water to the face, and she reacted instinctively, shoving the break pedal down to the floor. Rubber tires screeched in agony, but it was too late. Her car wasn't going to stop in time.

She yanked the wheel to the right, trees filling her whole vision as her car slid straight into a large oak.

Bam!

Pain seared across Audrey's face, her vision filled with the white of her airbag. With shaking hands, she managed to unbuckle her seat belt, open the door, and slide into the cool night air. She leaned against the side of her car, her legs threatening to dump her into the damp leaves below.

Her ribs burned with every breath, and when she ran her fingers over her numb face, they came away covered in blood.

Audrey stayed leaning against her car for a long time, and then she pushed herself upright and, slowly and painfully, walked back up to the road.

It was dark and empty in the moonlight, stretching away in both directions. There was no sign of the boy anywhere. But Audrey knew what she had seen, and she wasn't the type of person prone to fantasy . . . It had been *him*.

Audrey turned, her gaze sweeping the woods around her. Everything seemed too quiet, like the trees were waiting, and she had the uncomfortable feeling that something was watching her. Something that didn't care about her well-being.

Pressing a hand against her aching ribs, she carefully made her way back to her broken car and her cell phone and just hoped help wasn't too far away. She wished she had worn something a bit warmer than a business skirt.

She opened her door and slid inside.

"Hello, Mrs. Matsuoka," a voice said quietly.

Audrey started, jerking around, but there was no one there.

"You won't be able to see me unless I let you," the voice continued. *"But I can see you whenever I want . . ."*

"Who are you? What do you want?" She kept the quivering out of her voice.

"You know who I am."

Audrey could feel a faint whisper of breath on the back of her neck, and she shivered. She *did* know who it was: Aiden Price.

"As for what I want?" the voice continued. *"Well, just one simple little favor . . ."*

ACKNOWLEDGMENTS

The first seed of this story took root in our imaginations years ago, but it took the efforts of a lot of people to help it grow into the book you are holding in your hands now. Thank you to Sarah McCabe, our brilliant editor, who took our initial messy draft and helped us transform it into something much stronger. We owe so much to you, and to the rest of the Aladdin team who worked on this book, including Mara Anastas, Chriscynethia Floyd, Rebecca Vitkus, Tiara Iandiorio, Caitlin Sweeny, Alissa Nigro, Anna Jarzab, Savannah Breckenridge, Lauren Hoffman, Nicole Russo, and Christina Pecorale and her sales team. Also thank you to our truly amazing cover illustrator, Diana Novich.

We are fortunate in our writing friends, but we especially need to thank Alan Wehrman, who read the full draft plus multiple versions of the first fifty pages without complaining, and whose insight shaped the direction of the novel. And thank you to Maureen McQuerry, Stephen Wallenfels, Jeanette Mendell, Mary Cronk Farrell, and Amanda Divine, as well as our fellow Kidliterati writers: Suzi Guina, Katie Nelson, Jennifer Camiccia, Kaitlin Hundscheid, Liz Edelbrock, Taylor Gardner, and Tara Creel, who all had a hand in making this a better book.

We are very grateful for our agent, Jennifer Azantian, the best champion a pair of writing sisters could hope for. And even though it was years ago, we will always remember our Pitch Wars group: Liz Briggs, Stephanie Garber, and Teresa Yea—you encouraged us when we were first getting our author feet wet, and we couldn't resist writing the three of you into this story. Sorry that only one of you made it through in one piece, but such is the way of horror.

One half of this writing duo had a baby right around the time this book was due and would never have been able to make that deadline without the love and support of our families. Thank you to our parents, Rich and Rose Bartkowski, who traveled across the country twice in order to help with baby care. And thank you to parents-in-law Lyn and Bruce Lang for all the care in between and every day since, not to mention daily home-cooked meals. Also thank you to our siblings, Rosi and Ed Reed, and Jesse and Ashley Lang, for all your encouragement.

To our partners, Sean Lang and Nick Chen, it goes without saying that your support has made all of this possible . . . but we'll say it anyhow. And to Ember and Evelyn Rose, both of whom have taught us so much about time management.

Finally, thank you to our readers: we're so grateful you decided to join us on this journey. Buckle up, there's still a lot more story to come.

HEIDI LANG & KATI BARTKOWSKI

are a writing team of two sisters. Heidi is afraid of all things that go bump in the night but watches shows like *The X-Files* and *Stranger Things* anyhow. Kati enjoys reading about serial killers and the apocalypse but secretly sleeps with a night-light. They believe that the best way to conquer fear is to share it with as many people as possible, so between the two of them, they love creating stories full of all the things that scare them most. They are the coauthors of the Mystic Cooking Chronicles trilogy.